—— *In the* ——
HEARTLAND

A Story So Real It Might Be True

BUNK RUSSELL

PAGE PUBLISHING, INC.
Conneaut Lake, PA

First originally published by Page Publishing 2019

ISBN 978-1-64628-027-8 (pbk)
ISBN 978-1-64628-026-1 (digital)

Printed in the United States of America

A post-9/11 novel that features some facts and some fiction of a changed society in the heartland.

CHAPTER 1

"Okay, Marty, tell me again why you wanted this meeting today after all these years."

"We need you, Jonathan. This thing has got the Bureau buffaloed."

"What thing?"

"Now come on, you're not going to tell me that the infamous Jonathan Beck of twenty-some odd years in the bureau doesn't keep track of current events."

"Listen, Marty, I still watch TV but only on rare occasions, and when my radio is on, I'm mostly listening to country music or, believe it or not, El Rushball."

"Are you trying to tell me that you haven't heard of all of the murders of middle eastern men that have been occurring at random all around the country over the past two years?"

"Yeah, I have heard of them, but that's about as far as it goes. Marty, that's your job now and the rest of the assholes in Atlanta or wherever! You have evidently forgotten that I didn't voluntarily retire, you and your pinstriped pals forced me out via forced retirement and at a pittance of what I should have gotten."

"That was nearly five years ago now."

"Yeah, Marty, that's right, but at times, I must admit that it seems like yesterday. Now don't get me wrong—I am enjoying my retirement. I fish and hunt more now than ever. For five straight years now, I have been in a flooded rice field in Arkansas on opening day of waterfowl season to witness and to harvest the fall flight of mallards that migrate into and around Stuttgart. I have harvested around three hundred greenheads every season since my ousting from the bureau."

"Ousting? Now come on, Jonathan, you were not totally innocent of any wrongdoing. You call us pinstripes because you wouldn't wear a suit even to divisional meetings, and I still don't believe you ever read the mandates or the procedures manuals."

"Okay, Marty, let's cut to the chase. Why am I here listening to this bureau crap from you all over again? The Walleyes are moving up river, and I got a limit in less than two hours last night and I plan to go again tonight."

"The big boys and I have decided that you're our man."

"Your man my ass! Don't think for one minute that I would even remotely consider helping you or any of the other bastards for that matter. Put your suits on, read your damnable mandates and procedures manual, and go out there and catch whomever or whoever is killing these mop-headed camel jockeys. Get the waiter, Marty, I don't have time to listen to any more of your bullshit."

"See what I'm talking about, Jonathan? It's just that type of outburst and behavior that got you canned."

"Then why the hell do you want my help?"

"Because dammit, Jonathan, we're at our wits end and we don't want anyone else to die. The President is under a lot of pressure to fire the director if we don't stop this sicko."

"Why do you think it is a him or a sicko? David Head couldn't catch a cold in a hell storm, and his ass should be fired."

"I didn't say *him*. I said *sicko* because nobody in their right mind would go out and kill innocent people they don't even know."

"Well, you're barking up the wrong tree here, Marty. I am not interested."

"Believe it or not, Jonathan, it was David's idea for me to get up with you."

"Really? And he thinks that I would help save his ass after he canned mine? I have got to change how I comb my hair, Marty. Surely I can't look that stupid? I lost my wife when I lost my job, and my kids have to work their way through college because of that lazy fool. Politics, Marty—politics is what got me, and it will mostly likely be politics that will get David. Your ass is probably next, Marty, for David will use you all as scapegoats before he will admit his incompetence."

"David knew that you would object, so he gave me the authority to bring you back at full pay and full benefits."

"Nope! It won't work, Marty. I am not coming back for any amount of money. Besides that, I still can't figure why he would want me back."

"David thinks that you're his best bet to solve this thing. You've got to remember, Jonathan, it's been two years now and nine bodies, and we've made no progress at stopping this animal."

"What makes you think that it's just one person, Marty? It could be a group or still yet one person could have started the killing, and then now you have a bunch of copycats. After 9/11, there are a lot of people that hate those rag heads. I won't even buy gas at a convenience store if I see one of those bastards behind the counter."

"That's part of our problem—we haven't been able to establish a pattern nor a profile in this case."

"Well, I'm of no use to you for I am now retired from the bureau and I am also tired of the bureau so go dig up some other poor joker that David buried on his way up the ladder. There are some damn good men and women out there working in security in the private sector that David ran off over the years that might be able to help you and might also be willing to help you of which I am not one."

"Okay, Jonathan, I will relay this to David, and I am sorry for wasting your time."

"Oh, you haven't wasted my time. It has been enjoyable to learn that David needs me, and it has also been fun to tell him to go bite a wild hog in the ass. Yeah, tell him just that for me, Marty. I still can't stand that two-faced yahoo!"

Jonathan fishing for Walleye on Tellico Lake, near Knoxville, Tennessee

I love to fish for walleye in the early spring, I thought, as I boated my fourth keeper of the evening, an eighteen-inch beauty. Just one more and I will have my limit. The bait came up to the lights early tonight, I thought, as I looked at my watch to see that it was only ten minutes past midnight. I guess that the lake is starting to warm a bit, allowing the bait fish to rise to the surface sooner. It has been a rather warm spring in East Tennessee. *Pop, pop, pop.* There it is—the sound of walleyes hitting the minnows on or near the surface just outside the glow of the light. I raised my wrist to cast my ten-inch Redfin in the direction of the popping sound at the edge of the shadow then I stopped. Why rush things? The night is young, and I am only allowed one more fish. The slower the retrieve, the better for this technique. You must keep the bait on or near the surface as you give it a gentle twist. They don't hit hard; the line just gets heavy and moves downward or to one side or the other, then you set the hooks. It's great fun, and walleye is, by far, the best tasting freshwater fish found anywhere. I rate it above Crappie and Bream, both of which I dearly love. It's a white flaky meat with a gentle sweet taste that's so good your tongue will beat your brains out trying to get the last drop on its taste buds.

I laid my rod and reel down and leaned back into the captain's seat of my pontoon boat looked to the sky and started to think about my conversation earlier in the day with Marty Ashcroft at the 5 and Diner for lunch. No way that I will ever consider going back to the bureau, no fucking way. I love how I spend my days now and my nights, no more bars, no more adolescence fears, no more women to tell me what to do and when to do it. After three failed marriages, the broads just don't impress me much anymore. I just call up dial-a-hook about once a month and then I am good for a while. Some of my buddies make fun of me patronizing hookers, but I just respond to them by saying, "Hey, guys it's not the pussy that I am paying for—I am paying for them to go away when I am finished." That's right—it's all about me now. I don't have to worry about satisfying anyone anymore, and besides that, I probably couldn't anyway, so what the hell?

I really don't give a damn about those Arab bastards anyway. I couldn't care less if someone killed every damn one of them tomorrow. Our government says that we have declared war on the terrorists; however, it seems to me that all we're doing in the Middle East is pussy-footing around and getting our young men and women killed for nothing. It's Vietnam all over again, just on a smaller scale—at least for now anyway. You would think that somebody somewhere in our government would step up and say, "Hey, let's destroy the bastards and take the oil fields or get the hell out of here." One damn bomb would solve our entire problem in the Middle East, and then we could let them breed all over again. Maybe—just maybe—they might get it right this time and worship the right God too. But who am I to say? Just a lowly retired old fart that loves to hunt and fish, and I don't go to church much anymore myself anyway, so I guess that I should just drop the God thoughts too.

First it was the Hispanics that came here to take our jobs and live off our welfare system that they have never paid a penny into, I might add, and now you can't buy a tank of gas or stay the night in a motel without having to look at one of those mop heads and hand them your money. Now that really pisses me off. Especially since I read in the *Wall Street Journal* a while back that most of them are buying those convenience stores and motels with loans from our government interest free no less. Some damn declaration of war that is. I'm tired of the Japs. You can't buy an American-made car today that is not constructed to a great extent with Japanese made parts. I told a buddy of mine the other day that was bragging about his American-made Dodge Hemi that if he took out all the foreign parts in his Dodge, it wouldn't even start. The best damn thing the Japs ever did for the future of their country and their economy was to bomb Pearl Harbor because after we kicked their asses, we then spent billions to help them rebuild. Now they can outproduce and outprice us in most industries. How in the name of God does that make any sense? That's like giving a guy a stick to beat you with in a fight.

Nope, no way in hell this old boy will help them catch this guy or guys!

Johnathan back at home in Knoxville, Tennessee

"Hello. Ah, Marty?"

"Yes, Jonathan. Good morning!"

"Good morning, my ass. I didn't get home until daybreak I spent the night on Tellico Lake. What time is it anyway, and why the hell are you bothering me again?"

"It's nearly ten o'clock, Jonathan, and you have always been an early riser."

"I wish that you would get the hell back out of my life and leave me alone. I get up when I damn well please these days, and besides that, it is none of your business when I get up!" *Clang!*

Ring! Ring! Ring! Ring!

"What, dammit? I am trying to sleep. Would you please just leave me alone?"

"I have got a better deal for you, Jonathan—"

"I don't give a shit about any deal! I don't care what it is! I have already told you no!"

"David said for you to name your price, your deal, and your terms that will make this work."

"Make what work?"

"You know what I am talking about, Jonathan, we need for you to head up a team to find this sicko and bring him to justice soon."

"What if I told you that this guy or guys is my hero? Now how do you like those apples? I haven't lost a minute's sleep over the death of a single one of those bastards and you know it!"

"I know that you're a little redneck, and that you're an isolationist at heart. However, I also know that Jonathan Beck was one of the best agents and that you always went after mass murders with a vengeance. It was your overzealous techniques that eventually got you in trouble with the top brass. You would do anything, anytime, anywhere to anybody to get information to get a conviction whether it was justice or not somebody's ass was going to jail if Jonathan

Beck was in charge. Come on now, Jonathan. This is your chance to finally do things your way. You can't let this opportunity go by now, can you?"

"Watch me, you yahoo!" *Clang!*

I love the Waffle House, especially breakfast there in the mornings and breakfast there late at night. In the morning, I catch up on all the latest gossip and news from the local yokels no matter what town. A late-night breakfast will allow me the pleasure of talking to some old drunk broad trying to sober up some before going home to her old man or boyfriend.

On this day, it would just be breakfast in the morning, and I wasn't really interested in any local gossip or news. My thoughts kept going back to Marty's offer, and so I bought a paper and started to read about David's Thorn.

The national columnist in *USA Today* was trying to portray the killer as most likely being from the south or Midwest even though there had been very few of the killings in the Deep South—that is if you don't count the state of Florida as being part of the deep south, of which I don't. I told my son that you can drive either north or south on Interstate 95 and eventually end up in New York if you get my drift—just try to find a natural-born Floridian south of Interstate 10. It ain't going to happen today. There they go again—the elite media trying to pick on us poor Southern rednecks. They think that we're against about anything and anybody, I guess. Three had been slain on or near an interstate highway in Florida, so the feds and the state have been looking into the trucking industry for some time to no avail. Good idea, I thought, for right after 9/11, the trucking industry had covertly rid itself of any and all drivers of Middle Eastern decent. Now it wasn't done by the industry itself or by the trucking company officials; it was the drivers that acted swiftly after 9/11 in letting them know that their welcome had run out in the truck stops, in the rest areas, and anywhere else for that matter. In reality, I doubt if the truckers ever welcomed them. They just put up with them for a while, waiting on a good reason to run them out and 9/11 was as good as any. That said, I guess the trucking industry was a good place for David's boys to start looking; however, it wouldn't be easy for the feds to infiltrate that group.

The article went on to talk about the many hate groups that call the South and the Midwest home. There was quite a conglomeration located in a line from Alabama to Ohio and on through Missouri to Colorado. They ranged in thought and ideology from white supremacist to state rights to the now popular "Patriot" movement that was growing exponentially in scope and number nationwide. The writer gave very little print to this movement and ideology; however, several years back, I did a study for the bureau on these groups, and I was astounded at the numbers then, and I predicted that this was a movement that must be watched very closely. It wasn't the numbers that was shocking; it was the diversity of the membership of the followers. There are times that I even feel attached in theory to some of them. The only thing holding the Patriot movement back is the fact that they are not very well organized as a single group under a narrow leadership. Their base, however, is mostly highly educated and believe deeply in the basic tenants of the Constitution and they don't believe in any broad or so-called modern-day interpretations. They truly believe the wrong side won in the War Between the States, yet they're not racists for the most part; however, I would classify them as separatists, and there is a definite difference. These folks most definitely believe in closing the borders, and had they been running the country prior to 9/11 that would only be an insignificant date on the calendar today. I believe that and they know that, and so I am positive that they are at least planning retaliatory actions right now and probably already have some action at work. These groups should be prime suspects for the massive killings. The only problem is how do you infiltrate them and where? I know of law enforcement personnel on the state, local, and national levels that call themselves Patriots and of members of both houses of our government. Their call to arms is the famous quote, "Give me liberty or give me death!" Now how do you find fault in that when everyone knows that our liberties are being eroded away daily?

I paid the waitress and then went on my way back to the house for some more coffee, and then I thought that I might just venture up to the Clinch River for a little trout fishing. I love the Clinch, and I have written a lot about what I call my river and of its pristine environment. In a column that I wrote for *Sports Unlimited: In the South*, I once said that when I die, I want to have my body cremated and my ashes placed into the Clinch for at that time, it will be the trout's turn to eat me. God knows that I have feasted on their bounty for many moons. I have seen highways named after great politicians (if there is such a creature) and great athletes, and in my younger days, I thought that if I ever amounted to anything it would be nice to have a portion of my beloved Clinch named after me, lol. My only request would be, as if that would ever happen, is to please pick a section that is not frequented by those sissy-looking fly fisherman in their pastel-colored waders and faggot-looking hats. I have got enough issues in my current life to answer to in heaven without me cussing those tree-hugging bastards from above. That is, I hope from above, but as a second thought, you know I don't think that God would like them much either for everyone knows that he wasn't a catch-and-release sort of guy for he fed the multitudes with just two fish and a few pieces of bread. However, they might have an angle with the maker because they all think that they can and should be the only ones walking on—ah, excuse me, I mean in the water. As a side bar, to my best recollection, Jesus "got out of a boat" to walk on the water and a fishing boat at that; he didn't tip toe through the tulips and then walk on the water. Thank God for Jesus and "real men."

Back at the FBI office in Atlanta, Georgia

"Well, Marty, what do you think?"

"He'll take it, David, just give him a little time. You know how Jonathan can be these days."

"Yeah, I just wonder if we're doing the right thing by giving him so much freedom and power. Jonathan can't do this alone, Marty, he must have a staff."

"I know that, but let's wait and let that be Jonathan's idea."

"He must use bureau people, Marty. Do you think that he will object to that?"

"Yes! But he'll still do it—just give him time."

"I am afraid that we don't have much time, Marty. It's about time for someone somewhere to find another body."

Jonathan attempting to fish on his beloved Clinch River

The fishing was slow partly due to the slow bite but mainly because I was preoccupied. This damn thing with Marty was beginning to constantly bug me now. I could use the money, and I hate to admit it, but sometimes, I really get bored, plus it would be nice to put those bastards to shame.

I think that I might just go out to the White River for a few days and give my life and this whole damn thing some thought while doing a little turkey hunting in the morning and then fishing for trout in the evening with some old friends of mine. I like to stay in an old rundown cabin owned by an old friend that also owns a really great guide service on the White, the Red, and the Little Red. Jimmy, like me, drinks a little too much these days, but unlike me, he is worth a ton of money and is currently dating some good-looking dumb-ass blonde from Russia. I like to fish with Jimmy for he too hates fly fishermen even though he pretends to like the sissies when they frequent his lodge and pay outrageous guide fees. He and I love to just drift the scenic river and enjoy the beauty of its pristine shores, and every once in a while, we will cast out a line in between old war stories of all of the asses we've kicked and of all the women we've screwed. For three solid days, that is all we did. Jimmy never even called the lodge, and every time his cell phone went off, he would cuss the damnable thing and then proudly hit the Reject button.

The morning of the fourth day was the opening of turkey sea-son in the Ozarks so we hit the local restaurant early for coffee and a sweet roll, and that is when Jimmy informed me that he would have to pass on the hunt because of some pressing business issues. He had gone at least three days without a piece of Russian ass, so I guess that was the real pressing issue. That was all right with me, I said, we could go after a long beard in the afternoon or the next morning for I needed to spend some time alone anyway. After easing down three or four cups of Java, we went our separate ways and agreed to meet at the same restaurant about three in the afternoon. I went back to the cabin to spend some time alone and to give some serious thought to Marty's proposition.

Back at the restaurant waiting on Jimmy

"Hey, big guy," Jimmy said in a loud and boisterous voice.

Yep, just as I thought, I said to myself, *the old boy got that piece of ass.*

"Are you ready to go after the old man of the forest?"

"Sure am," I replied, "do you know a good ridge to hunt?"

"Yes, just past Crater's bluff where the Red and the Little Red meet. Miles Stewart said that no one hunted that area this morning and that he has been seeing some really nice long beards."

Jimmy got one with an eleven-inch beard that evening, and early the next morning, right down by the river, I got one with two eight-inch beards and three-quarter-inch spurs. After lunch and some more chit-chat, I was on my way back to Knoxville, still undecided about my future but feeling very relaxed. Why should I give up this type of freedom for the rat race of the bureau and all its bullshit?

The money, I guess, and you can bet your ass it will cost them if I come back! I will demand a cool two hundred and fifty thousand in cash up front and another one half million when I catch the bastard, dead or alive. I will also need all expenses covered including motels, meals, booze, and we must not forget the hookers too. David won't mind the hookers because he will think that just might keep me away from Margaret when I am in Atlanta. Oh yes, Margaret is his lovely wife who is oversexed and underscrewed most of the time, and she might just hate the bureau as much as I. David is extremely jealous of her; however, he doesn't have the time to keep her satisfied. In my younger days, I helped the old boy out every now and then when he was called out of town or out of the country for long periods. He never caught us, but he always suspected that I had it in for him when he was away, in more ways than one. That, I think, is at least in part why I was fired even though he would never admit it.

I don't really need the damn money, however, it would be nice to take care of the kid's future, especially their education. There's no chance in this country for young white kids to make it in the labor market. The Wetbacks will work for nothing, and then our government gives so much free money to the so-called Arab-Americans, most of which aren't even citizens of this country, in terms of free loans to start small businesses. That's what really pisses me off—they're out there trying to destroy our country, and then we support them and even educate them. Their Bible, the Koran, teaches them to hate and then to kill us, and then the 'talking heads' on the news talk about the Radical Islamic, not the peace-loving patriots of America Islamic. I just don't get that type of thinking. They *all* hate our asses and everything we stand for in this country. They want our milk and honey and all our money, but that's the extent of their love.

After settling in at home in Knoxville,
Jonathan called Marty in Atlanta

"Hey, Marty, I'm back!"

"Well, did you catch many fish?'

"We did okay—I was mainly just trying to get away and let my mind clear up a bit while I pondered your proposition."

"Did you hear about the body?"

"No, what body?"

"They found it just this morning near Springfield, Missouri, floating in a stream. This bastard has dumped over half of his victims in lakes or streams. This one was evidently found just a day or two after it was decapitated."

"Decapitated?"

"Yes, didn't you know that all but a few had been beheaded?"

"No!"

"Yeah, must be some type of way of mimicking the way they have killed our people over there. In a few cases, he has made his victims eat their own excrement as their last meal. Now isn't that some sick shit?"

"Jesus, Marty, spare me the details!"

"Okay, but after you get on this thing, officially, I will need to fill you in on all of the facts and even the gory details of how this sick bastard operates. Most of the victims have been either owners or operators of hotels or convenience stores."

"Well, that didn't take any masterful detective work. Hell, that covers ninety percent of the bastards with the remaining ten percent being American-educated doctors. You would think that they would go home to help their own sick and suffering, but no, they want to stay here so they can milk our retirees and the Medicare and Medicaid system for all it's worth. It's a damnable shame, Marty."

"Maybe, Jonathan, but we don't make the rules we just enforce them."

"Where did you get the 'we shit' white man? Have you got a mouse in your pocket or something? Maybe you have forgotten that I make my own rules now. I get up when I want to, I go to bed when I want to—no wife, no kids, no shit. The only problems I have these days is when it is raining too hard for me to fish or hunt."

"Come on, Jonathan, we have got to get this thing done. I don't want another person to die before we get a team together."

"A team?"

"Yes, a team. Jonathan, you can't do this by yourself and you know it too."

"I pick my own team, right?"

"To an extent, maybe?"

"Bullshit, Marty. I have to have full autonomy or I won't even consider it!"

"Come on, Jonathan. This is government shit, remember?"

"Hey, Marty, you came to me, remember? I can just walk away now without giving it another thought."

"Hey, Jonathan. You came to me this time, so I at least know that you have some interest, right?"

"Maybe?"

"Okay, here's the deal, I want two hundred and fifty thousand up front in cash tax-free on deposit in my savings account at Bank of America and all expenses paid and—I do mean all. I work outside the bureau, and I work alone with the only exception being that I have access to all of the bureau's data and technology and personnel if and when needed."

"Come on, Jonathan—!"

"Wait, Marty, I am not finished. After I catch the killer, I get a half-million dollars tax-free to be split between my son and daughter."

"Geez, Jonathan, you know they won't go for that type of arrangement. Besides, I am not sure they could even do that if they wanted to, the bureau has to answer to Washington, and everyone else for that matter. I can't take this to David—he'll throw me out of his office."

"Well, tell him to catch the bastard himself! That's my deal, Marty, plain and simple—no ifs and/or buts!"

"Look, give me something that I can tell David that will give him some control even if it's just on the surface. I have got to sell this to him and then he must sell it to others."

"That's it, Marty, I won't take it under any other setup. Hell, Marty, I might end up dead trying to catch this guy."

"Okay, Jonathan. I'll run it by David Saturday on the golf course. He is much easier to talk to in a golf cart."

Chapter 2

Back at the ranch, I decided to start doing a little research into the killings to determine just what was there and what the media had to offer. The Internet would probably be a good place to start. The Yahoo search engine listed thousands of sites when I typed in the phrase *Islamic killings*, so I had to search again under American mass murders, and again, thousands of sites appeared. Finally, I got it narrowed a little by typing in the name of the most recent victim, Suleman Ai-Tajir, he was a student attending the University of Arkansas, on some sort of government grant. He had become the killer's tenth victim if there was only one killer, a fact believed by most of the researchers on the case but doubted by me. Just like in the Ted Bundy case and that of the Green River killer, copycats get involved, and that skews the accountability factor, and it's very difficult if not impossible to get straight answers from the killers that have been caught. Most of them will exaggerate the kill; it's part of their psyche and thought process. They all want to become the best or the worst at what they do. Gary Ridgeway, the Green River Killer, preyed on prostitutes because he thought that they were the scum of the earth and a menace to society. He had sex with most of them; however, he didn't consider that rape, and at some point during his interrogation, he stated that he hated rapists and that they all should be put to death. He was a killer and proud of it, and he actually believed that he was helping society out by getting rid of these misfits. I think that he claimed to have killed over fifty women; however, most of us believe that there was at least one if not more copycats involved in a goodly number of the killings a fact or fiction that may not ever prove to be right or wrong.

From most of the pieces that I found, a pattern had really not been established as of yet in these killings. The easy things had pretty much come to light with labels like Hate Crime and Racist being the most used by the mainline printers, and of course the paramilitary group finger pointing that is always there today regardless of the crime. The bureau must have some specifics by now. I thought, I will get Marty to let me review them soon. I need to have a starting point on this thing.

As in times past, when I was one of the "suits," it amazes me just how long it takes the so-called experts to get a pattern and/or a line on these people. You've got to determine early on when and where they hunt their prey if you have a snowball's chance in hell of catching them before the number of bodies get so high. However, it's usually the large numbers that act as a catalyst for them to look back in retrospect.

I spent the better part of the evening looking for some good nitty-gritty data and found none, just innuendos and opinions, which are like assholes. Everybody has one, and in this case, it was no exception. Most of the printed information was really not information at all, just tons of verbiage describing and slamming this maniac for the carnage. They just can't get past the carnage in these cases and that slows down the process and makes it to where they can't see the forest for the trees. Historically, it has happened time and time again from the most famous cases down to the pimp gone mad. Bodies have to be stacked up like cord wood before they get the picture. However, there is always some lonely low ender on the investigative totem pole that "gets it," but no one listens to him or her, and I bet that he or she is out there somewhere in this case too and I must find them.

Back near Atlanta at the Atlanta Athletic Club

"Dammit, Marty! You have got to stop talking during my backswing."

"Ah, I'm sorry. It's just you don't stop talking so you can listen to me when we're in the cart."

"Maybe I don't want to listen to you, Marty?"

"Well, that may be true. However, if you want to get Jonathan involved, you have got to eventually listen to me."

"Let's play golf right now, Marty, and then I will listen to you in the clubhouse over a few beers after eighteen."

Three or four hours later at the Nineteenth Hole

"Bullshit! Marty! Jonathan has lost his frigging mind. There's no chance—and I do mean no chance—that we can or will pay him that kind of money or give him that much control. The man's a damn idiot! Waiter! Get over here and bring me a double Scotch on the rocks. To hell with this beer. What the hell is wrong with you, Marty? You know better than this shit!"

"It was your idea to get Jonathan, and it was your orders that sent me to talk with him so you can't put this off on me! Besides— and I know that you don't want to hear this—but if it works and he gets this guy, you would pay him twice that much money and…you and I both know that!"

Several minutes went by before David broke the silence as he twisted the ice cubes around and around in his drink. "You know that I hate the bastard, don't you?"

"Which one, the killer or Jonathan?"

"Both! And Jonathan with a purple passion—it pisses me off just to look at him."

"But—"

"I know—he is still our best bet to get this monkey off my back before I, you know, lose my job. Everybody from the President to my wife is on my ass over this thing. However, he may be a bigger problem than the killer. In some ways, Jonathan is hard to control and to predict."

"If you don't go with Jonathan, what are your options?"

"I'm not sure that there are any right now. Can you get the money? You know, from a slush fund or something? Don't need to have the higher-ups discover this until we get some results."

"It's hard to do that today with everyone breathing down our backs and with Congress getting tough on white-collar crime and all, but I might have an idea."

CHAPTER 3

Back at Jonathan's home in Knoxville, Tennessee

"Hi, Dad. I'm glad that you called. You did remember my birthday this year!"

"How's things?"

"Pretty good I guess."

"Driving all the young boys there crazy I'm sure. Are you still wearing the T-shirt that I gave you when I took you to Florida State that first day?"

"No!"

"Do you remember what it even said?"

"Yes! 'My dad will kick your ass!' It was such an embarrassment to me when I took it out of my suitcase and my roommate saw it and told every guy on campus."

"How's the job going?"

"Okay, I guess. It limits my ability to take the amount of hours that I would like to take. However, it keeps me busy and out of trouble."

"Not much time to date?"

"*Dad!*"

"Well, I just wanted to call to wish you a happy birthday and to let you know that you do have a small package in the mail and a small check. Maybe it will help a bit. Has your brother called today?"

"No! He'll think about it in a week or so and then call to apologize and to borrow some money. Are you going to make any of his hockey tournaments this season? You do know that he is the starting goalie this year and they're ranked in the top ten and some of the analysts are picking Colorado State to make the Frozen Four."

"I hope so—however, there is something else I was going to tell you. I have been taking with the bureau recently, and they want me to take on a special project."

"No way, Dad. Tell those, ah, folks to bug off, not after the way they treated you, not to even mention the fact that they're the main reason you and Mom split."

"Not really, baby. Your mom and I were destroying ourselves from within."

"Yeah, but it all started after they dumped you and our finances got tight."

"I'll admit that didn't help things. However, our romance had died out years before. I think she was just holding on until you and your brother went off to college."

"Have you talked with her lately?"

"Nope! There really isn't any reason to, with her remarried and all."

"Oh, I can think of two pretty good reasons, but I know that you don't want to go there, so just tell me a little about this special project."

"It's nothing much, just a little murder case that has David's ass in a bind."

"Tell him to kiss off and leave his ass in a bind. It's nothing too dangerous, is it, Dad?"

"Oh no, just paperwork and research mostly, but it will start taking a ton of my time."

"Oh well, it's not that you spend much time down here anyway."

"Come on now, girl. Things have been tough on me, and I do love you so very much. If this thing goes well, I may have some extra funds to send you and your brother's way."

"It's not the money, Dad. I would just like to see you more often."

"That may come to pass. Take care and I will call you again soon. I love you!"

"Okay, Dad, and I love you too!"

"Hey, Junior!"

"What's up, Dad?"

"For one thing, your sister's birthday!"

"Damn, ah, I mean darn it, I just can't remember dates very well."

"Oh, I think you remember them pretty well when they have names in front of them instead of numbers behind them."

"Not really. It's hockey season, so I don't have much time for the girls these days. By the way, we're ranked in the top ten right now, and I had a great game the other night against Michigan in front of the Avalanche scouts."

"Great! I guess you still plan on making it to the NHL?"

"You got it. I'm better than most of the starting goalies there now."

"Well, I see that you're still not short on confidence."

"That's right, and I am six feet tall now and in great shape, so my size is not an issue anymore. I have always played big anyway. Are you going to make any of my games this season?"

"Sure!"

"Oh yes, let me guess you will be here for the Colorado game and the game with Army?"

"Why those games?"

"The only ones you ever make are on the two weekends that bring you out this way every season, the opening week of Elk season, and the opening day of pheasant season in Kansas, and those are the weeks we play Colorado and Army."

"I promise that I will get out for another one or two more this year. However, son, it's not like you went to Huntsville like I wanted."

"Huntsville? Dad, why would you go there when you can play for Colorado State?"

"Well, for one thing, they offered you a partial scholarship and they're located close to home."

"Oh, here we go again with the money thing?"

"Not really, son. Just give your sister a call, and don't tell her that I called you."

"I won't, but she will know anyway, and she will rag my ass over it too."

"I love you, son, and don't let in any easy ones!"

"I won't, Dad, and I love you too."

"I guess that I should have told him about the bureau, but I didn't. He'll find out soon enough—I guess that is if David comes across with the funds. I wonder when our monster will strike again?"

Back in Atlanta at the FBI offices

"Look, David, I think that I can swing the funds. It will be a bit difficult, but I do have a few debts out there that I can call due!"

"Okay, Marty, I just hope that we're making the right decision. Get the bastard his front money as soon as possible."

"Consider it done! Now what about his request for access to our files, et cetera?"

"Give it to him, but have someone follow behind him to make sure he doesn't abuse his privileges. Has he told you whom he might want to work with him?"

"No, but I can guess."

"Who?"

"I would say 'Lay Down' Sally Evans and most likely Rodney Fischer."

"I can understand, Sally, but why, Rodney? He is retired too, for Christ's sakes."

"Birds of a feather!"

"Shit! I've heard of the A-Team, but this son-of-a-bitch will be the F-Team, fucking for them and fired for me!"

"You can call it off anytime you wish, David!"

"Yeah, but he won't give back the money."

"That's right, when I give him the cash, consider it gone, baby!"

"Look! I'm tired of talking about it. Give him the cash, and tell him to catch this pervert dead or alive."

Marty and Jonathan Met at the Holiday Inn Express in Marietta, Georgia

"Go ahead, Jonathan. Count it out to make sure it's all there."

"Nope! I trust your math. Now what about my team and my access to your files?"

"Name them and you have it!"

"I want Rodney Fischer and Beth Lewinski!"

"I can't believe it, a retired fibbie and a Jewish woman?"

"I just knew that you would want Sally Evans."

"No, I am too old for her sexual energy, and besides that, she doesn't have it anymore. Sally couldn't catch a fish in a bucket with a dip net."

"Rodney, Beth, and I will make a great team. Rodney has great instincts and Beth is the techno nut, and me…well, you know!"

"That's my concern, Jonathan. You're the variable I don't know!"

"I work like hell and I play like hell, but I will have your man by Christmas."

"Don't get too confident, Jonathan. There have been some heavyweights working on this thing for a long time now."

"Who has the lead on the case now, Marty?"

"Blake Whitney has been and will continue to be the official lead—however, he knows that David is making you the unofficial leader and you will be working independent of all of the others in the bureau."

"When do we get started?"

"Whenever you're ready!"

"Okay, I will need access to the files in the morning so that I can see what you have before I bring in Rodney and Beth."

"Do you want David or me to tell them that they're the chosen ones?"

"No! I will drop by Beth's office tomorrow after I spend a few hours in the files and the lab. You guys have got to have something, and I will most definitely need a jumpstart, a direction, or at least a menu of leads. Blake is no dummy—in fact, he should have David's job as far as I am concerned."

CHAPTER 4

Jonathan at the FBI offices in Atlanta

Damn, is this all they have? I thought as I sat for my eighth hour in the Task Force room going over file after file of the same shit. The best definition of an idiot is someone that keeps doing the same thing over and over again thinking that they will somehow get a different result, and believe me, the bureau has its share of them. Case after case after case, they just keep doing the same old thing and coming to the same damnable conclusions. I sold out for far too little money. I could have easily gotten a million dollars up front, if not more now, definitely later. I need to get into the field and speak with some of the grunts—that's where I will get some meaningful answers and some dependable leads. The brass are sitting on their asses too much to solve this case.

"Rodney!"

"Hey, Jonathan, what's up?"

"Just you, big guy, what's shaking?"

"You know there are rumors floating around that you might be getting involved in the serial killing case."

"Which one?"

"Don't be coy with me, son. You know exactly the one that I and everyone else in this country and around the world are talking about these days, the Rag Head Massacres."

"You had better watch how you talk, Rodney. This room is most likely bugged, and you of all people know that! That slang is worse than using the *N* word these days with all the political correctness bullshit. Just prior to leaving the bureau, I got written up for calling a Jap a Jap—can you believe that shit? We're getting our kids killed daily over there in a war *that we won* five years ago, and the deadbeats in Washington are still concerned with the political implications of our every move or statement about those bastards. However, while we're on the subject, what do you know about the case, and why do you have an office here while in retirement? I came back too, just to help on a temporary basis with some of the massive paperwork here—however, I have not been doing anything with respect to this case. I spend about twenty hours a week here transferring file data onto computer files."

"Why do you ask?"

"Well, I might just need some help if—and I did say *if*—I get involved."

"Really, I would love to work with you again, especially on this case. This thing has the entire bureau buffaloed, Jonathan."

"Okay then, you're on. So now let's go see Beth."

"Beth? Beth Lewinski?"

"Yep!"

"Great, let's go. Her office is just down the hall now right next to David's."

"Oh shit, I don't want David to overhear anything, so why don't you go get her and let's have lunch?"

* * *

Jonathan was afraid to even talk in the cafeteria at the bureau, so they walked across to a sandwich shop just down the street.

"Okay, Beth, what's the scoop here? Who's the closest to the case out in the field? Please don't say that it is Blake!"

"Well, Blake has the lead as I am sure that you already know. However, there's a guy out in Memphis that has been on the front line and has viewed every corpse and every crime scene. However, he has not gotten the attention nor the ear of any of the bigwigs at the bureau. I do believe that he is the person that you should visit first."

"What's his name?"

"Mitch Blalock—he is a young guy that reminds me a lot of the stories I hear about you from your younger days in the field. He's a real bloodhound and another hound of sorts too, if you get my drift? Works all day and half of the night and then plays the other half. I don't know when the bastard sleeps."

"Do you like him? Yeah, kind of, I guess. He is cute."

"Can you work with him without mixing business with pleasure?"

"Yes, dammit, and I don't believe that to be a fair question! All I said was that he is cute, not that I wanted to sleep with him."

"Then let's go to Memphis!"

"When?"

"Go home and pack, and I will meet the two of you at Hartsfield at midnight. Our flight departs at two a.m."

"What?"

"You heard me go pack!"

"How did you already know about Mitch?"

"I have my contacts in and out of the bureau. You know I just needed for you to confirm his worthiness and willingness to help us on this case."

That afternoon, David rushes into Marty's office

"Look, Marty. Jonathan is already spending money and doesn't have the first lead."

"You have got to let it go, David, if this thing has any chance in the world of working out with Jonathan."

"Okay, I'll sign the disbursement documents, but I can tell that this is going to get expensive. He had better produce some results early."

"He said that you would have your man by Christmas."

Jonathan, Beth, and Rodney at the Atlanta Airport
boarding a Delta flight to Memphis, Tennessee

"I can't believe we're flying first class, Jonathan."

"I'm not a young guy anymore, Beth. I need some leg room. Besides, it's all on David anyway."

"Tell me about this Mitch guy, Rodney, how does he operate?"

"Sort of quiet but thorough, spends a lot of time on the net, and has developed close ties to some of the groups under surveillance. His expertise is under cover covert surveillance, and he has all the traits of a chameleon."

"Has he spent too much time on this case in public view to work his chameleon magic here?"

"Maybe, however, I do believe that he can help us even if only from afar."

"I think that he has some information, guys, and he has expressed to me at least an interest in getting more involved. He too believes that the road to solving this case runs through one if not several of the so-called Patriot groups."

"That's what scares me, Beth, about this case for those folks have very few enemies among regular citizens, and I believe that it will be extremely difficult to infiltrate them, and even if you get it done, you may be infiltrating the wrong wing or movement. This killer may be a socialite in Washington, DC or a hog farmer in Iowa or some aborted combination of the two. He may be a guide on the Columbia River in the summer and a scuba diver instructor in Hawaii during the winter months or just a traveling salesman pedaling his wares and his insanity."

"So we've ruled out women?"

"Yes, absolutely, positively! This is not their type of crime, and from what I have read so far in the bureau files, I see nothing that would change my thinking. Now I have not ruled out more than one perp nor have I ruled out a conspiracy."

"Why a conspiracy, Jonathan? I don't understand the hate."

"There has always been a certain isolationist-type attitude among the electorate in this country, and in this post 9/11 era, it has only grown."

"Yeah, but there is a big difference here, Jonathan. I haven't heard any of the isolationist or a Patriot advocating the killing of a race of people."

"No, but believe me, Beth, things have changed since 9/11. Even with these guys, they want our borders sealed and sealed now at any cost even if it means that we have to shoot anyone crossing the borders illegally. Listen to your guy O'Reily on Fox. A night doesn't pass that even Bill talks about the need to use our National Guard to protect and to seal our borders."

"But not to shoot people!"

"Then why does he advocate the use of the guard?"

"Okay, I guess that we have to look behind every door."

"When we get to Memphis, we'll go straight to the motel and get a little shut-eye, and then in the morning, I want you and Rodney to meet first with Mitch, and then I will join you guys in the lobby at about ten a.m. for a summary."

CHAPTER 5

Beth, Rodney, and Jonathan meeting with Mitch in the lobby of a small motel near the airport in Memphis

"Tell me about this Beck guy, Beth. Is he for real, and is he competent?"

"Yes, on both accounts, and he has a quick eye for leads and an energy level of a man half his age. However…"

"However what?"

"He is unpredictable and whimsical in his style and manner. He does, however, have a long, storied, and successful background in the bureau. This will be his biggest challenge to date, and right now, he is trying to just gather information from anyone and everyone closely or even remotely involved in this case. That is why he needs to talk with you today."

"Isn't he in retirement?"

"Yes, however, he has agreed to help…or I guess I should say *lead* the investigation on this case."

"Okay, here he comes now with coffee in hand."

"Good morning, guys, and I presume that you are Mr. Blaylock?"

"Just Mitch to you, sir, and it's a pleasure to make your acquaintance this morning."

"Well, let's cut to the chase. Tell me everything you know about this case. Beth, let's all order the breakfast bar so we can keep it simple. Put the tab on my room and add a twenty percent tip."

"Twenty percent?"

"Yes, I didn't stutter, did I?"

"It's like this, Mr. Beck—"

"Drop the *mister* stuff! It's just Jonathan."

"Okay, Jonathan, it's like this. We really don't have much. It's like these people are invisible."

"People? So you think there is more than one perp?"

"Yes, the murders are too organized and cover such a broad range of geography. I also think that they have done this before—at least in some fashion. This is not just some guy out there that just learned to kill or to hate. This may not necessarily be the work of one of the so-called patriot groups. However, I can definitely say that it is the work of a person or persons that in their own mind believe this to be an act of patriotism. Therefore, they have done nothing wrong, so their conscience is clear, and that will make them harder to catch. Another thing that bothers me is that there are few clues and very little evidence available from the crime scenes. The bodies are most often found in some type of water—a lake, river, or stream. I am not sure if this tips us off as to the habits of the perpetrator or perpetrators or of the victims. Again, this is a very complex case, Jonathan, that crosses many time zones, and to tell you the truth, we are not getting much help from the local authorities. It's almost like the local authority, in each case, either doesn't give their case much priority or they just come right out and tell us in private that they don't want the bastards in their community anyway, so maybe this will make them all sell out and move. It is very similar to what I have read about the mentality in the South prior to and during the liberation of the blacks in the South."

"Have we got anyone besides you in the field up close and personal to the killings or is this still a behind the desk case?"

"Ah, there are others. However, I do think that I am your man to take the point!"

"All right, if you had the point, as you call it, what would you suggest that we do first starting today?"

"We have got to get the local police to be more cooperative, and we have got to get some agents on the ground under cover in and around Salt Lake City."

"Why Salt Lake?"

"There seem to be a lot of White Supremacist groups there, and since the bodies have been found in and around water, that may be their way of leaving us a clue. I do believe that in all mass killings the perp or perps always leave clues."

"Always?"

"Yes. Always they want us to know who they are and what they are, and I truly believe that they want and need to be caught."

"Can you take that lead in Salt Lake, or have you already been exposed too much?"

"Yes, I am still able to do undercover work in certain areas and especially in a case like this one that has had very little to no undercover work done to date."

"Great, then you go there in the morning and get a list of the known groups that you think might be capable of perpetrating this type of crime and then get back with me via my cell in a week or so."

"What about my expenses et cetera?"

"I'll call Marty after breakfast and have him send you two credit cards and five thousand dollars in cash via Western Union along with an open-ended two-way first-class plane ticket to Salt Lake. Oh yes, are you armed?"

"Yes, I have an eight-shot Smith, a Glock .9 mm, and my old 357 from my dad."

"Okay, Mitch, here is a phone number of an old contact of mine in Salt Lake. His name is Jim Swenson. He owns a pawnshop on the west side, and he can and will supply you with all the credentials you might need to take on a new identity: social, driver's license, passport, or whatever. He can even supply you with foolproof receipts from any place anywhere in the world to back up any story you might need to tell or defend after you have told it. He will be invaluable to you while you're out there, so please use his services. He is loyal and trustworthy."

"Should I travel with him, Jonathan?"

"No, Beth. I will need you with me!"

"What should I do, Jonathan?"

"Rodney, I need you to go back to Atlanta to coordinate things from the office at first. I still think that we're missing something there or it is being withheld from us and others. The evidence that has been gathered to date is sketchy at best. I think that there is something wrong with the investigative process within the bureau. I realize that David does not seem to have anything to gain by back shelving this case, however there just doesn't seem to be enough progress being made on this thing. You will also need to be there with Marty, making sure that we have no delays in the funding process in the field."

"Beth and I will stay here a couple of days gathering information. I think that we will then go to Springfield to research the site of the last murder."

"Beth, I will also need for you and Rodney to stay in close contact so that you can keep our efforts organized and filed in your laptop as we go. Do all of you have voice mail and text messaging abilities?"

"Yes, and the bureau can track our every movement via satellite through our cells."

"I, ah, don't think that is a good thing! Beth, can you jam that process when needed?"

"Yes!"

"Great then, let's get started."

Jonathan and Beth in Springfield, Missouri

Our first stop in Springfield was a visit to the original Bass Pro Shop location. I had a great time, and Beth was bored, as I should have expected. After about an hour, Beth came to me with a copy of the local paper. "Look, Jonathan, you have to go four pages in before you see anything about the recent murder, and then it's only three paragraphs saying a whole lot about nothing."

"Let's pay a visit to the local sheriff's office to see what they may have on the case."

On the way to the sheriff's office, my mind began the process of profiling the killer or killers—just call it instinct, or the thoughts of a borderline criminal. That's right—all of us on the law enforcement side are just that, borderline criminals. There's a fine line between us and the perps. The thoughts of the perp or perps in a case like this must be that of a patriot. Internally, he is asking himself, *Why? Why are these bastards here in the first place? Why? Why? Why?* That has always been the underlying question when it comes to modern-day immigrants, and it becomes magnified when we as a nation go to war with their homeland and with their basic philosophy of life. 9/11 magnified this ideological difference even more as we as a nation look back at our dead. Most of the everyday citizens in this country still wonder why. Why are we fighting this war with restrictions? Do we not remember Vietnam?"

"Jonathan!"

"Yes?"

"Well, we're here!"

"Okay, let's go in and see what we can gather, if anything, about this latest murder."

My first question to Sheriff Hutchinson was, "How many detectives have you assigned to this case?" As expected, my question was answered with a bunch of mumbo jumbo and with no specific answer. According to the sheriff, everyone on his staff was involved, which meant that in reality, no one was specifically involved. We spent the better part of an hour chatting with Mr. Hutchinson but gathered very little useful information. It was clear, however, that this case was not getting nor was it going to get top priority from his detectives. On the way out, I stopped to flirt a minute with his secretary who was quite busty and was clad in a very tight and short mini skirt with a lot of bright makeup, just my kind of gal. She informed me that the sheriff's brother had been killed in Vietnam and that he had lost a grandson in Iraq. That pretty much explained to me his lackadaisical approach to this case.

Beth listened and watched with a critical eye as I talked to the lady about how beautiful she was and about how lucky the sheriff was to have her in his employment.

She quickly informed me to feel welcome to call her any time I needed to get an update on their investigation. I then responded with a request for her name and phone number. Her name was Suzy, and she not only gave me her office number but also her cell. As Beth and

I departed, Beth said, "You know, sometimes you make me sick with all of that bullshit!"

I just laughed and got into the car without making any further comment.

CHAPTER 6

Back in Atlanta at the FBI office

"David, Rodney would like to meet with us later this afternoon if at all possible?"

"Have they got a break in the case?"

"I don't think so. However, I do think that he needs to ask us a few insider questions."

"Okay, let's meet in the south conference room at 3:00 p.m. sharp."

"Great!"

South conference room, 3:02 p.m.

"Have you got something for us, Rodney?"

"Not really. Just a few questions. I am concerned over the lack of information available here at the bureau concerning these murders! Do we just not have much, or am I missing something?"

"I have told everyone in records and everyone that is and that has been associated with this case to give you full cooperation and access."

"I think that I have seen everything available and it just isn't very complete. Is that right, Marty?"

"I think so, Rodney. However, I will review with you what you have and then follow up to see if we have missed something."

"Blake Whitney has been in charge of this thing from the get-go, right?"

"Yes."

"Well, I know him to be good, efficient, and thorough! There has to be more here!"

"Well, Blake is still the official lead on this case. Why don't you guys get together and compare notes and files?"

"Good idea. When can he be available?"

"Anytime. What about tomorrow, afternoon?"

"That works."

Beth took off a few days to go spend with her mother, so I decided to spend some time analyzing what we had and then making a few phone calls to Rodney and to Mitch. I then started to make my analysis as I drove back to Memphis. War does funny things in the minds and the hearts of men. The sheriff's lack of concern was of really no surprise. I think back to the change within the populace of this country during the depths of the depression of the Vietnam War. Basic patriotism didn't change; however, the support for the war eroded tremendously during the last few years as the body count got larger with no sign of victory in sight. Victory—now that's another vague term in the context of the wars of today. We no longer have surrenders, nor do we see any spoils of a so-called victory. In fact, the so-called losers often get the spoils. I noticed just last week that my new Rockport shoes were made in Vietnam, and I have been told that a lot of furniture is even manufactured there today. Just the other day, I read where we were prosecuting a man for selling some type of trade secret to China. However, our own government sells them weapons, and over 80 percent of the items on Walmart's shelves come from there. To the average Joe, that just doesn't make any sense; therefore, he has a problem understanding why we are waging war against an enemy on one front and then supporting and protecting them on another. Tracking this killer or killers will be an enormous task since most of us have most likely thought of doing the same thing ourselves. We just don't look at people of Middle Eastern decent today in the same way as we did prior to 9/11—that is the populace I am speaking of. Our enemy does not wear uniforms today, so their style of dress, their accent, and the color of their skin become a mark or uniform, if you will, in our minds. Is this type of thinking discrimination or is it not? I guess that this is a gray area again, further complicating our ability to distinguish between the known enemy we see carrying guns and killing our people on the TV news shows and that of the same-looking character walking down our streets, shopping in our stores, and being educated in our schools and taking over our jobs and our professions. The thinking can become "If it looks like a duck, walks like a duck, and quacks like a duck, then chances are it is a duck."

"Rodney?"

"Yes!"

"What have we got there?"

"Not much yet, Jonathan. The information is thin, and I cannot really find any sign of how this thing has gotten much more attention here than anywhere else. I do believe, however, that something is being held back. I just can't decide what it is nor who might not be forth coming at this time. It would seem to me that no one here could benefit from not wanting this killer found as soon as possible. I know that David's job is on the line for sure. I have discovered a ballistics file on the weapon that is being used in most, if not all, of the killings."

"Ballistics? I didn't realize that they were being shot?"

"Yes, that is in all of the cases where the body had not decomposed too much before being found, and of course, you already know that some of the bodies had been decapitated with no visible wound being found. I think that we can assume from what information we have that they too must have been shot since the others were. Ballistics indicate a small caliber rifle, most likely a .22-caliber or maybe even a .25-caliber, so if and when we get any suspects, we can try to run a ballistics match on any and all rifles and pistols of those calibers that they may have in their possession, own, or have access to in their lives. Of course, ballistics is of no use if we have no suspects or suspect weapons."

"Have you spent any time with Blake?"

"Yes, and even though I know him to be a good man, he just doesn't seem to have the data that he should have. That said, he does seem to be more interested now and is doing everything that I ask of him and doesn't seem to have any hidden agendas."

"Okay, keep up the work and let me know if you get anything new. I think that I will get up with Mitch to see what he is up to in Salt Lake."

Jonathan, now in Memphis, Tennessee

Memphis is not a bad town to spend a day or two in a motel. For a single man, old or young, the barbecue is good, and I have always loved the blues-styled music, especially that of the deep South. Being a great fan of Elvis, whose music was so dramatically influenced by the blues, I think, that is why he chose to call Memphis home instead of the place of his birth, Tupelo, Mississippi. I decided to call a lady detective friend of mine to ask her out for dinner. I have not seen nor heard from her since my retirement and her divorce.

Mary Ellen was standing at the door of her fancy downtown suite when I arrived thirty minutes late as usual. She is a strikingly beautiful woman for fifty-two years of age. Her belly protrudes a little now, but that's all right with me. I like a woman with a little meat on her; you don't fall off as easily.

We ate at a small BBQ place on Beal Street that is owned by the son of an old high school friend of mine, and it is the only one in the area with a true Southern flair with sweet sauce, Brunswick stew, and crackling cornbread. Mary Ellen was more in the mood for wine; however, she was willing to settle for beer, at least for the meal. She is a classy attorney during the day with high-buttoned blouses and below-the-knee business suits who loves three-martini lunches; however, in the evening hours and with the right guy, she is willing to show a bit of her redneck roots. On this evening, I think that we both were more interested in getting back to her place for a little R and R and, yes of course, "S."

The next morning, Mary Ellen was more relaxed than I had seen her in years. She even called her secretary to inform her that she would not be in until later at an undetermined time. Mary Ellen even talked about retirement and of her desire to spend some time in the near future traveling around the country and possibly the world. I guess that being a divorced empty nester just isn't very entertaining. I then began to tell her about my new venture at the bureau.

"Now, Jonathan Beck, you told me just last year that you would never ever go back to the bureau."

"Well, I guess that the old saying is true: 'Never say never'!"

"Why the sudden change of mind?"

"I guess that it is mostly the money and a little bit of a challenge, and if I would admit it, I was getting bored."

"You don't need the money!"

"Well, things are not always as they seem, and the kids could use some more help from my end with college and all. Their mother did call me a lot for help, however, with me never returning her calls, she has finally given up on me doing anything other than directly with the children. It would be nice to surprise them all with a nice deposit to their bank accounts when this thing is said and done."

"Have you got any leads?"

"Not really, with a case like this, everyone is a suspect."

"Huh!"

"You tell me one person in this country today that cares anything about anyone in the Middle East after 9/11."

"You can't mean that you approve of the killing of innocent people in this country just because of their heritage?"

"I did not say that. However, I cannot say that I have any love for them either. The ones who live in this country today do very little to endear themselves to the average every day Joe either. A friend of mind that owns a furniture store in Atlanta says that he hates for anyone from the Middle East to shop in his store. He says that they are arrogant, smart-ass cheapskates that are always saying, 'What's my price?' I am telling you that the government's continued support for the immigration of these people with government-sponsored education programs and financial aid to their start-up businesses and so on is not helping. Couple those facts with our political handling of the so-called 'war on terror' after 9/11 and you are creating a menu for trouble within our border. I still say that we will get another attack on our soil soon, and it will most likely be bigger and badder."

"What is your plan for catching these creeps?"

"I have a good team put together, and they are doing most of the grunt work for me, but with that said, we have got to first infiltrate some of the so-called hate groups. After that, we will just have to follow our noses and also keep looking in our own backyard at the bureau for more leads and info. It is still very strange to me that there isn't any more information on file there, and I am not sure what that means if anything. I do know that I cannot leave out the possibility of FBI and/or CIA involvement."

"What?"

"That's right—during my twenty-some odd years in the bureau, I saw some very strange and confusing happenings. Don't forget Oliver North and the CIA involvement in the Latin American countries prior, during and after the Reagan administration, and the Bay of Pigs incident in Cuba during the fifties, and our CIA direct involvement in the removal of Batista and the empowerment of our supposedly friend Castro."

"Yeah, that worked out just great, didn't it?"

"Just my point. It may not seem logical—possible FBI or CIA involvement in this thing. However, if you know anything about American and world history, you just can't rule it totally out of the realm of possibility."

"I can tell you a story about Watergate and of a possible China connection that has never hit the news media to this day."

"I tell you what, Jonathan—let's catch breakfast and then go back to my place and you can do just that."

"What about your obligations at the office?"

"Fuck'um, I need and deserve a break."

"Waffle House okay?"

"Yeah, let's go there. I won't have to dress. I can go in my sweats."

Back at Mary Ellen's place

"Hey, do you know what a *morner* is, Mary Ellen?"

"I shouldn't say this, but what is a morner?"

"It's the same thing as a nooner but sooner!"

"Okay, you got your morner, so there will be no nooner. Now get on with your story."

"Okay, but pour us a drink first. I like to drink in the mornings—it just jump-starts your day."

There was a time back during the happy days of my marriage that I did some public service work on my own at the Union Mission. My wife and I helped over five families a year get into government housing and off the streets. The homeless has always had a place in my heart for I have always felt that except by the grace of God, it could have been me several times in my life.

We met all types of folks from all walks of life, including all the professions from lawyers, to educators and even doctors, all of which were either singularly homeless, having been ostracized by their families or homeless with their families. Bad luck, illness, alcoholism, or business failures do not discriminate; they hit people in all walks of life, in all neighborhoods, and in all stages of life. One particular individual we met was a doctor named Gary Monroe and his son Junior, a brilliant guy with impeccable credentials. His story doesn't fit into any of the aforementioned categories; in fact, it stands in and of itself even to this day.

His son spoke fluent Portuguese and absolutely no English when I first made his acquaintance. He was a very hyperactive child of some seven years of age at the time. However, he was very respectful of me and his dad. At first, I asked no questions. I just tried to help them get off the streets and into some type of housing. Finally, we found a very nice apartment, and I gathered furniture and toys from around the community so that they could get back to a normal life. Over many weeks, Gary and I developed a sort of friendship, and both of us started to share personal stores and personal experiences in our lives; however, I always kept the fact that I was employed by the bureau a secret. He was not the first nor the last to never really know of my vocation. For some reason, the three capital letters FBI had a tendency to spook people. Most often, if people in my casual life insisted on knowing, I would just say that I was a consultant and then come up with some romantic story always emphasizing how smart I was. This tended to intimidate them, and very quickly, they would change the subject, letting me off the hook.

One day, right out of the blue, while the two of us were enjoying a cup of coffee, Dr. Monroe pulled out a set of x-rays out of his side table and showed me a square-shaped object in his skull just behind his eyes.

"What is that?" I asked, and then Dr. Monroe started to explain.

He first just said that it had been planted there in Canada after he had been kidnapped by what he thought was the Canadian government; however, he later discovered that it was a far more covert operation than that. Of course, I just sat there for what seemed like forever in a daze, then I asked why.

"Do you want to know the entire story?" Gary asked, and of course, I said yes.

"Well, it all began when I became employed by some of the guys who later became involved in the Watergate mess. I traveled a lot between Washington DC and China in those days delivering packages from our government to theirs. On one of my trips, I met the eldest daughter of Mao Tse Tung, and after many trips there, we fell in love—mistake number two, I guess. The first one was becoming employed by our government and not really knowing what I was doing. All I really knew was that it paid well and foreign leaders treated me like royalty. I even slept with her in the dictator's mansion on several occasions before we wed. She was a very passionate woman in bed and she loved Americans, so I was a prize catch—or so I thought. Later, she and I found out that I wasn't what she nor I thought I was. To this day, I really don't know why I did some of the things our government asked me to do except for youthful ignorance and the intrigue. I thought that I was a James Bond of sorts, I guess. Now you must remember this was in the heyday of the Nixon years prior and during his historic trip to China, a trip which I almost exclusively paved the way for, behind the scenes of course. It was not until years later that I realized why I was never a part of any of the public displays or celebrations in Washington or in China. At the time, it really did not seem important. I was having a ball, spending unlimited rolls of cash, sleeping with the dictator's daughter and anyone else I desired. I was on top of the world—or so I thought.

"I can't remember the date, but it was just days prior to the Watergate break in that I received a call from Washington wanting me to go that very hour to China and to personally deliver a package to Mao Tse Tung. I reported directly to Charles Colson, picked up the package and fifty thousand in cash and travelers' checks, along with my Delta Airlines tickets to China. I had no difficulty moving that quickly for I had a high-security government passport, and almost everyone at the airlines knew me by my first name. Upon my arrival at the dictator's mansion, I learned of the fact that his daughter was pregnant with my child so a wedding took place immediately. It was either that or my head. I loved her deeply, so it was a blessing, I thought, and not a problem. Little did I know at the time that I would never see my child born nor my wife again. The wedding was fabulous, and even President Nixon sent over some tenth-tier dignitary. Less than a week later, however, the world was shocked by the news of the Watergate ordeal, and I was called backed to Washington immediately.

"I was ready to step up and defend my country and my president for in my mind he had performed miracles abroad and was second to none in the new world order. Nixon was a genius on the political and foreign fronts. He held the world in his hands and had helped to establish this new world order and I loved him dearly. I was energized and excited when I arrived in Washington. Just like a Marine in uniform, I was ready for the fight to defend my president. However, as I departed my flight, five guys whom I had never met shuffled me off the plane and into a limo and drove me to New York City with no explanation as to what was happening. In New York, they hustled me through Laguadia onto a private jet and gave me a new passport, a new driver's license, and a social security card. The same five goons flew first class with me in the middle of them. I did not and could not have any contact with anyone other than these five nameless and speechless goons. I kept waiting for some sensible explanation, but it never came. Finally, we arrived in Miami and were again greeted by four or five total strangers. The others handed me off to them like a baton in a marathon race, and then they were gone. At this point, I was at my wits' end and mad, so I began to object and even punched the smaller guy in this new group of goons. He immediately pulled a gun and stuck it halfway down my throat before a heavy-set Latin American-looking dude pulled him away. I then grabbed him and demanded an explanation of what was going on or I was going to cause even a bigger scene in front of God and everyone.

"He then said, 'Let's go to my place and I will explain.'

"Not really having a good alternative at this point, I agreed and crawled into another limo. This one, however, was better equipped than the other, with a bar, llama fur floor mats, and even a marijuana cigarette to help calm my nerves. *Ah ha*, I thought, *things are starting to look up for me*, especially when we arrived at this huge mansion on some beach with scantily clad beauties everywhere and one hanging onto my arm as we entered. She immediately escorted me poolside and poured me my favorite drink, scotch, straight up.

"A short time later, a Kojac-looking fellow came over pulled up a chair and started calling me by the name you know me as now, Dr. Gary Monroe, and without explanation informed me that I was now in an official witness protection program and that I would be flown out to Idaho sometime tomorrow. I was also informed that all of my past had been erased, and as far as anyone would ever know, I had never existed on this planet as Dr. Wesley Adams. I protested greatly at first and immediately informed them that I had a wife back in China with a child and that I was a very important American diplomat. Over the next several hours, he proved to me that in fact, except to me, I was no more. He even had me call my wife, and she denied knowing me and spoke wonderfully of her husband, David Niles of San Francisco, and of her soon-to-be-born child and that I had evidently had some time of dream or had been in a coma or had experienced some type of amnesia.

"In the span of twenty-four hours, I had been transformed into a person that even I did not know.

"American Falls, Idaho, is a nice town but small in comparison to the cities that had been accustomed to living in as Dr. Adams. I was given the title to a nice farmhouse on one hundred acres. Idaho does not have a lot of water. However, I had a nice stream. The next five years went by rapidly, and I tried not to read the papers very often. I was tickled shitless when I discovered that old Chucky boy had gone to the pen. I almost forgot that the government had set me up in a practice in American Falls. It was a family practice fully equipped and with a local bank balance of $200,000. It did not take me long to get bored with that, so I added acupuncture and massage therapy to my bag of tricks. I had learned the science and art of acupuncture from the great *shu shi wama* in China. I also stocked and sold a wide variety of health foods and healing herbs. That part of my practice really began to grow. However, it did draw a queer eye from the AMA from time to time. My massage therapist was a wonderful girl, some fifteen years my junior, and we eventually fell in love. She was a graduate of the University of Nebraska and a truly good person. Oh yes, Jonathan, I almost forgot to tell you I was also ordered by the goons to never take on a life partner nor to marry. At first, my government visitors were not too concerned about our relationship, but as the talk of a possible marriage surfaced, panic set in quickly.

"It was on a Friday, I do believe, that after my last patient left, I went to lock the doors when in walked the famous fivesome along with Kojac. He said that I was to announce that I was going on a two-week vacation to close my practice for that period and to fire Kathy, my massage therapist and new love. I told them to go to hell, pulled out a double-barrel shotgun, and ordered them off my property. In a matter of weeks, my life was again in shambles. My mother died of a sudden and unexpected illness, and Kathy was killed in a head-on accident with an eighteen-wheeler caused by brake failure on her vehicle. Two of my patients had filed suit against me for medical malpractice, and the state was starting to take action to have my license revoked.

"'Why?' I asked. I just could not understand why. Of course the government jerks would also show up at the funerals with their condolences and each and every time advise me that I needed a vacation. Kojac said that if I did, my life would get better if I just cooperated and got a little rest. It was about this time that I decided that they were right, except one little minor detail. I wanted to have my vacation and R&R without escorts.

"I had met a guy in China from England that was a missionary in South America and lived with the natives on the Amazon River. I contacted him via the English consulate and immediately made plans to join him. He was very anti-government and had no problem with keeping all of this a secret. I emptied my bank account that had built up to nearly a half-million dollars, took on an assumed name, got a fake passport, and booked a flight to Lima, Peru. There I met up with William Tate. We spent the night in Lima and then took a small plan to Pacallpa and then scared the hell out of a bunch of wild chickens when we landed in this pasture or field. From there, we traveled on this so-called road to a dense forest along the shore of the Amazon somewhere between Inqitos and Manaus. At that point, my life took another complete and total metamorphosis, but life was sweet in a weird sort of way—no government, no goons, and no Dr. Gary Monroe. My latest passport read 'Levy Strause.' All right, I know that is not original, but give me a break. If you have nine lives like a cat, it ain't easy coming up with names. I spent the next fifteen years there living off the land and water. I thought that maybe the government was not concerned with me anymore, so I just preached to the natives, got really into Christianity, and met an absolutely wonderful girl from Portugal. Life was great.

"You know, Jonathan, I can't really put everything in chronological order or even remember the number of years or even the year anything happened in that part of the world. Time just stands still.

"However, I eventually met up with a French guy from Canada. I can't even remember his name now. And after a year or so, I got permission from Madeira, Junior's mother, to travel to Canada with Bernard. Yeah, that's his name, Bernard. I do not know why I wanted to go. I guess that I just needed to see civilization again for at least a month or so. Madeira finally became apprehensive of us leaving, so she decided to travel with us to Canada.

"Montreal is a great city, and Bernard's folks were great, but the homes there are small so Madeira, Junior, and I got a small temporary furnished apartment of our own on a weekly rental basis.

"We were just about to make plans to go back to South America when Madeira, Junior, and I were traveling on a toll road in the direction of the old world's fair site from 1967 when a police siren sounded behind us and then the butterflies came back as my blood pressure rose and my heart rate spiked. It couldn't be, I thought, no way I must have been speeding or something. I tried to settle down as I pulled over. However, it was obvious that I was nervous and scared. This made the cop nervous and suspicious, so he started to check all our credentials. That is when everything started to unravel again in my life. Madeira didn't speak much English, and the whites—as she called them—always scared her anyway, so she was a basket case and was holding onto Junior with dear life.

"To make a long story short, we were held on improper credentials, and I was separated from Junior and Madeira. Several days went by without any of us being booked, and I was afraid to object too vociferously, so I just waited for it all to work out. Then one day, a doctor came in and wanted to draw some blood from me again. I did not like the idea. However, I did not want to raise any red flags, so I went to a clinic with him.

"That was the last thing I knew until I awoke abandoned on the side of a highway in the middle of Montana with no money, no clothes, and yes, no Madeira and no Junior. Bernard never came to see us, and to this day, I do not know where he went. I tried the phone number I had for him, and it was not his anymore, and the people there now speak only French and have never heard of a Bernard."

"Damn, Gary, that is some story!"

"Oh, I am not finished yet. It gets even better—or worse, depending on your perspective.

"I was now homeless in Montana with no money, no cell phone, and of course, no food. Again, I took on an assumed name and started to pick up odd jobs around for cash. It was now my guess that Madeira and Junior had been deported or killed. I could not account for nearly a week in time, so anything was possible, and I was suffering from severe headaches. It took me about a month of bumming around to get enough money together so that I could travel south to

Miami and then eventually back to the Amazon basin. It was there that I discovered that Maderia and Junior had been deported and were living in the village, and both of them had presumed that I had been killed by the CIA or the FBI.

"My headaches continued and actually got worse over time. The local doctors could not isolate a cause, so we all just thought that I had developed migraines. Maderia developed some sort of sickness, and again, the local doctors could not determine what it was, and she refused to return to the United States for treatment after my many requests. One night, she went to sleep not feeling well and just never woke up. This devastated Junior, and I miss her to this day. However, it prompted us to return stateside to try to determine what happened to us in Canada. I was convinced now that her death and my head-aches were related to our capture and the missing week in Canada.

"We first arrived back in Miami and then traveled to Washington, DC. I was more brazen on this trip and went straight to the veter-ans' hospital there about my headaches. I almost forgot to inform you that I am also a decorated Vietnam War veteran, and that in part helped to get me the opportunity to work for President Nixon. The doctors there confirmed that there was an implant. However, they had no idea of its type or origin. One of the doctors said that it appeared to be similar to a type of implant being experimented within Europe to help blind people regain a portion of their vision. They all then started to ask me questions about my time in China and if I had had any vision problems in those days. I wasn't buy-ing their make-believe ignorance nor their story about the studies in Europe. It just seemed to me that as soon as they made their ID of the implant, they immediately began to fabricate an explanation. I was released quickly with no further appointments, and when I asked about having it removed, they advised me to contact the doctors that had inserted the implant. Of course, I then went off on them about the fact that I had no idea and that I believed that it had been placed their after I had been kidnapped in Canada and that I believed that there had been some type of involvement by the CIA or the FBI or possibly both. When I tried to tell them the story that I am telling you now, they then referred me to psychiatric.

"I then applied for some type of social financial aid so Junior and I could eat and have a place to sleep to no avail. It was after that when I decided to travel back to Miami. However, I was broke and now considered by the VA to most likely be insane, so I hitched a ride for Junior and me with a trucker heading south, and that is how we ended up in Knoxville, Tennessee. I met you and your family, and the rest is now history, I guess, except for the fact that I still do not know what this thing is that you can plainly see on my x-rays."

"Well, Jonathan, that is as far-fetched a story as I have ever heard," replied Mary Ellen, "without it coming from a novel. You didn't give this story any real credence, did you? After all, this guy is most likely a psycho and made the whole thing up."

"Maybe, but maybe not. You see, I had a friend of mine with the sheriff's department in Knoxville make a contact with the FBI office there with no direct connection to me, and he had them check out this Dr. Monroe."

"And?"

"About a week later, I went to visit the good doctor and Junior, only to find the apartment that I had arranged for them and all the furniture and all of Junior's toys in place, however, there was no doctor nor no Junior."

"What happened?"

"I don't know—they just vanished from the face of the earth and have never been seen nor heard from again."

"Don't you guess that they just up and hitched another ride to another town to panhandle off of some other kindhearted folks like you and your family."

"Maybe, however, it was strange in that they left everything— and by everything I mean everything, except for their persons—and Gary's medical files they were all gone too. Another thing—this was in the middle of the winter with below-freezing temps and they didn't even take a jacket or a change of clothes."

"Did you follow up any after that?"

"For a while, however, I then got too involved with assignments they too seemed to have picked up about that time as if the bureau was trying to occupy my time. I was also having trouble at home about that same time so I gradually just stuck the whole thing in the back of my mind and went on with my life. From time to time after that, I would do some computer searches, however, I never did get a line on either one of them."

"What do you think happened?"

"I really don't know. However, the possibilities are scary if you think about them very much."

"Do you think this Dr. Monroe was lying?"

"I don't know that either. However, I do believe that he believed what he was telling was the truth, and I believe that he would have passed a lie detector test."

"Guess?"

"I think that there is a good possibility that he was telling the truth and that he had a more detailing account of Watergate and of the story behind the story of Nixon's China connections. Just think about our relations today with China—hell, they control our domestic and foreign policy because of our dependence on them for cheap labor and for cheap products. This country would go into a depression if China got mad and just stopped the container flow to Walmart alone."

"So what makes you think of a possible CIA/FBI connection to the murders?"

"Oh, I don't think that there is…however, it is not out of the realm of possibility."

"This thing in the Middle East could eventually involve China, and who knows what else is out there as a possibility? You do remember the now-proven CIA involvement with mind control in the fifties and early sixties, and speaking of the CIA and the sixties, you do know who invented LDS?"

"Tiny Tim?"

"No, it was the CIA!"

"Really?"

"I am damn glad that I am in law and not your line of work, and to think that the average Joe thinks that my profession is crooked."

"If you study that era in detail, you will find that the CIA was involved with radiation experiments in Oak Ridge on human guinea pigs, many class-action and individual lawsuits are still pending in the courts on some of those experiments by surviving relatives based on the recent studies and findings by Vanderbilt University."

"The CIA was also implicated in the deaths of John and Bobby Kennedy and Martin Luther King."

"Oh well, Jonathan, it sounds farfetched to me. However, you are the FBI guy."

CHAPTER 7

Mitch in Salt Lake talking with a patriot group leader

"Look, I need to be involved in something so that I can vent the frustrations that I have for all foreigners in this country. I really did not realize just how much of an isolationist that I had become until many things started to come to me in the years following 9/11. I firmly believe that if something is not done quickly, then we are going to lose our country to the United Nations, or even worse, we could lose it at the ballot box."

"I know that you have been attending our meetings here in Salt Lake for a while now, however, we still don't know enough about you to let you into our entry circle. There is stuff going on out there today that we are involved in either directly or indirectly to try to stop this madness and to try to save our country for the white Anglo-Saxon Americans, the heritage of which founded this country, and to tell you the truth, we need more people like you involved."

"Hey, I have sources and resources at my disposal. You just tell me when and where—I have the cash."

(Of course, I was speaking of the monies that I hoped that Jonathan could get to me via David. I had spent weeks trying to get close to the guys; however, I was not getting very far until I started to mention the magic word *cash*!)

"Let me give it some more thought and I will let you know something after next Thursday when our inner sanctum convenes again."

Back in Memphis, Jonathan talking with Mary Ellen

"Jonathan!"

"Yes!"

"Mitch here!"

"How goes it?"

"Okay, I think that I am getting closer to making some inroads out here. However, it's tough all of these folks are so paranoid of strangers. I tell you something else—I think that we have more murders on our hands than we realize. I have picked up accounts of at least a dozen murders of Islamic Americans just here in Salt Lake alone since 9/11. Now they don't fit our research MO of our supposed serial killer. However, they are still dead."

"Don't get sidetracked. We have got to stick to our plan, and we have got to get someone arrested soon."

"Jonathan, you had better start to prep Marty and David now because this thing ain't going to get done by Christmas—at least not by Christmas of this year."

"Okay, I'll deal with them. Get to some specifics on how I need to help you move quicker."

"Next week, I may be able to get in with what I think is a group that is most likely not involved with the murders, but through them, I might be able to find out if this thing is actually an organized and orchestrated effort on a broad scale. I need to obtain another cell phone—one issued through maybe a group in upstate New York or something so that I can show them some past and current involvement. My parents are from that area, and I think that Beth has some connections with a rat or two up there so it should be believable and doable. In short, I need a trail of involvement and of attachment and commitment to a cause."

"Consider it done. I will get with Beth as soon as we hang up, and I will call you back tomorrow. After that, I will be out of touch for a while."

"Oh damn, I almost forgot I will need a sizable amount of cash that seems to speak louder than words with these guys."

"I will instruct Marty to take care of that so you can contact him directly."

Mary then asked as she looked at Jonathan, "What was that call about?"

"I have got to leave you now and get back to my FBI work."

"Okay, just give me call anytime that you are going to travel through this part of the world."

"I will, hun. You take care now."

The following Thursday just after midnight

"You know, we do need some more support from guys like you. However, we must be very careful these days. We have already found over ten government informants in our midst since 9/11. You must also understand that we have had nothing to do with any of the malicious actions taken by some groups against Arab-Americans or any other Middle Eastern race since 9/11. We would love to deport all of the Rag Heads and the Mexicans too. However, violence is just not our style. Our numbers are down since the millennium debacle. Even the militias have decreased drastically over the past six years. This has decreased our cash flow tremendously. However, the Patriot movement is alive and well. Our main effort now is to try to get as many Patriot sympathizers elected to political office as possible and to set up our own governments when and where we can."

"Oh yes, Mitch. It just came across the wire about twenty minutes ago that another Muslim had been slain and the body was found in or near a river on the Canadian border."

"Damn!

"Uh!"

"Auuh! It's just that I can't seem to be at the right place and at the right time."

"You're for real about getting involved!"

"It's them or us, I tell you, and our government will not address this phenomenon."

"Look, Mitch, I think that you might be a little too radical for our cause here. However, I can recommend you to a group in

Washington state near Whatcom County. They're a hybrid KKK group with militia-type arms and leadership."

"I don't know. That type of group is too visible, don't you think, and I am not going to wear a white robe."

"They're little different today in their approach and leadership, and the robes are only worn in private, and I don't know of them burning any crosses of late either. Their leader, Robert Pierre is more like that David guy down in Louisiana that became a senator. He is very polished and says all the right things. However, the hatred of blacks, Jews, and any and all modern-day immigrants, especially those of non-Caucasian descent, has not changed."

"From your brief description, it doesn't seem to me like they are any more assertive than you guys."

"Not directly. However, I know for a fact that they have killed before."

"Really?"

"Yes, but that is all that I can say right now."

"Okay!"

"How was this latest Muslim killed?"

"Same as the others, I think? Let's try to find something out about it?"

"Sure, no problem. I will call the sheriff he is an active member of our group and a true White Supremist at heart."

Back at the FBI offices in Atlanta

"I have called you guys in because Jonathan is missing again!"

"Look, David, what is strange about that? Jonathan has gone on his little binges for years, and that in part led to his divorce…even though he will tell another story."

"Yes, I know, Beth. However, why would he do it now? We are several months into this thing and have nothing, at least to my knowledge."

"I have known and worked with Jonathan for years, and I can tell you that he is an equal-opportunity offender. That said, however, he is also the best in the business, but he does come with a price and some baggage, and all of us knew this going in, including you, David."

"I know, Rodney. Sometimes I wish that I had not told Marty to get him for this."

"I still believe that he is *your* best bet in getting this thing solved through your office!"

"That is exactly why I got him, Rodney. It's just at times I can't sleep knowing that my future is in his hands."

"Have any of you heard from Mitch?"

"Yes, I wired him some cash this week, and by the way, he is undercover as Allen Herrick."

"So is he making any progress in Salt Lake?"

"Well...he is actually in Washington State now, embedded in some Neo-Nazi/KKK hybrid."

"What?"

"I actually think that he is getting somewhere out there and has actually become knowledgeable of more murders, murders that neither law enforcement nor the press have linked to our serial killer."

"Great, all that is going to do is muddy up the waters and make it more difficult to get to some kind of closure here real or not."

"Jonathan has instructed him not to get off track and for him to do just that."

"I guess that is all I have for now. However, when any of you hear from our Johnnie Walker Red boy, have the son of a bitch give me a call immediately."

A few hours later in Beth's office

"Have you heard from Jonathan?"

"No, Rodney, I haven't."

"I have!"

"Why didn't you tell David it might help to keep Jonathan off the hot seat and the rest of us employed?"

"I don't think so. You see, Jonathan is leading all of us in one direction, and he is going in two directions."

"I don't understand."

"He still thinks that the CIA and/or the bureau are involved."

"Really?"

"He has discovered that the FBI, no less, are using the Patriot Act to organize a covert operation to build support for the war in the Middle East and to create chaos at home."

"That doesn't make much sense to me. I don't see what we have to gain or the administration."

"I am not sure myself. However, it wouldn't be the first foolish blunder for this administration or any other for that matter. Another thing—did you not find it strange that David didn't mention the latest killing to us in the meeting?"

"It hadn't really crossed my mind, but it does seem a little weird. However, I am not ready to make the leap to concluding that means FBI involvement here."

"I just don't know at this point."

"Look, Rodney, we had better abandon this type of thinking and get to the task at hand."

"Okay, I agree!"

Jonathan on some highway near the Pacific Northwest answering a call from Mitch

"Ah, Mitch…or, ah…is it, Allen? How goes it?"

"Okay, Jonathan, where have you been?"

"I have been doing a lot of thinking and a little fishing up north. What have you got?"

"Not a lot. There is, however, a nationwide web of Neo-Nazi/ Patriot/militia/White Supremist groups that are overtly or covertly connected operating within our communities and our governments that I have discovered, and I believe somewhere within this network lies our answer. The problem is it may very well be nearly, if not totally impossible to isolate an individual killer. One of these groups, the Michigan Militia, has some type of connection to the White House and even helped or offered to help during the immediate days following 9/11…however, I don't believe them to be involved with this thing."

"You get me to the organization responsible or even seemingly responsible for this, and I will find a way to first hang the blame and then the noose on an individual just like we did with the child killer in Atlanta in the eighties. We have got to have closure, real or unreal, to this thing now just as we did then."

"This web is coast to coast, Jonathan, and intertwined in and out of society and government."

"Just get us to a group or groups of groups that could be responsible and that has killed in the past, and then I will find a pervert that has a believable past and possible connection and fry their ass. All I need is one person that has killed or tried to kill even and remotely resembles the MO of our perp the government, the press, and the public are ready to believe anything at this point all we need to do is give them a reason."

Back at the FBI offices in Atlanta

"Rodney!"

"Yes, Jonathan, what's up? I won't even ask where you have been."

"Good, I have an assignment for you."

"Great, I am getting cabin fever stuck in this damn building."

"Well, what I need for you to do is to start a computer database on all the victims to date, logging all of their personal and business data, including but not limited to any or all trips that may they have taken in the year prior to their death, in and out of the country. I also need their personal and business banking information, including but not limited to any and all of their transfers for money in and out of the country. Get with Western Union and all the other money transfer specialists in their regions of the country to see if any of them have moved funds through their networks in the last five years and to where and to whom did this money transfer. Once you have all this data entered in a database, let me know and I will then give you additional instructions. Oh yes, I also need for you to get with David and tell him that you need to access the public library files of each of the victims. I need to know what books they have been reading during the last year of their lives."

"Jonathan, I don't think that we have the legal authority to do that."

"Hey, if I didn't know that this information could be obtained, I would not ask for it!"

"Jonathan, the Patriot Act does not allow us to access that type of personal data without due process."

"Look, stop trying to play lawyer. We have had the public libraries all over the country get this information for us years prior to the stupid Patriot Act. The FBI knows every time some wacko checks out any and all books related to making pipe bombs, etc. That is exactly why they have not been removed from the libraries. I laugh every time I hear some dumb-ass politician start crying to get Congress to remove any and all terrorist books and materials out of the libraries."

"Okay, Jonathan. I will get right to it, and I will call you with updates and questions if any."

"Great, and while you're at it, see what, if anything, the guys in Atlanta have already got in this regard. This information should have been readily available when we were called to action, don't you think?"

"Possibly. However, if they had done all of this, we may have never been needed."

Man Gets Thirty-Nine Years for Firebombing Temple

Associated Press in Washington Post Oklahoma City. A federal judge on Tuesday sentenced a man to thirty-nine years in prison for firebombing a Jewish temple and later trying to send a racist later to the congregation. The defendant raised his hand in a stiff-armed Nazi salute as the judge left the court.

Sean Gillespie, twenty-one, of Spokane, Washington, was found guilty in April of three bombing-related charges for hurling a Molotov cocktail at Temple B'Nai Israel a year earlier. The act, which caused minor damage to a brick wall and a glass door, was captured on a security videotape.

Gillespie's sentence was lengthened because of the letter he attempted to send to the temple after his conviction. The letter, which was read in court, expressed hatred toward the Jewish people and a desire to spark a racial holy war.

Temple B'Nai Israel's Rabbi Barry Cohen said the attack sparked fear and anger among temple members.

"There was little physical damage to the building, but there was clear psychological damage," Cohen said. "In this country, we can't be afraid in our places of worship. That's just not acceptable."

Gillespie, who once belonged to the white supremacist group Aryan Nations, asked Judge Robin Cauthron for leniency on grounds he had a troubled childhood.

Federal sentencing guidelines called for a minimum of thirty years in prison, but Cauthron said a greater sentence was warranted, citing the letter and the nature of Gillespie's crime.

"What you've done is not an act of vandalism, it's an act of violence," Cauthron said.

Elsewhere Tuesday, a federal grand jury indictment unsealed in Eugene, Oregon, charged three men with various crimes after rocks engraved with Nazi symbols were thrown through windows at a synagogue during a service in 2002.

Two brothers, Jacob A. Laskey, twenty-five, and Gabriel D. Laskey, twenty, and Gerald A.

Poundstone, twenty-seven, all were charged with conspiracy to violate civil rights. Jacob Laskey faces other charges including solicitation relating to attempts to kill potential witnesses.

Trial was set for October 26.

Prosecutor William Fitzgerald said the case remains under investigation.

What is this? I thought. I realized that it was an e-mail from Mitc—ah, I mean Allen—but what was its meaning? I mean about the killing of Jews?

Mass Slaughter In Our Schools: The Terrorists' Chilling Plan?

By Chuck Remsberg

Probably the last place you want to think of terrorists striking is your kids' school. But according to two trainers at an anti-terrorism conference on the East Coast, preparations for attacks on American schools that will bring rivers of blood and staggering body counts are well underway in Islamic terrorist camps.

The intended attackers have bluntly warned us they were going to do it.

They're already begun testing school-related targets here. They've given us a catastrophic model to train against, which we've largely ignored and they've learned more deadly tactics from.

"We don't know for sure what they will do. No one knows the future. But by definition, a successful attack is one we are not ready for," declared one of the instructors, Lieutenant Colonel Dave Grossman. Our schools fit that description to a tee as in terrorism and threat.

Grossman, the popular law enforcement motivational speaker, and Todd Rassa, a trainer with the SigArms Academy and an advisory board member for the *Police Marksman* magazine, shared a full day's agenda on the danger to US schools at a recent three-day conference on terrorist issues, sponsored by the International Association of Law Enforcement Firearms Instructors (IALEFI) in Atlantic City.

They reminded the audience that patrol officers, including perhaps some with their own children involved, will inevitably be the first responders when terrorists hit. And they documented chilling descriptions of the life-or-death challenges that likely will be faced.

In Part 1 of this three-part report on highlights of their presentations we focus on what's known about the threat to our schools to date, why terrorists have selected them as targets, and what tactics you're likely to be up against in responding to a sudden strike.

In parts 2 and 3, we'll explore Grossman's and Rassa's recommendations for practical measures you and your agency can take now to get ready, including some defensive actions that don't require any budget allocations.

Why Schools? Two Reasons: 1. Our values. "The most sacred thing to us is our children, our babies," Rassa said. Killing hundreds of them at a time would significantly "boost Islamic morale and lower that of the enemy" (us). In Grossman's words, terrorists see this effort as "an attempt to defile our nation" by leaving it "stunned to its soul."

2. Our lack of preparation. Police agencies "aren't used to this," Rassa said. "We deal with acts of a criminal nature. This is an act of war," but because of our laws, "we can't depend on the military to help us," at least at the outset.

"Indeed," Grossman claimed, "the U.S. is the one nation in the world where the military is not the first line of defense against domestic terrorist attacks. By law, you the police officer are our Delta Force. It is your job to go in, while in most other nations, cops will wait for the military to come save their kids."

"School personnel," Rassa said, "are not even close" to being either mentally or physically prepared. "Most don't even have response plans for handling a single active shooter. Their world is taught to nurture and care for people. They don't want to deal with this."

The American public, "sticking their heads in the sand, can't be mentally prepared," he said. "They're going to freak when it happens," their stubborn denial making the crisis "all the more shocking."

Noting that "sheep have two speeds: 'graze' and 'stampede.'" Grossman predicted that "not a parent in the nation will send their kids to school the next day," perhaps for many days after a large-scale terrorist massacre. If day care centers "also on the terrorists' list" are hit as well, "parents will drop out of the workforce" en masse to protect their children and "our economy will be devastated."

How We Know They're Coming Al-Qaeda has publicly asserted the "right" to kill two million American children, Rassa explained, and has warned that "operations are in stages of preparation" now. He played vivid videotapes confiscated in Afghanistan, showing al-Qaeda terrorists practicing the takeover of a school. The trainees issue commands in English, rehearse separating youngsters into manageable groups, and meet any resistance with violence. Some "hostages" are taken to the rooftop, dangled over the edge, then "shot."

"Any place that has given [Islamic terrorists] trouble, they've come after the kids," Grossman said. Muslim religious literature, according to Rassa, states clearly that the killing of children not only is "permitted" in Islam but is "approved" by Mohammed, so long as the perpetrators "are striving for the general good" as interpreted by that religion.

He cited instances in Indonesia where girls on their way to school have been beheaded and in other countries where children have been shot, mutilated, raped, or burned alive.

In this country, this year (2006), Rassa said, there have been several school bus-related incidents involving Middle Eastern males that raise suspicion of terrorist activity. These include the surprise boarding of a school bus in Florida by two men in trench coats, who may have been on a canvassing mission, and the attempt in New York State by an Arab male to obtain a job as a school bus driver using fraudulent Social Security documents. The latter gave an address in Detroit, home to a large colony of fundamentalist Muslims.

Rassa claimed that floor plans for half a dozen schools in Virginia, Texas, and New Jersey have been recovered from terrorist hands in Iraq.

The Terrorists' Tactical Model A "dress rehearsal for what terrorists plan to do to us" has already taken place, Rassa and Grossman agreed. That was the brutal takedown in 2004 of a school that served children from six to seventeen years old in Beslan, Russia.

Some one hundred terrorists were involved, nearly half of whom were discreetly embedded in the large crowd of parents, staff, and kids who showed up for the first day of school; the rest arrived for the surprise attack in SUVs, troop carriers, and big sedans. Across a three-day siege, seven hundred people were wounded and 338 killed, including 172 youngsters.

If a similar assault were launched against a school in your jurisdiction, how would you and your agency respond? Consider this modest sampling of challenges that were deliberately planned or arose from the ensuing chaos at Beslan, as outlined by Rassa:

- The school was chosen because it was one of the taller buildings in the area and had a very complicated floor plan, making a rapid and effective counter assault by responders extremely difficult. Offender weaponry included AK-47s, sniper rifles, RPGs, and explosives, with everything the terrorists needed carried in on their backs. RPGs were fired at a responding military helicopter and at troops.
- More than one thousand men, women, and children, including babies, were penned in an unventilated gym and a cafeteria. As the days passed without food or water and inside temperatures rose to

115 degrees, survivors were eating flowers they'd brought for teachers and fighting for urine to drink out of their shoes in desperation. Women and some children were repeatedly and continuously raped.

- Adult males and larger male students were used as "forced labor" to help fortify the building then shot to death. Bodies were thrown out of an upper-story window, down onto a courtyard. Attempts at negotiation by responders were used by the terrorists strictly as an opportunity to buy time to solidify their fortifications.

- Surviving hostages were surrounded by armed guards standing on dead man switches, wired to explosives. All entrances to the building as well as stairwells and some interior doorways were booby-trapped. Youngsters were forced to sit on window sills to serve as shields for snipers. "Black widows" (potential suicide bombers) were rigged so their bomb belts could be detonated by remote control when leaders considered the timing was right. The terrorists stayed cranked up on some type of amphetamine to keep awake.

- Armed, outraged parents and other civilians, some of them drunk, showed up and started "rolling gunfights" outside in a futile effort to defeat the takeover. The crowd identified one embedded terrorist and "literally ripped him apart." The media was everywhere, unrestrained. So many people were milling around that responders often could not establish a clear field of fire.

- When troops finally stormed the school in a counter-assault on the third day, pure pandemonium reigned. Soldiers and the kids they were trying to rescue were gunned down mercilessly. Explosions touched off inside started multiple fires.
- Responders who made it inside had to jump over trip wires as they "ran" upstairs under fire from above. By then, terrorists were holding hostages in virtually every room. Rescue teams were subjected to continual ambushes. Gunfights occurred predominately within a six-foot range, with some responders having to fight for their lives in places so cramped they couldn't get off their hands and knees.
- Some children successfully rescued from the building were so crazed by thirst that they ran to an outdoor spigot and were killed by a grenade as they filled their hands with water.
- Terrorists who escaped during the melee ran to homes of embedded sympathizers who hid them successfully and were not immediately suspected because they were considered "non-strangers" in the community. Some townspeople who volunteered to help as stretcher bearers for the injured were, in fact, embedded terrorists.
- During the siege, "at least four people or agencies claimed to be in charge. Actually, no one was in charge and no one wanted to be."

"Osama bin Laden has promised that what has happened in Russia will happen to us many times over," Grossman warned. "And Osama tries very hard never to lie to us."

What's Likely Here Probably not so many terrorists involved at a single location. Moving that big a contingent into place would likely attract too much attention and thwart the attack. Grossman describes a more likely possibility, in his opinion:

Terrorist cells of four operatives each might strike simultaneously at four different schools. They may pick elementary schools, or middle schools with no police officers on site, where the girls are "old enough to rape" but students are not big enough to fight back effectively.

The targets may be in states "with no concealed-carry laws and no hunting culture" and in communities where "police do not have rifles." Rural areas could be favored, where thirty minutes or more might be required for responders to arrive in force.

The attackers will probably "mow down every kid and teacher they see" as they move in to seize the school. They may plant bombs throughout the buildings, and "rape, murder, and throw out bodies like they did in Russia." Emergency vehicles responding and children fleeing will be blown up by car bombs in the parking lot.

In all, one hundred to three hundred children could be slaughtered in a first strike.

Terrorists capable of this are already embedded in communities "all over America," Grossman and Rassa agreed. More will probably gain entry surreptitiously from Mexico, making southern California potentially a prime target.

No Time for Despair It's a grim picture for certain. "But if we think there's nothing we can do to prepare, that is a defeatist mentality," Rassa said. "We ought to be trying. If we're not trying, we're failing. We may as well give up our guns and surrender now.

"I can't think of a better thing to train up for than protecting our kids. If we try but fall short, look at how much else we'll still be able to handle than we can now.

"What made most of us do active-shooter training? The killings at Columbine. Are we going to wait for something far worse than that before we do the most that we can to stop the terrorists who are coming for our schools?"

"Note, Jonathan, this is a copy of a real study done by well-meaning leaders that is now being used by some of the groups that I am working in and with to justify their violence and potential violence. Of course their goal is to kill or export all Middle Eastern and Middle Eastern-looking people for that matter.

"I am learning a lot about how some of these radical fringe elements have made their transformation from moderate to sometimes violent radicalism.

"On the movement's moderate side, are conservative Christians opposed to the liberal establishment. More radical participants include both Christians and non-Christians who deny their US citizenship, drive without licenses, and refuse to pay income taxes in an effort to live outside "the system." Interspersed among these two groups are the most dangerous patriots: Klansmen, neo-Nazis, and Christian Identity believers (i.e., White

Supremacists who blend pseudo-Christian beliefs with racism and anti-Semitism).

"The glue binding this wide assortment of persons is a lethal compound of four ingredients: an obsessive suspicion of their government; a deep-seated hatred and fear of federal authorities; a belief in far-reaching conspiracy theories; and a feeling that for all intents and purposes Washington bureaucrats have discarded the US Constitution. Most of the individuals in this antigovernment community also feel that a cold war of sorts is being waged between freedom-loving patriots and federal officials. Belief that this Cold War will escalate into violent conflict is so great that many patriots have organized themselves into heavily armed militias, most of which function contrary to state laws prohibiting private armies.

"To complicate matters, religion and/or racism are the impetus for large segments of the movement. These two powerful forces have created an unholy alliance between racists on the one hand and some conservative Christians on the other. Their common ground is apocalypticism, the belief that the present world will one day end through cataclysmic confrontation between God and Satan, out of which will emerge God's righteous kingdom.

"A high level of paranoia gripping many participants in this movement makes the situation even more explosive. An ocean of pamphlets, newsletters, videotapes, and audiocassettes has flooded patriot minds with far-fetched plots the likes of which are usually associated with paperback spy novels. For instance, patriots believe the American government is now serving an insidious scheme hatched long ago by behind-the-scenes internationalists whose ultimate goal is world domination."

My only reply was, "I am not interested in a history lesson. I need a murderer!"

Allen had also attached some pictures of some of the meetings he had attended highlighting some of the members and players that he thought to be suspicious. He had handwritten in the margin, "Get what you can on these guys," and then I noticed check marks by three men. The pictures seem innocent enough, and all were smiling and by all pictorial indications they could have been in Sunday School class. However, I did remember that pictures can be very misleading. I remembered the faded family albums that I still had of my family in days gone by when Helen and I seemed so together even though I knew that things had already changed between us prior to the date on some of the pictures however the pictures hid that fact. Pictures are referred to by some as "snapshots in time"; however, they sometimes hide more than they show. Pictures do lie.

I immediately forwarded them to Beth for her and Rodney to analyze ASAP.

I continued to look at them, however, and I could visualize Richard Nixon in his last days in office pictured smiling and denying the inevitable truth of Watergate and of a picture not long ago of George Bush smiling and declaring that the war in Iraq was over and that we had won, yeah right!

CHAPTER 8

Mitch talking to himself on his way to the
Double Dribble Sports Bar in Spokane

Jonathan just doesn't understand that this takes time and that if I rush
too fast and make the slightest error, I too will become one of the dead in
this murder mystery. I think that mostly likely the answer to this thing can
be found in or around one of these groups; however, their membership is
extensive and covers the entire United States. However, I do believe that
the heart of the conspiracy—if it is a conspiracy—lies somewhere in this
Pacific northwestern pattern of White Supremacy-focused militia groups.
I need to learn more about the Lake Hayden area of the panhandle of
Utah since several Christian-Aryan Nations compounds are located in
and around this pristine area. One of the most suspicious of these claims
to fame is "to tell the people across America there is yet white men and
women who do not bow toward the east!" Since Lake Hayden is only a
short forty-five-mile drive from Spokane, I should be able to get some
general information here and I bet the girl at Double Dribble should be
just the source. Double Dribble is a great little sports bar that I frequent
often for the great drinks and to flirt a little with Rachel.

"Hey, Allen, where have you been of late?"

"Ah, I been out of town on business."

"By the way, what is your business?"

"Furniture sales…now get me my usual, girl! What do you
know about Lake Hayden?"

"Oh, Allen, it is so beautiful and has some really great bed and breakfast inns. One of the best was built by the Spokane capitalist F. Lewis Clark. I would love to go there sometime—it sits on twelve beautiful acres that border Hayden Lake."

"What about this weekend?"

"Is this your attempt at a date?"

"I don't know about a date, but would you like to go there this weekend?"

"I normally get to know someone a little more than I know you, before I spend the weekend somewhere with them. I might need to think about it a while."

"Whatever? I do need a tour guide and some company, and you just said that you have always wanted to go there."

"Oh, what the hell, Allen! Let me talk with my boss to see if I can get off with this short of notice."

"Okay, I will call and make the reservations on my way home."

"Just a minute, I am not sure that I can get off," I said.

"No problem, I am going anyway. However, I would love for you to be along with me. I will call you tomorrow to confirm."

"Are you not even going to take me out somewhere tonight or between now and then before we spend a weekend together in a romantic bed and breakfast?"

"Ah…no! I will call you tomorrow and I will pick you up Friday about 5:00 p.m."

"Damn, you're weird! But call me tomorrow."

"See ya!"

FBI office, Atlanta, Georgia

"Yes, sir, Mr. Director, I have a full and highly competent staff working on this as we speak both in the field and in Atlanta and all over for that matter. You have got to understand this is not your typical mass-murderer case. These bodies are not isolated to any specific area, and I also believe that for the first time since the FBI got involved, that progress is now being made."

"Look, David, I don't think that I have to say this, but I am. Your job and my job are on the line here, and I can't speak for you, but my wife and I like our standard of living that this job provides our family. If you need more manpower, get it. If you need more funds, requisition it, understand? The President is tired of reading about this every morning. It is complicating his domestic and foreign policy agendas. His exact words to me just this morning were, 'Those fucking Arabs are starting to compare the US situation now to Israel.' Now how do you think that is helping the peace talks? By the way, I want a full written report on our progress on my desk by Monday morning. I have got to have something to turn over to my writers and to the press secretary so that they can present it to the public in a palatable manner next week. I have to convey the message that we are about to solve this national tragedy. Goodbye!" *Click!*

"Those stupid sons of bitches don't understand that they started this shit and that it can't be fixed overnight especially with the fucking war in Iraq raging every goddamned day."

"Jane!"

"Yes, sir?"

"Get Jonathan on the damn line!"

"Yes, sir!"

"Rodney."

"Yes, David?"

"Get me everything that you and Beth have now!"

"But, sir!"

"Don't *sir* me!—You heard me!

"Have you got Jonathan yet?"

"No, sir, but I will keep trying. It seems that both of his cells are turned off!"

"That fucking figures! I should have never got him involved. Get Mitch on his Allen cell phone!"

"Yes, sir!"

"Sir—"

"Yes, Jane, it seems that Mitch's cell is also turned off!"
Clang!

It seems like every time I go somewhere, it is always raining. In this state, it has either just finished raining, just starting to rain, or it is raining. Maybe I should have called Rachel back? However, after giving it more thought, even though I would love to spend a couple of days all snuggled up in some romantic bed and breakfast after getting Jonathan's call last night, now is probably not the time. I hope she is not too mad. Oh well, what the hell; she will get over it! It's not like we're involved or anything like that!

My overnight stay of choice now would be the Affordable Inn, not the Clark House. The area is absolutely gorgeous. Jonathan would love to visit here just for the fishing. My mission now was to get an idea of what was happening here (underground, that is) and where. It is hard to believe that anything of a sinister nature could go on here in this picturesque town with a resident population of under four hundred people. However, I knew better from my, brief as it was, undercover work in Spokane they have talked of a twenty-acre compound in or near Hayden Lake. That was the home of some of the most radical Neo-Nazi/Christian/White Supremacists. I thought that during this visit, I might be able to get familiar with the area and all, for in time, I was hoping to get close enough to the insiders in Spokane to get an invite. My greatest fear is that I might not hide my real personality and my real political views well enough and that at any point, I could get made for I truly hated these people of hate even though some of their basic tenets sound good and even righteous at times. Their real goal was genocide. Genocide of anyone and everyone not like themselves. 9/11 and the Iraqi war were just excuses and now a catalyst to justify their wrongs. I am different from Jonathan and from a different generation; he is sympathetic with these people and their cause.

This assignment scares me more than any of my other undercover work since leaving the Marines, graduating from the FBI facility near Miami and then coming under the employment of the FBI. This is the first time that I have been assigned to a case where the villain or villains were not clearly identified. All I had to do in the past was get prosecutable evidence on the bad guy or guys. I guess that I need to keep what Jonathan said in mind. All he wanted was someone to convict. He doesn't seem to give a damn if they're totally guilty or not just that they are prosecutable. I know for a fact that the government in this case has ignored some killings and that the murders are more widespread than they want us to know. They seem to concentrate on a select few that carry a specific MO and then they package these as the problem. I guess that gives them an easier track to follow and, therefore, an easier way to get an arrest made and then what they call "closure." These Patriot types may not be natural-born killers; however, they do hate the government, and more importantly, they fear the government, especially the "initial" branches, i.e., FBI, CIA, etc. God help me if my cover gets blown! That in and of itself is not any different than some of my drug work. However, in those instances, it was easier to become a chameleon.

After checking into the motel and then spending several hours getting familiar with both Hayden Lake and Hayden, I ended up drinking beer in Sergeants Restaurant and Lounge on West Government Street. In this part of the world, it isn't difficult to strike up an anti-government or anti-immigrant conversation. While I sat at the bar the jokes being told by the bar keep and the local yokels and yours truly started with Hispanic and ran the gamut ending with an untold number of rag head and camel jockey tales. One guy sort of quoted George Carlin saying something to the effect that the president needed to bring in the 1.1 million illegal aliens, issue them a rifle and a back pack, and then send them to Iraq to replace our native-born citizens and have our citizen soldiers patrol the borders of this country upon their return. After the Iraqi conflict is resolved then let the illegals become legal for their service there; however, he went on to vent that they would most likely then return to their own country because they would be like the rest of us then and have to start paying taxes, paying for their education, and etc. We all got a good laugh and then went on for hours about how ole George had a damn good plan. About midnight, I started to test the limits of their beliefs and theories by taking my feelings to the limit by saying such things as that where I come from, we shoot the bastards on sight, and how I respected whomever it was that was slaughtering the damnable rag heads all across this land for as far as I was concerned, they had not even begun to pay for what they did to us here on our own soil on 9/11. My ranting and raving got all kinds of applause and accolades even from patrons not directly involved in our fun. One particular fellow setting at the opposite end of the bar from where I was seemed to really be getting off on this type of talk and keep yelling "Hell, yeah!" every time any of us talked about any type of violence against any minority, especially the Middle Eastern varieties. At one point, he said that's right by God and we should behead all the bastards. That comment got my attention for he then started talking about several of the killings and with knowledge. He either had inside information or did one hell of a lot of reading and research about them.

I immediately offered to buy him a beer and then moved to the stool closest to him and then prodded the conversation deeper and more grotesque. At that time he seemed to get nervous, went to the restroom, and then disappeared for the night. "Damn it," I said to myself after discovering that he was gone for I had not even gotten his name. The barkeep then informed me that he was a regular and a weird sort of guy that keeps us on our toes when he is here. Another guy chimed in by saying he sure got involved when you started talking about shooting those bastards! "You did say that, didn't you?"

Now that was a question that I was not prepared for, so I thought it best to move on to another subject. I started to inquire about the fishing and of the water sports of the area and of how beautiful I found Hayden Lake. With that, one of the ladies at a nearby table had her waiter send me a beer on her. I decided to join her if for no other reason than to get off the conversation at the bar. After all, I was trying to fit in and not trying to get ostracized from their midst. She was a nice-looking lady in her mid-thirties, I guessed, however she was wearing clothes more suited and fitted for a nineteen-year-old. Her mini skirt keep working its way up her thigh so that at times, I could see her black and white panties underneath and she seemed to like that. Her tits were of the CC or DD variety and kept pushing partly out of her T-shirt. The shirt had a picture of a shark on it and the words "man eater" under the picture. She was wearing too much makeup. *Damn, she was beautiful!* I am a lot like Jonathan in that regard. I like my women a little on the trashy side, and this broad surely fit the bill. I then decided that I should just cool it for the night and to turn my attention to trying to get into this broad's pants, and I did just that.

The next morning, I awoke in this gigantic poster bed in a cathedral-type room with a ceiling that seemed to be a hundred foot high. My first thoughts were where in the shit am I? It was immediately apparent that I had too much to drink. The sun was shining brightly through the sky lights a mile above the bed, it seemed; however, I was still having trouble focusing. The posters on the bed seemed to run all the way to heaven like the beanstalk in the old-time storybook tale my mama read to me when I was a kid. I just knew that something was wrong. Had she put a drug in my beer or what? I started to remember her escorting me into her home, apartment or something. However, the lights were out and my mind was more on her than on my surroundings. I wobbled out of bed and noticed a set of French doors with one side partly open, leading out onto a veranda, so I staggered in that direction. The closer I got, I could see her sitting or more accurately lying on a lounge chair looking out over her pool. It then hit me that I did not even know her name.

"Well, good morning, handsome!"

"Good morning to you," I responded, still thinking, *Hell, lady, I don't even know your name or where I am and again realizing that Budweiser can still get me into more trouble that I can get out of at times. However, I was not ready to ask her name, so I just asked for coffee.*

"It's on the way," she said as she set her cell phone on the veranda by her chair. James will be here momentarily.

James? I thought to myself. *Who is this broad? I hope to hell that I have not gone home with the governor's wife.* As my eyes began to focus a little better, I could see that she was wearing a very expensive-looking see-through gown. My time in Spokane had produced enough results for me to know that I was at least in the right part of the country, and with the right people, all I needed now was to learn the ropes, gain their trust, and get involved. I looked out over her large and beautifully landscaped pool and courtyard, realizing that this was most definitely a detour from my urgent goals and then James showed up with my coffee.

"Thanks for the coffee," I said to her and to James, a very muscular, blond, tanned, and young man of possibly Swedish descent.

I then told her that I was expecting her servant to be more mature and black.

"You sound just like my husband," she replied and then said, "What woman in her right mind would want an older servant and especially a nigger!"

"Husband? Well, I guess that I had better be on my way."

"Don't worry. He is held up on his island off the coast of Vancouver with more than one young thing."

"Are you divorced?"

"Hell no. I can milk him for more this way. I let him have his island castle and his horde of hot bodies and he lets me have my pleasures too! It's not a bad arrangement. Really, I just married him for his damn money anyway, and I have all I need under this setup."

"What is his occupation?"

"Shipping! He controls most of the west coast in the same manner as Steinbrenner does the east coast. After listening in on your conversations and carrying on at the bar last night, what makes you think I would hire a nigger?"

I immediately discovered that she must be one of them and that I needed to be guarded in how I answered this question. "I just thought that up here everyone must own one!"

She then burst out in loud laughter and then knew that I had responded correctly. "Does your husband employ a lot of immigrants?"

"No! But when he has to, he sends them on the most dangerous and most risky assignments and then hopes to hell something happens to one of the wetbacks."

"Great," I said, "then he is helping us cleanse this country. I think that I might just move out here."

"Where are you from, Allen?"

Damn, she knows my name and I still don't know hers. I still did not want to ask for I had just spent the night in her bed and was sitting here talking and staring at her nearly nude body. I just could not own up to the fact that I didn't know or remember her name.

"Tennessee, Memphis, as a matter of fact."

"You sure have a lot of niggers there.

"So you have visited our fine state."

"Yes, Larry and I went to visit the king's mansion a few years ago."

"So how did your husband like the BBQ in the area?"

"My husband? How in the hell should I know?"

"Oh, I am sorry, I thought—"

"No, Larry is one of my lovers. He plays hockey for a minor league franchise team connected to the San Jose Sharks. He hopes to get called up soon."

We talked on for several more hours and then I decided that I needed to get back to my motel room and back to my FBI responsibilities. I bid my farewell and thanked her for the evening and then was on my way and as I drove down her long drive to the highway. I smiled as I thought, *That damn broad still has not put on any clothes!* Oh well, I guess everyone needs an aversion from time to time especially in my line of work of undercover espionage.

CHAPTER 9

Back at my room, I put together a report that Beth had asked for several days ago and then dropped it into the Fed-Ex box in the lobby of my motel and then took two Tylenol PM and turned in early. The next day, I thought that I might try to find out something about the twenty-acre compound that was the home of a very radical arm of the Neo-Nazi/Christian/White Supremacist organization that I believe to be involved directly or indirectly with the murders across the country.

Back at the FBI offices in Atlanta

"Dammit, Rodney," David exclaimed as he burst in on him and Beth as they were working up the profiles for Jonathan and on trying to get a pattern on the movement of the killer or killers. "Where in the hell is Jonathan?"

"I don't know," Beth said as David threw the morning paper into Rodney's lap.

"Look at this fucking headline in the *New York Times*, no less: 'FBI at a Standstill in the Horrendous Murders of Middle Easterners'! The damn nitwit that wrote this crap has not got a fucking clue about this case or what we are doing or what we are not doing. It goes on to say that I have refused interviews and that undisclosed sources have said that the case is not getting worked properly. Beth, you call the *Atlanta Journal* immediately and schedule a press conference for ten in the morning. I am not going to take this shit sitting down.

And one more thing, find that damn Jonathan! The director is on my ass over the lack of results in this and over the adverse publicity. That bastard had better have some answers, and he had better have them pronto. I robbed the Denver mint to pay the son of a bitch, and to date, I have nothing to show for it except a bunch of fucking receipts. If they shift this case to New York, I will be fired!"

Mitch was now at a meeting in a compound near Spokane.

The meeting hall was quiet this night as the secret conclave met for the first time in weeks on this rainy night in the hills of the Pacific Northwest. All were present with the exception of one; however, the slow movement of tires over the gravel road could now be heard as their secret leader drove up the driveway of the twenty-plus-acre estate. He entered the meeting to a quiet reception and was slow to speak as tears arose in the corners of his eyes. "It is always a sad occasion when one of our kind is lost in this war against Islam. However, I hope that some of what I tell you today will put your conscience at ease." The president's own assertions about the peaceful nature of Islam were briefly interrupted when the state department issued the annual report required by the International Religious Freedom Act of 1998. This year, as in the past, our Muslim world partners in the so-called coalition against terrorism were prominently featured among the most violent and most intolerant regimes in the world. Religious minorities are persecuted in over twenty states where Islam is the official or dominant religion. The million Christians who have fled the Muslim world in the past five years were hardly seeking sanctuary from the peaceful face of Islam.

With shocking regularity, human rights group report the death of Christians at the hands of Muslim militants in Africa, South Asia, and the Middle East. In Pakistan, Islam has been the official religion since 1973, and over the years, the state department has urged our ally to appeal the Section 295 of the penal code there. This is the section that stipulates the death penalty or life in prison for blaspheming Mohammed, and the state department notes that it "contributes to the interreligious tension, intimidation, fear, and violence." A Christian Pakistani, Ayub Masih, was jailed five years ago on a blasphemy charge and he has now filed his final appeal against the death sentence imposed on him. Masih is alleged to have said, "If you want to know the truth about Islam, read Salman Rushdie." An accusation by a Muslim neighbor was enough to secure the blasphemy conviction. Under Pakistan's "Hudood ordinances," the legal testimony of religious minorities is accorded half the weight of Muslims. The testimony of a non-Muslim woman is halved again.

Most recently gunmen from the Army of Omar opened fire on a Protestant congregation worshipping at St. Dominic's Catholic Church in Bahawalpur, killing sixteen and the Islamic party leaders in Pakistan immediately claimed that the massacre was a conspiracy to defame Muslims.

Furthermore, the state department has now changed their position from diplo speak by saying, "Freedom of religion does not exist in Saudi Arabia." Christians have been flogged, imprisoned, and executed by the Saudi government that prohibits non-Muslim worship even in private homes. Any Muslim there that converts to another religion is subject to the death penalty by beheading. That is why we have often seen the same thing happen to American Muslims in recent time.

Nigeria is another nightmare. The Center for Religious Freedom, part of the Freedom House, maintains a New Martyrs List to call attention to the most horrific cases. In one bloody week in May, over two hundred people were killed in Kauna. Among the dead was Rev. Clement Ozi Bello, a twenty-six-year-old former Muslim who had recently been ordained a Catholic priest. The young priest was attacked by a mob that dragged him from his car tied him up and gouged out his eyes before leaving him dead on the side of the road. In another incident, churches and Christian-owned shops were gasoline-bombed in an area of Kaduna now adorned with pictures of Osama bin Laden.

I could go on and on delineating similar instances of violence and murders against our Christian brothers all over the world and especially in the heart of our so-called alliance. There are many stories to be told of these in Nigeria, the Philippines, Egypt, and the Sudan. "John, would you please hand everyone a copy of these for them to read of the specific details at their leisure?"

In closing, you might say that the American Muslims do not hold the same beliefs. Well, that is just not correct, and I can quote you some statistics just recently mentioned on the Rush Limbaugh show. Thirty-one percent of American Muslims believe that suicide bombings are justified, and 58 percent support the al-Qaeda cause. I might also add that our government is not the only one with embedded spies.

Back at the FBI offices in Atlanta, Georgia

David was reading the *New York Times* in his office on this fine morning as he periodically looked out over the Atlanta skyline, wondering if all of this could really be happening in this country and at the same time, knowing that if he didn't get a handle on this thing soon, he would most likely lose his job and his way of life. The phone rang, and it was Martha, his wife, calling from Miami. She had decided to take a couple of weeks' vacation just to get away from the pressures of it all. David had never been easy to live with, but now it was worse as he brought everything home with him on a daily basis now.

"Hey, sweetie, how is Miami?"

"Just great, and I have really been enjoying the beaches, and the night life here is phenomenal."

"Night life?"

"Yes, South Beach is wonderful. However, I have found a couple of back street places near Fort Lauderdale that cater more to our age group."

"Our age group?"

"Oh...ah...I mean, you know, like you and I, honey!"

David thought for a minute. It had been like forever since Martha had called him honey. Maybe this trip will help her? However, he still worried about the "our" phrase; however, he was afraid to ask any further questions even though her answer was a little weak and vague.

"By the way, I think that I might stay over a few more days to give me a break and you a little space."

"Okay, just be careful."

David then went down to Rodney's office and found them studying several charts and graphs. The bureau has always been big on paperwork and thick files.

"What is it looking like, guys?"

"You know this case all too well, sir. It is impossible to get a definitive pattern because the murders are so widespread geographically and demographically. I do believe that we are making progress by having Mitch—ah, I mean Allen—embedded out west. Even though most of the murders have been committed in the south and southwest. I still believe that the hierarchy of the Neo-Nazi/ Christian/White Supremacist groups and affiliates are centered in the Pacific Northwest, with maybe the most militant factions in the state of Washington. That said, I should still emphasize the fact that all these organizations have cells located not only nationally but also internationally and all of them are capable of committing these types of acts on their own anytime and anyplace. This mobility factor and the fact that most of the members are hard to identify in their regular day-to-day routines of life, make profiling difficult. The last time I spoke with Mitch, he was feeling very good about his work out there. I believe that he is getting close to something. While he was in Salt Lake, he felt that he was moving in the right direction. However, he was nervous and concerned over being identified as a spy. He told me that he could not trust anyone in that region because even the known innocent citizens were highly suspicious of our government and very sympathetic toward these fringe elements. 9/11 and the border issues have galvanized support for these movements nationwide. He spoke of a twenty-acre compound that was home to an extremely radical and violent faction of the Neo-Nazi/Christian/White Supremacist sect somewhere near Spokane that he felt was our best bet as to finding the center of power and maybe even the call to order for most of the immigrant and Muslim murders. This sect seems to be better financed and better organized that most of the others. Mitch also informed me of the murder of an embedded FBI agent from DC; however, I have not been successful in determining his identity or even if the murder actually occurred.

"Hold on a minute, guys," Beth said. "I just received a message over the hotline that another murder was reported today when a body of a Muslim man was discovered in some water in or near Alligator Alley in Florida. I also have Jonathan on the line, and he wants to speak to you."

"Jonathan! Where in the fuck have you been?"

"That's not important, David. However, I am on my way to the site of the newest murder."

"Are you in Florida?"

"Yes, Fort Lauderdale to be exact. However, I am now just about an hour away from our scene."

"I bet that you have been in Tallahassee with your daughter instead of working."

"I wish, but actually, I have been occupied for the past week in Fort Lauderdale working on your problem, and now I find myself very close to the latest find, so evidently, my work is paying dividends. Oh yes, I have been trying to get up with Mitch and to no avail. Have you guys heard from him recently?"

"Rodney talked with him last a little over a week ago."

"That's not like Mitch. We need to hear from him soon. Why don't you get Beth on that immediately?"

"Sure thing! Call me on my direct line or on my cell after you investigate there."

"Will do, bye!"

Damn that Jonathan! He is hard to pin down. When you are wanting to give him a good ass chewing, he seems to always have an answer or a way of getting you off topic. Beth, go ahead and start trying to locate Mitch through our normal channels and contacts in the region. Rodney, why don't you check on the possible connection between Spokane and the Midwest specifically the Michigan area? I would like to know where it branches from there.

"You do realize, David, that…wait a minute, that's it!"

"That's what?"

"Water!"

"Water?"

"Yes! Water! Water is the most occurring common denominator in the killings. It's right here in black and white, there have been a few exceptions in the ones we have chosen to look at internally. However, most of the victims have been found in or near water. That's our key—we must use that as the link!"

"What kind of a damn link is that? Over 75 percent of the globe is covered in water!"

"I know, however, we must work from that point of reference. It has to be our key. All mass murders have a common thread or point of reference. For ours, it is water!"

"Okay, we know that many of them have been beheaded, and we figure that is a way of mimicking the way many of our people have been killed, and several have been burned, and we figure that ties to 9/11. How in the world can water be tied to these?"

"I don't know, David, but it is, and we must determine how, but more importantly, why?"

A couple of hours later, Jonathan calls David from the latest crime scene.

"What's happening there, Jonathan?"

"You would not believe this, David." This man was disemboweled and his intestines sliced up in front of his eyes. He was emasculated and watched as those body parts were destroyed…fingers were chopped off and his nose and mouth and anus were sliced open. His last name is Necati, and he was stabbed 156 times, and finally, his throat was cut, practically decapitating him. His legs are missing, and some are speculating that an alligator was probably to blame there.

"Rodney thinks that water is playing a key role of some sort in these murders. What do you think?"

"I don't know how that could come into play. However, come to think of it, most of the bodies have been found in or near water."

"Beth thinks that it is just a coincidence."

"I don't know? Let me go for now so that I might get some information from some of the locals."

David went straight to Beth and Rodney and gave them what few details of the latest murder that he had just received from Jonathan.

Beth responded by saying, "Well, there's another connection. The last known American soldier that was kidnapped and killed in the Middle East faced the same type of torture, execution-style death almost to a tee."

"Rodney, what do you think? Could this be a hint that might be pointing us to ex or present military?"

"Could be…or maybe Navy SEAL since water is involved? You do know that most of the more militant Neo-Nazi/Christian/White Supremacist group memberships are ex-military?"

"Yes! And again, that will be a difficult avenue to follow for most of their files are sealed. I have tried on more than one occasion in the past, on other cases, to get background on Vietnam vets with absolutely no success."

"What we really have now is three points of interest—the water factor, the possibility of present or ex-military, and we almost forgot the fact that many have been shot by .22-caliber rifle."

"That's right, Beth. Have you seen the ballistics yet?"

"Yes, and they were all fired from the same rifle, believed to be Marlin."

"Interesting? I wonder why our wonder boy has not yet put this together?"

"Oh, I believe that he has, David. You must remember he ordered the ballistics test, and he has always felt that there was a governmental, military, political influence, if not out-and-out involvement. I will check with him when he calls me and make sure that we are all on the same page."

Jonathan lying in a bed resting at a small named motel near the crime scene

I have often wondered about life, how we got it, where it came from, and precisely what are we to do with it! Oh, I know all of the religious stuff about creation and of all the evolutionist theories; however, that is not what I am thinking about. It's the everyday things that puzzle me. I find myself now staring up at a corner in my motel room at a spot where the ceiling and two walls meet, and I think, *What if it were not there?* That's right—what if that physical point on a physical object not only did not exist but never did exist? What if I did not exist? What if I was just the figment of someone's or something's imagination? Am I a good person or a bad person? Or you might even ask if there is a difference. This type of thinking that I find myself in the middle of at times reminds me of a book I once read. I cannot remember the title of it for the life of me, but it was about a man institutionalized for a mental problem. He often asked himself and the prison guards, *Where are all of the supposedly insane people? Which side of the wall do they reside? Why do things come at us so early in life?* We have to make decisions about things like careers and marriage long before we are ready and our passions don't last forever. Our task in life, it seems, is not to conquer them but to merely survive them. Have I survived my passions of life, or have they consumed me? Why am I doing this? I could be floating the river, watching my son play hockey, or just lying on the beach with my daughter. Where are my passions today, or more importantly, what are my passions today? There is an old John Cougar song that says, "Life goes on, long after the thrill of the living is gone," and that, in part, is why death scares the middle-age man more than it does the old because for us, the thrill is gone.

CHAPTER 10

Jonathan's son at Colorado State University

"What does your dad do for a living?" I asked my friend as we lay on our beds in the dormitory at Colorado State.

"I am not sure he does anything 'for a living.' He has worked hard all his life…however, I am not sure that he has ever 'made a living' and yours?"

"Well, he was retired FBI, but he is back at it again."

"Maybe that is why he did not make any of your games this season?"

"Yeah, probably. He always has some excuse for not being here when I need him or for sister either for that matter. I am really worried about him. This time they have assigned him some really complicated case and he is the lead investigator on the mass murder case."

"What mass murder case?"

"You know, I saw you reading about it the other day and joking with Yosif about it at lunch."

"Oh, the murders of the Arab people."

"Well, not just them—it seems that there is some sort of world-wide hatred against them and others that has grown since 9/11 with the—quote un-quote—'War on Terror'—escalating here and abroad. I think that the president is more right than my dad thinks he is. However, I am not sure that we can be the peacekeepers to the world, at least not without a very high price to pay. I just wish that my dad would have stayed retired."

"Why didn't he?"

"I think that they are paying him a ton of money and that he is funneling most of it to my sister, and me, in addition to that, I think that even as much as he loved hunting and fishing so much the past few years, he got bored."

"Your dad was evidently really good at what he did in order for them to pay him so much to come back."

"Yes, however, it took its toll on our family, and I am not so sure the money was really worth that."

"He must have a lot of fame too?"

"Not really—most of his work is behind the scenes. His superiors get most of the credit and all of the press."

"Then let me get this straight—you're mad at your dad for doing this for you and your sister and at the same time you criticize him for not thinking more of you and her? That seems to be paradoxical to me, if not out-and-out wrong."

"It's not that I am mad with him or that my sister is mad—it is just that we have always wanted to have more of his time, yet he has always thought that it was all about the money."

"Just remember it is always easy to discount the importance of 'the money' as you call it when you have it! A poor man's time doesn't pay many bills. Believe me, I know that truth firsthand."

"I guess you're right. We are probably too hard on him, but there is another side to my concern, and that is his life. I am afraid that this assignment will get explosive, and I don't want him to get himself killed."

Back in Atlanta

"Beth, Jonathan here. Have you got anything on Mitch?"

"No! Not yet, however, I have contacts in Utah, Spokane, and throughout the Pacific Northwest on it as we speak. You must remember that he is undercover, and it is normal for him to disappear for long periods at a time. Sometimes it is a must."

"I know. However, it is different this time. I gave him specific instructions to stay in contact with some of us at all times, and he has two cell phones and the Internet at his disposal."

"That is all well and good. However, when you're undercover, there are times the rules and directions have to play second fiddle or you can lose your life."

"By the way, what is this water thing David keeps talking about?"

"It was not, David. I came up with that one while working on your profiling project. There is a combination of things that interest me now besides the water. There is the .22-caliber that has been involved in most of the cases, if not all, and ballistics confirm it to be out of the same rifle, and there also seems to be a military or ex-military connection."

"What is the military connection?"

"I don't really know exactly. It's just that so many of the groups that I have been researching both for you and Mitch have a heavy concentration of ex-military members, especially Vietnam War veterans. Right now, it's just a theory, and I am just noting anything and everything that turns up frequently in the murders and in my research of the individuals and groups of interest. To date, these three, the water, the .22 rifle, and the military connection seem to be the forming part of a picture that could end up identifying a specific individual or at least narrow or suspected groups of interest down to one or two, a far cry from where we have been. The water may just be coincidental. I truly believe that we are now making some decent progress. Mitch may very well connect a few more dots for us."

"I am still worried about Mitch. See if you can get Rodney involved in locating him too. Maybe we should start back in Memphis with some of his professional and non-professional colleagues. Oh yes, please inform David of the progress that we are making!"

A few days later…

Back at the Bureau in Atlanta

"All right, dammit. I am not saying that we are making good progress, just progress! It was Beth that originally said that *she* believed that we were making 'decent progress'! Look! What about you being part of the solution instead of part of the problem, David! All I hear from you is bitch, bitch, and bitch! Get the bigwigs in Washington active on this shit instead of spending so much of the taxpayers' time and money in lobbying Congress for more of their time and money. You answer to the attorney general. What the fuck is he doing? Fishing of the coast of Costa Rica, I would imagine, while supposedly being involved in influencing their government to help us on various agenda and fronts."

"The attorney general that you spoke of called me just yesterday, threatening to pull the responsibility of this case out of my department and into the Department of Counterterrorism if we cannot show him some sizable progress, but more importantly, he needs publicity about us making quality progress. Listen, I think that you have already determined that it really has not received priority status up and until now. I do not believe that neither he nor the bureau chief really gives a fuck about the killing of Arabs. It's his job and mine that we are concerned about. I need for this case to stay right here under our watch so get me something that I can give to them to get them the publicity they need to get the liberal media and the Arab American groups off their ass. By the way, where is Mitch?"

"That's a good question! I have Rodney and Beth both working on getting up with him from two different fronts. I expect to hear from him anytime now!"

"Get back with me soon, Jonathan, and as for disappearing, I don't need to go days with hearing from you either."

"Okay, see you later, boss! No wonder his wife has such a hot box for a lady her age. I would not fuck that bastard either! I wonder if she is still in Miami? I only spent two nights there."

Double Dribble Sports Bar in Spokane

"Where is your buddy from Memphis, Rachel? I have not seen him in here for a while."

"He is not my buddy. Hell, he asked me to go to the mountains with him for a weekend a while back, and I went to a lot of trouble to get off, then the bastard stood me up. I guess that he made the trip to the Hayden Lake area and then went back to Memphis or something? In reality, I just do not know! Why?"

"Nothing, really. I just like his politics, and he plays a damn good hand of Texas Hold 'Em!"

A week later in the Atlanta offices of the FBI

"David! Jonathan just called and he wants to go undercover to track Mitch!"

"No! Absolutely not, Beth…that is totally out of the question here! It would be just too dangerous to consider."

"Jonathan is worried about Mitch, and he is afraid that maybe his cover got blown."

"I will send someone out of Atlanta. You tell Jonathan to spend his time getting me an up-tempo progress report so that I can go to the press immediately."

"Okay, I will tell him, but you know, Jonathan, it would not surprise me if he is not there already. Historically, by the time he asks permission to do something, he has most likely already started or finished whatever it was!"

"You get him on the phone now and then patch him through to me."

One hour later

"Well, why have you not called Jonathan yet?"

"Oh, I have called him on all of his cells, at home, and I have sent two emergency emails, all to no avail."

"Bastard! I knew that I could not trust him for this mission!"

CHAPTER 11

Somewhere in northern Michigan, this newspaper article was passed around at a meeting of the *American Dissident.*

We Must Not Single Out Arab Americans
Anonymous

As an African American, I am outraged by the singling out of Arab Americans and Muslims following the terrorist attacks.

Throughout the country, there have been reports of the harassment, beatings, and killings of Arabs and South Asians. Muslim women and children are afraid to leave their homes and wear their traditional clothing in public for fear of becoming the targets of racial violence. And men deemed to be "Arab-looking" have been removed from airplanes after passing through security checkpoints.

Outside of Detroit, a 45-year-old US citizen originally from Yemen was shot twelve times in the back by his girlfriend's former lover. The suspect reportedly told the victim, "I'm going to kill you for what happened in New York and DC."

The FBI is investigating the murder of Waqar Hasan, a forty-six-year-old Pakistani grocer in Dallas, and authorities cite racial hatred as the motivation behind the killing of Balbir Singh Sodhi, 49, an Indian Sikh gas-station attendant in Mesa, Ariz. When he was arrested, the suspect in the Mesa killing reportedly said, "I stand for America all the way!" The FBI is also investigating the killing of an Egyptian-American grocery-store owner, Adel Karas, 48, who was shot to death in his store in San Gabriel, Calif.

In Seattle, the federal government has charged a man with shooting at Muslim worshipers and attempting to set a mosque on fire. In Salt Lake City, a man was arrested for allegedly setting fire to a Pakistani restaurant. And there have been several other cases.

Rep. John Cooksey, R-La., did not make things better when he declared on a radio show that "someone who comes in that's got a diaper on his head and a fan belt wrapped around that diaper on his head, that guy needs to be pulled over." Cooksey later apologized.

On a Northwest Airlines flight from Minneapolis to Salt Lake City, three Arab-American men were expelled from the plane because of their ethnicity. Northwest removed the three men when the other passengers refused to fly with them. In Orlando, Fla., two Pakistani businessmen were removed from a flight they had boarded after the pilots insisted on their expulsion due to their perceived ethnic background.

In times of war and national crisis, Americans often have felt the need to find a scapegoat. Typically, these scapegoats have been members of racial and ethnic minority groups.

At the height of the Civil War in 1863, armed mobs took to the streets of Manhattan in protest of President Lincoln's federal draft order. The mob of poor white laborers ultimately directed their wrath toward African Americans, who as noncitizens were exempted from the draft and competed with poor whites for the lowest-paying jobs.

African Americans were lynched and beaten in the streets, and a black church and a black orphanage were burned to the ground. The Civil War draft riots claimed at least 105 lives.

After Japan's attack on Pearl Harbor during World War II, President Roosevelt signed Executive Order 9066, which led to the internment of 112,000 residents of Japanese descent, two-thirds of whom were US citizens, according to the *Los Angeles Times*.

More recently, in the aftermath of the 1995 Oklahoma City bombing, Arab communities in the United States were harassed. However, the public soon learned that the person responsible for the bombing was Timothy McVeigh, a 27-year-old white male. Yet no one suggested that the government harass and target the nation's young white men on the grounds that they pose a threat to national security.

So why are Arabs and Muslims branded as terrorists?

"The American popular culture has been poisoned by the vicious racism of Hollywood and the op-ed pages of American newspapers," according to Hussein Ibish, communications director of the American-Arab Anti-Discrimination Committee. "Arabs and Muslims have been portrayed in movies and TV in almost exclusively negative terms, as terrorists or oil sheiks. We have been telling the entertainment industry for years that if they refused to show any positive or neutral Arab or Muslim characters, this could lead under the right circumstances to a rash of hate crimes."

Ibish's sentiments are confirmed by recent polls. A Gallup Poll found that 58 percent of Americans supported more intensive airport security checks for Arab passengers, even those who are citizens, and 49 percent supported special identification. A Zogby poll presented a more positive view of Arab Americans, with 62 percent of Americans holding a favorable opinion of Arab Americans, although 38 percent of its respondents believed that Islam encourages "fanaticism."

In both polls, African Americans, the primary targets of racial profiling by police, were ironically the group most in favor of intensive security measures for Arab Americans.

Americans cannot respond to terrorism by inflicting their own brand of terror on fellow citizens and residents, simply because they are or appear to be members of a particular ethnic, racial, or religious group. The singling out of people based on ethnicity or looks must stop now.

"As your leader I stand before you today and say that not only is this a crock of shit it is further proof that we need not forget our war against the niggers! We are the true leaders in this so-called war against terrorism because *we know who our enemies are*, and it ain't just the fucking rag heads! If this nigger were a true American, he would not publish this anonymously and he would also speak out against the rag heads and not for them." The meeting of well over one hundred men and women cheered loudly for well over two minutes after this statement.) We must join with all our Patriot friends regardless of their militia or other patriot ties in this "war" against all minorities and immigrants in and out of this country that threaten the sanctity and purity of the White/Christian/Anglo-Saxon race here and abroad. Heil Hitler!"

Again, the meeting hall burst out in applause of support.

"I now refer you to the second article in your packet, an article trying to justify the existence of the so-called non-militant Muslim population in this country. However, the killing of the Muslim bastard is proof that our fellow Hoosier brothers have it right!"

> Muslim Man's Killing Hate Crime, Sons Say
> Police Investigate as Fear Rises in Northwest Indiana
> Advertisement
>
> Tribune staff reporter
>
> Northwest Indiana restaurant owner Naseeb Mohammed attended prayer services at his mosque on Friday, where local and federal law enforcement officers assured Muslims that they would be on guard against hate crimes as the latest anniversary of the Sept. 11 attacks approached.
>
> Mohammed, 60, of Munster, Ind., was killed the next morning as he prepared lentil soup in his Middle Eastern restaurant, Aladdin Pita, in Merrillville. Employees arriving at about 10:00 a.m. found him dead of a gunshot wound, police said. Police said they do not know whether the slaying is a hate crime. They said no evidence, such as vandalism, was found to suggest a hate crime.
>
> But Mohammed's sons insisted hate must have been a motive because only $150 was taken from the restaurant even though more was avail-

able. They also said it does not make sense to rob a restaurant in the morning before it opens, when more money would be available after closing.

"This is someone who wanted to bring grief to the Muslim community, and that's what they did," said his son Bassam Mohammed, 25.

"This is just another act of terror," said his oldest son, Ghassan Mohammed, 28.

As softly weeping women filed into the family's home Sunday afternoon, chairs were arranged in the garage and beneath a canopy for solemn-faced men, who were served strong black coffee in accordance with tradition. Sugar would not be appropriate during mourning, Bassam Mohammed said.

The murder has made Muslims in northwest Indiana more wary and fearful than ever, one community leader said. Imam Mongy Elquesny of the Northwest Indiana Islamic Center in Merrillville, where the meeting Friday with law enforcement was held, said he expected 60 children for Sunday school but only 20 showed up.

"They have a kind of fear for their children," he said of the reasons parents gave for keeping their children home. Elquesny said there have been several meetings with law enforcement since 9/11, with community members invited to ask questions.

The meetings have helped ease some fears, he said. While about 150 families were registered with the Islamic Center before 9/11, now there are about 250. Elquesny said the increase is because of the good reputation the area has for being safe and welcoming for Muslims. After the community meeting on Friday, two FBI officials went with Elquesny to Mohammed's restaurant for a meal, said Elquesny and FBI Special Agent Wendy Osborne.

Now the FBI is helping with the murder investigation, Osborne said. The Northwest Indiana Major Crimes Task Force has brought together investigators from more than a dozen jurisdictions.

"The Arab community is part of our community," said Detective Jeff White, a member of the task force. White would not comment about the factors that make Mohammed's sons think hate motivated the murder. But he said those factors have been considered by investigators, who are still unwilling to say the murder is a hate crime.

"They don't want the Muslim community to be angry," Bassam Mohammed said of comments by police. "We have a pretty decent-size community, and for them to be angered, it's not in their best interest."

On Sunday afternoon, the restaurateur's sons greeted visitors who came to offer condolences at Mohammed's home. Naseeb Mohammed left his native Palestine shortly after high school, spending about a year in Kuwait before coming to the United States.

"He had to support his family," said Bassam Mohammed of his father's reason for leaving Palestine. "There were no jobs there. You cannot support a family in Palestine." Gesturing about the home in the upscale subdivision, the son added, "He wanted to support his family comfortably and, as you can tell, he succeeded." It was hard work, achieving the American dream. "He worked as a cook," Bassam Mohammed said. "He worked as a dishwasher. He worked as a stock boy."

Bassam Mohammed said that in the years since 9/11, he and his family have suffered varying degrees of racism and mistrust.

"I was born and raised and went to college here," he said. "I'm as American as any American. For someone to tell me to go back to my country, it doesn't make sense. This is my country. But I've had that happen to me in college, in the restaurant and in the bowling alley."

Services for his father, who leaves a wife and seven children, will be on Monday.

"The horrible day that it is," Bassam Mohammed said. "It's going to be sad because of what happened to the twin towers on Sept. 11, and for me it will be even worse because it will be the day we bury my dad."

"I think that we are all in agreement here that this type of activity needs to occur on a daily basis throughout this great land of ours. To hell with the sand niggers, the regular niggers, and let's not forget the Jew bastards." To that comment, the place got so loud with cheers it would have reminded you of a Southeastern Conference football game. "Which now gets us to the third article in your possession, entitled 'The Anthrax Murders,' published by one of our own.

"Superficially, this essay comes to a different conclusion than I do about the culprit in the anthrax murders. However, both could be true. Bush had intimate ties with the Israeli neocons through Cheney, Perle, Wolfowitz, Abrams, Kristol, Feith, Rumsfeld, Libby, Bolton… My comments are shown in green.

"This study is based on an article in the latest National Vanguard print magazine, 'The Anthrax Mystery: Solved.' It is one of the most compelling and important stories we've told since this program began in 1991. The anthrax murders, which began shortly after the 9/11 terror attacks, remain officially unsolved. Was this bio-terrorism a case of an Arab attack on Americans because 'they hate our freedom'? Was it the work of a 'domestic terrorist' motivated by hate of the US media or government? You're about to hear the evidence, and the evidence points to none of these things: Instead it points to the anthrax attacks being an operation of a foreign intelligence service with capabilities and motives identical to those of the murderous Israeli Mossad. Listen to the evidence and decide for yourself as American Dissident Voices presents 'The Anthrax Murders, the Israeli Connection.'

"On October 4, 2001, reporters in Florida announced the first case in twenty-five years of a person contracting the deadly bacterium anthrax. The following day, Robert Stevens, the photo editor of the Florida-based tabloid *Sun*, died. His death was the beginning of the Anthrax Mystery, America's worst—and most baffling—case of bio-terrorism. Days later, four other persons in the New York City and Washington, DC, areas would die from anthrax spores that leaked from tainted letters sent through the mail. Seventeen others would become infected, and hundreds of millions of dollars would be spent on cleaning up contaminated office buildings and postal facilities. All these events came just a few days after the tragedy of September 11. It appeared the terrorists had struck again, but this time, the attack was biological.

"Investigators believe seven letters containing anthrax spores were mailed. Four of the seven are thought to have been mailed on the same day and addressed to major media outlets in New York City: ABC News, CBS News, NBC News, and the New York Post. Of these, only the NBC and New York Post letters were recovered. Letters believed to be addressed to ABC News and CBS News offices caused two persons to develop anthrax infections. One was a seven-month-old boy brought in by his mother, a producer at ABC News; the other was an assistant to Dan Rather at CBS. These letters were never found.

"The two recovered letters did not have a return address but were postmarked September 18, 2001, in Trenton, New Jersey. They contained identical messages tending to indicate that the perpetrators were Islamic terrorists. The notes read, '09-11-01, THIS IS NEXT,

TAKE PENACILIN [sic] NOW, DEATH TO AMERICA, DEATH TO ISRAEL, ALLAH IS GREAT.'

"It is also believed an anthrax-laced letter was mailed to the *National Enquirer.*

"Interestingly, hoax letters claiming to contain anthrax were mailed days later from St. Petersburg, Florida. However, instead of anthrax spores, these letters contained a harmless substance described by some as looking like talcum powder. One of these hoax letters was again addressed to NBC News in New York City. In addition, Judith Miller, the author of a book on bio-terrorism and a reporter on the Middle East for the *New York Times*, received an anthrax hoax letter at her office. The St. Petersburg Times and Fox News also received similar hoax letters.

"The mailing of the hoax letters cannot be considered the work of a copycat. For example, the NBC News hoax letter was mailed on September 20. This would have been two days after the NBC News letter containing anthrax was mailed from Trenton, New Jersey. The remaining hoax letters were mailed between October 5 and 9. News reports naming media outlets that received the original anthrax letters were on October 12 and 13. A copycat mailer could have acted only after October 12, when the public first became aware of the media anthrax letters. The apparent purpose of mailing the hoax letters was to foster the anthrax scare and create a media frenzy.

"The mailings of anthrax-laced letters from New Jersey and the Florida hoax letters that followed were probably coordinated. The mailing sites of Trenton, New Jersey, and St. Petersburg, Florida, were chosen, perhaps, to emphasize an Arab or Islamic connection in the minds of Americans. Trenton is the home of a large Arab-American community. Also, several of the September 11 hijackers had lived in both areas. The mailers of the anthrax and hoax letters wanted the public to think that remnants of al-Qaeda were still around and active.

"However, the mailing of the anthrax letters shows a degree of media savvy that would be unusual for foreign Islamic terrorists. The persons who sent the letters knew which media outlets would have the greatest influence on the public. Even today, with the advent of cable and satellite television, the three major television broadcast networks remain as the primary source of news for most Americans. *The New York Post* and the *National Enquirer* are tabloid papers and were likely chosen for their sensational headlines. Of all the papers in New York City, the *New York Post* would have screamed the loudest concerning the threat from Islamic terrorists. For Americans who don't follow the news, the *National Enquirer*, with its presence at every checkout stand in America, would convey the message. The desired effect in choosing these media outlets was to alarm the public and to remind them these terrorists wanted to destroy both America and Israel.

"But only five of the seven anthrax letters were sent to media outlets. The remaining two were addressed to members of the United States Senate. These letters were posted on Tuesday, October 9, exactly three weeks from the first anthrax mailings, and four weeks from September 11. The letters were addressed to two of America's most liberal Democrat Senators: Tom Daschle of South Dakota and Patrick Leahy of Vermont.

"An aide opened the Daschle letter on October 15. A puff of powder quickly flew out of the letter. Capitol police were called, and a Hazmat team sealed off the Senator's office. This letter had a different note that read, '09-11-01, YOU CAN NOT STOP US. WE HAVE THIS ANTHRAX. YOU DIE NOW. ARE YOU AFRAID? DEATH TO AMERICA. DEATH TO ISRAEL. ALLAH IS GREAT.'

"Once tests confirmed the Daschle letter actually contained anthrax, all Capitol mail was stopped and impounded for further investigation. The Leahy letter would be found on November 16 in the impounded mail. It also contained anthrax spores and an identical note. It is believed the Leahy letter was delayed and misdirected due to an initial misreading of the letter's zip code.

"The Senate letters had a fictitious return address indicating they came from schoolchildren. The return address read, '4th Grade, Greendale School, Franklin Park NJ 08852.' Apparently, it was thought a letter coming from schoolchildren would have a better chance of reaching the intended targets without raising suspicions.

"The envelopes and notes have yielded few clues leading to the true identities of the persons who were responsible for the anthrax attacks. Obviously, the senders tried to mask who they were and to hide their true motives. Investigators turned to analyzing the anthrax material itself.

"Anthrax is a spore-forming germ, *Bacillus anthracis*, and can be found in livestock such as sheep or cattle. Analysis of the spores from the letters revealed them all to be of the same strain. This particular strain, known as the Ames strain, was first researched at the Army's Medical Research Institute of Infectious Diseases (USAMRIID), Fort Detrick, Maryland. This strain of anthrax bacteria originally came from a single cow that had died in Texas in 1981. Ames has the reputation of being deadlier than other anthrax strains. Some have called Ames the 'gold standard' of anthrax.

"From Fort Detrick, the Ames strain was sent to researchers in at least fifteen laboratories within the United States and six laboratories abroad. It is not known how many other universities and labs may have had access to the strain, but according to one law-enforcement official, 'more labs than you think' could have obtained the Ames strain.

"In the past, microbiologists attending conferences on infectious diseases would take vials of various strains and simply swap them with each other to aid in their research. Martin Hugh-Jones, a scientist at Louisiana State University, stated that during this period deadly pathogens were traded 'like playing cards.'

"Investigators examining the anthrax spores within the letters found them to be of different grades, with the best among them considered by some to be 'weapons-grade' material. A modern spray drying technique was used in preparing these spores, instead of the older method of milling. Also, radiocarbon dating found the spores to be relatively newly created—not more than two years old.

"This indicates to me that whomever sent the anthrax had more than casual access to weapons-grade anthrax. Otherwise, the materials would have been identical.

"Of the two anthrax letters that were recovered in New York City, the *New York Post* letter was found unopened and still contained the anthrax material. The NBC News anthrax letter tested positive for anthrax, but only a trace amount remained after it was opened. Major General John Parker, with the US Army Medical Research and Materiel Command, said one of his scientists described the *New York Post* sample as, 'looking like Purina Dog Chow.' It had coarse brown granules but was densely packed with anthrax spores and highly concentrated.

"In contrast, the anthrax in the Daschle letter was like a fine white powder; General Parker compared it to talcum powder. Under the microscope the Daschle sample was ten times denser in anthrax spores when compared to the *New York Post* sample.

"A team of scientists at the Fort Detrick lab opened the Leahy letter on December 5. This letter also contained a very fine powder, which was easily made airborne. The Leahy letter had particles that were smaller and more uniform in size compared to the Daschle letter. This made the anthrax spores in the Leahy letter even deadlier: Smaller spores of a uniform size have a better chance of entering the respiratory system and causing death.

"It was reported the quality of the anthrax spores found in the Leahy letter surpassed previously known state-sponsored bio-weapons programs. According to *Newsweek*, 'the Leahy anthrax' was coated with a chemical compound unknown to experts who have worked in the field for years; the coating matches no known anthrax samples ever recovered from biological-weapons producers anywhere in the world, including Iraq and the former Soviet Union. The anthrax in the Leahy letter has proven to be a superior product. Bio-defense experts assisting the FBI have so far been unable to duplicate the anthrax material through any reverse engineering processes. Investigators are left with the uncertain choice of deciding if this was the work of a lone brilliant scientist—or a state-sponsored bio-weapons program, pointing toward someone with high-security clearance as the culprit. This indicates to me that whomever sent the anthrax intended primarily to kill Leahy, Daschle, and Bob Stevens, with the other attacks being more smokescreens.

"So who sent the anthrax? Some, like Barbara Hatch Rosenberg with the leftist Federation of America Scientists (FAS), have a suspect. In her report, 'Analysis of the Anthrax Attacks,' Rosenberg presents her profile of the anthrax attacker, accompanied by her own political biases. Rosenberg believes the attacker has connections with the US government. She believes he is being protected by the FBI and has information on secret programs the government does not wish to be disclosed.

"In her profile, Rosenberg identified the attacker as a bio-defense insider with a doctoral degree. He is a middle-aged American who is skilled in working with dangerous pathogens. She boldly claims he is also a CIA contractor based in the Washington, DC, area. There is no mystery as to the identity of Rosenberg's suspect. Her suspect is the person around whom she has built her profile: Dr. Steven J. Hatfill.

"Barbara Rosenberg began her mission to 'bring Dr. Hatfill to justice' by giving a series of lectures and media interviews accusing the FBI of stalling the investigation. Eventually, she was able to arrange a meeting with Senate staffers and FBI agents in attendance. Several of the staffers worked for Senators Daschle and Leahy, the recipients of the anthrax letters. Without revealing his name, Barbara Rosenberg indicated to everyone there that her suspect, Dr. Hatfill, was responsible for the anthrax attacks.

"A week later—apparently as a result of Senate pressure—the FBI brought Dr. Hatfill into public view. In an investigation that had previously been out of the spotlight, the media were now alerted to the FBI's scrutiny of Rosenberg's suspect. When the FBI searched Dr. Hatfill's apartment, the media, with helicopters overhead, covered it live on national television. The whole world was now aware of the public pursuit (and some would later say the public persecution) of Dr. Hatfill.

"In response to this attention, Dr. Hatfill was forced to hold two press conferences and declare his innocence. On August 11, 2002, Dr. Hatfill said, 'After eight months of one of the most intensive public and private investigations in American history, no one—no one—has come up with a shred of evidence that I had anything to do with the anthrax letters.'

"Whatever their motives, the FBI was certainly having problems connecting Dr. Hatfill to the crimes. They could not place Hatfill in Trenton, New Jersey, at the time of the mailings, and no residue of anthrax material could be found anywhere he had lived or visited. There was no physical evidence whatsoever connecting Dr. Hatfill with the anthrax mailings.

"Hatfill is said to be one of perhaps thirty scientists who could have carried out this attack.

"This is ridiculous. Surely all these thirty people have signed a waiver that allows them to be interrogated with lie detectors to narrow down the suspects. Why has this not been done? This implies complicity in the attacks by the administration.

"His background as a former researcher at Fort Detrick placed him on the list. However, Dr. Hatfill claims to be an expert on viruses such as Ebola and Marburg, and not on anthrax bacteria. Dr. Hatfill has publicly stated that he has never worked with anthrax.

"The FBI initially interviewed Dr. Hatfill in January 2002, apparently as part of the investigation's broader look at scientists with a connection to the bio-defense community. At that time, Dr. Hatfill took a lie-detector test in an effort to clear his name. The agent who gave him the test reportedly said, 'I'm satisfied. I believe you had nothing to do with the anthrax.'

"Steven Hatfill studied biology at Southwestern College in Winfield, Kansas. During this period, he left his studies and traveled to Kapanga, Zaire, where he worked with Dr. Glenn Eschtruth as a medical missionary. After graduating from Southwestern in 1975, Hatfill enlisted in the United States Army. In October 1976, he married Caroline Eschtruth, the daughter of his mentor.

"It would be only a few months after their marriage when Cuban-led mercenaries based in Angola attacked Dr. Eschtruth's mission. The mercenaries captured Dr. Eschtruth and later executed him, a tragedy which left a strong impression on Hatfill. He and his wife Caroline were divorced in May 1978. Shortly thereafter, Hatfill returned to Africa and continued his medical education.

"Hatfill attended the Godfrey Huggins Medical School in White-ruled Rhodesia, graduating in 1984. While in Rhodesia,

Hatfill claims to have served with the Selous Scouts. The Selous Scouts were Rhodesia's crack counterinsurgency troops used against the terrorists who wanted to overthrow the white government. In 1980, as a result of international pressure, Rhodesia was turned over to the black Mugabe government, which still rules there today. The country would later have its name changed to Zimbabwe. In 1984, Hatfill moved to the Republic of South Africa to further his medical studies and research.

"While in South Africa, Hatfill was in contact with Aquila, the paramilitary wing of the Afrikaner Weerstandsbeweging (AWB) or Afrikaner Resistance Movement. The AWB was the largest white resistance group active in preventing the black takeover of South Africa. Some have labeled the AWB a 'neo-Nazi' organization. One has only to look at their political banner to come to this conclusion: It is very similar to National Socialist Germany's swastika flag but, instead of a swastika, uses a triskelion—an ancient symbol which resembles three 'sevens' arranged in a spinning design.

"A colleague of Hatfill's at Stellenbosch University's radiobiology laboratory saw a newspaper photo of AWB leader, Eugene Terre'Blanche, surrounded by Dr. Hatfill and members of the Aquila Brigade. This colleague—in an apparent effort to expose Hatfill—placed the photo on the lab's notice board. When confronted, Hatfill made no secret of his AWB ties. The colleague claimed, "This photo was put up on the lab notice board-and led to Hatfill boasting that he was the weapons trainer of the Western Cape Branch of Aquila." Since that time, the photo has not been seen by the public.

"Several amazing coincidences have contributed to the intense interest in Hatfill shown by investigators. They also help to explain why some, like Barbara Rosenberg, are so convinced Dr. Hatfill was responsible for the anthrax attacks.

"One coincidence concerning Dr. Hatfill and his times in Africa is the Greendale School reference that appeared as the return address on the anthrax letters sent to Senators Daschle and Leahy. There was an upscale suburb of Salisbury, Rhodesia, known as Greendale; the neighborhood school there was informally known as Greendale School. The school was actually named after White Rhodesian patriot

Courtney Selous, after whom the Selous Scouts were named. As mentioned previously, Hatfill claims to have served with this group.

"Another coincidence involves Dr. Hatfill's commissioning William Patrick, an expert on weaponized anthrax, to write a report on the proper procedures to be used if an anthrax letter arrived in the mail. Hatfill's employer at the time, Science Applications International Corporation (SAIC), saw a need for emergency responders to know exactly what to do if this were ever to occur.

"In the SAIC report, written two years before the anthrax mailings, Patrick describes how a few grams of anthrax spores could be sent in envelopes and details the proper emergency procedures that should be followed if this were to take place. The report was provided to the Centers for Disease Control and Prevention in Atlanta. They, at the time, were working on a similar report and provided the information they assembled to police and fire departments via the Internet. Dr. Hatfill's attorney Victor Glasberg denies the Patrick report was any type of blueprint for an anthrax mailing. Glasberg said, 'There is zero data in the report. It shows you what you do after it happens.'

"Perhaps the most suspicious coincidence was the mysterious anthrax hoax letter mailed from London, England, in November 2001, and addressed to Senator Tom Daschle. Within the envelope were a powdery substance and a threatening note. At the time of the mailing, Hatfill was in England training to be a United Nations bio-weapons inspector for a future mission in Iraq. As previously mentioned, several anthrax hoax letters were mailed to media organizations. This hoax letter was the first and only one sent to a senator. Some within the FBI wonder if the London letter may have been an attempt to frame Dr. Hatfill.

"One outfit that has spent a great deal of time and energy in blaming Dr. Hatfill for the anthrax attacks is the Jewish Defense Organization (JDO). This group has labeled Hatfill a Nazi because of his ties to the Afrikaner Resistance Movement. In the *Weekly Standard* article 'The Hunting of Steven J. Hatfill,' David Tell claims the JDO is responsible for spreading many of the damning accusations that now surround Dr. Hatfill. The JDO is an offshoot of the terrorist Jewish Defense League, founded by the late Rabbi Meir Kahane. Today, the JDO spends most of its time feeding reporters and commentators hateful and misleading information concerning Dr. Hatfill. Tell describes the JDO as the 'central clearinghouse of Hatfill demonology.' He claims mainstream reporters will use the JDO material on Hatfill but will never acknowledge their source. It is interesting that a small extremist group like the Jewish Defense Organization appears to have been the first to document the background and personal history of Dr. Steven Hatfill.

"The evidence is mounting that Dr. Hatfill is an innocent man and had nothing to do with the anthrax attacks. Reporters and investigators will realize this when those responsible for the anthrax mailings are identified."

Part 2

"In addition to Dr. Hatfill, whom we regard as innocent, there are two other bio-defense scientists who have received some attention in the anthrax investigation. But unlike Hatfill, these scientists have rarely been mentioned in the press.

"On October 3, 2001, Dr. Ayaad Assaad, an Arab-American scientist and a former researcher at USAMRIID Fort Detrick, Maryland, was called into the Washington, DC, offices of the FBI and was confronted with an anonymous letter that accused him of being 'a potential biological terrorist.' The author of the letter claimed to be a former colleague of Dr. Assaad, and accused him of having a vendetta against the government. The meeting between Assaad and the FBI took place two days before it was known that Robert Stevens, the first victim of the anthrax attacks, had died. The letter was postmarked September 21 and was addressed to 'Town of Quantico Police' in Virginia. Quantico is twenty-five miles south of Washington, DC, and is home to both Marine Corps and FBI facilities.

"A number of questions have arisen surrounding this letter. The timing of the letter is suspicious, given that it was written before there was public knowledge concerning the anthrax attacks. Dr.

Assaad believes the letter was devised to implicate him in the coming attacks and to set him up as the 'fall guy.' He believes the person who sent the letter may also be responsible for the anthrax attacks. The FBI determined Dr. Assaad was not involved with terrorism and that the accusatory letter must have been a hoax.

"The author of the letter clearly had inside knowledge of who's who in the US bioterror program.

"But Dr. Assaad had reason to be concerned. A decade earlier, he, along with two other Arab-American scientists, all of whom were working at Ft. Detrick, were targeted and harassed by another group of scientists working there. The group that was harassing the Arab-Americans called themselves the Camel Club. One of the Camel Club members was Dr. Philip M. Zack, lieutenant colonel in the United States Army. The apparent objective of the Camel Club was to drive the Arab-American scientists out of the bio-defense facility.

"Shortly after the Persian Gulf War in 1991, Dr. Assaad found an eight-page poem in his mailbox authored by the club. The poem contained lewd and obscene remarks and was written in an attempt to harass and mock the Egyptian-born scientist. Dr. Assaad reported these incidents to Fort Detrick's commander, who at the time did little or nothing to stop the harassment. Dr. Assaad later sued the army, claiming 'discrimination.' Was this a case of racism—or of something going on at the lab which the harassers might not want an Arab scientist to see?

"The Hartford Courant has been the only paper to have covered this story in detail. They reported that 'Zack left Fort Detrick in December 1991, after a controversy over allegations of unprofessional behavior?' The paper later reported Dr. Zack was observed entering the lab after hours on January 23, 1992. A surveillance camera recorded Dr. Marian Rippy, one of the 'Camel Club' members, letting Dr. Zack inside the building.

"Lab technicians noticed a late-night intruder was tampering with their equipment. A 1992 inquiry found someone was conducting unauthorized research involving anthrax during the evening hours. An audit of the lab showed twenty-seven sets of specimens—including anthrax spores—were unaccounted for or missing. One former commander at the facility said he did not believe any of the missing specimens were ever found.

"Dr. Zack is said to be Jewish, and for some this makes him the leading anthrax suspect, particularly among those in Internet discussion groups. They see the harassment of Dr. Assaad, the late-night research on anthrax, and the accusatory letter all pointing in Dr. Zack's direction.

"Ed Lake, the leading amateur investigator of the anthrax attacks, has done some important research concerning the letter sent to the authorities naming Dr. Assaad as a potential terrorist. Lake found that, after September 11, a great deal of speculation ensued concerning the possibility of another terrorist attack. The consensus was that the next attack would likely be biological in nature, and anthrax could be the weapon of choice. Lake did an analysis of how many times the word *anthrax* appeared in Internet discussion groups from September 8, 2001, to October 7, 2001. Not surprisingly, discussions concerning anthrax and a possible biological attack increased dramatically after September 11. Lake concluded, given the circumstances, it would not be unusual for someone to warn authorities concerning potential terrorist activity.

"This is the most likely explanation for the anonymous letter. A former colleague of Dr. Assaad sent the letter out of genuine concern in preventing a biological attack. This person may or may not have been a participant in the Camel Club shenanigans but could have been influenced by them. It is unlikely Dr. Zack sent the accusatory letter, since it would have brought immediate attention upon himself and his suspicious activities a decade earlier. Also, it is equally difficult to believe Dr. Zack was responsible for the anthrax mailings.

"So what other suspects remain? Our best-known suspect or 'person of interest' is Dr. Steven J. Hatfill. But after an extensive investigation by the FBI, no physical evidence connects Hatfill with the mailings. Other possible suspects can be dismissed as easily as they are mentioned. Iraq and al-Qaeda are not responsible, even though some within the administration and the news media would like to blame them. There have been suggestions the CIA could have sent the anthrax letters, if a hidden bio-weapons program existed within the agency. But what purpose would such an attack serve? It is hard to imagine a motive for the CIA to commit such an act. Were neo-Nazis, anti-abortionists, or right-wing militias the culprits? There are plenty of off-the-wall theories about possible suspects— even one involving a pagan cult in the Midwest—but nothing has panned out. There is, however, another possibility that needs to be considered.

"'Who had the means, the motive, and the opportunity to have brought about these attacks?' is a basic question that needs to be asked.

"An extensive and well-developed biological warfare program exists within Israel today. A motive for the anthrax attacks could be to blame Arab terrorists or a 'rogue nation' for this atrocity and to help launch the United States into war against Israel's enemies. Lastly, Israel had prior knowledge of the planned attacks on September 11.

"Israel's bio-weapons programs date back to the earliest formation of the Zionist state. Dr. Avner Cohen documents Israel's program in his paper, 'Israel and Chemical/Biological Weapons: History, Deterrence, and Arms Control.' Cohen begins by describing how Zionists during the 1948 war poisoned the wells and water supplies of Arab villagers. According to Israeli military historian Dr. Uri Milstein, the typhoid epidemic that spread throughout the coastal town of Acre in May 1948 was the result of Zionist Jews contaminating the Arabs' water supply. In Gaza, the Jews failed in a similar attempt. The Egyptian Army found four Jews disguised as Arabs near the water wells. The four terrorists were caught with a canteen filled with dysentery and typhoid bacteria. All four were tried, convicted, and hanged within a three-month period. Dr. Cohen questions if the two incidents were isolated or part of a larger program of bio-warfare during the 1948 war.

"Israel's bio-weapons facilities are located at the Israel Institute of Biological Research (IIBR) in Ness Ziona (also Nes Ziona, Nes Tona) a few miles southeast of Tel Aviv. In 1952, the IIBR consisted of a single building hidden in an orange grove. Today, the IIBR has grown into a massive fourteen-acre compound with several hundred employees surrounded by high walls and electronic sensors. What goes on behind those high walls is something Israel would prefer to be kept secret.

"Dutch journalist Karel Knip has researched the IIBR and came up with some interesting findings. Knip began by going through medical literature he found on the Internet. Specifically, he focused on the papers of 140 scientists affiliated with IIBR over the last five decades. With the help of experts on chemical and biological weapons, Knip developed an overview of the various programs that exist at IIBR. Knip found IIBR research began in the 1950s involving plague, typhus, and rabies. Dr. Avner Cohen discusses Knip's findings in his paper and states, 'a significant number of studies at IIBR focused on anti-livestock agents, following the path of other national BW [bio-weapons] programs at the time.' *Anti-livestock agents* is Cohen's cryptic reference to Israel's anthrax programs."

NTA

A motive for Israel in launching the anthrax attacks would be to bring America into war against Iraq and to remove that country as a potential threat to the Jewish state. When Iraq invaded Kuwait in 1990, the United States Senate was thrown into a heated debate as to whether or not this country should go to war. Senator Tom Daschle took the lead in being against American involvement. In order for Israel to achieve her war objective, this time, Senator Daschle would have to be removed—or turned toward Israel's position. Either way, Israel would win.

Likewise, Senator Patrick Leahy ran afoul of the Israelis when he introduced his Leahy Amendment to the Foreign Operations Appropriations Act. The Leahy Amendment, also called the Leahy Law, prohibits American arms sales to foreign security or military units that systematically violate human rights. The Israeli military routinely tortures Palestinian prisoners, assassinates Arab political figures, and fires American-made rockets and missiles into civilian crowds and apartment buildings. If an American administration ever decided to enforce the Leahy Law, Israel would find herself under an arms embargo. Eliminating or "turning" her senatorial adversaries—a gamble she couldn't lose—would be powerful motives for Israel to target Senators Daschle and Leahy for political assassination by anthrax. Remember also, as we discussed last week, there was a qualitative difference in the anthrax sent to the senators and that sent to media figures.

"For Israel to have initiated the anthrax attacks, prior knowledge of the al-Qaeda plot was essential. The Mossad, Israel's external intelligence service, has made it their mission to track Arab terrorists around the world. Indirect evidence of Mossad's surveillance of the al-Qaeda hijackers prior to September 11 can be found in the Drug Enforcement Agency report, 'Suspicious Activities Involving Israeli Art Students at DEA Facilities, and in an investigative report from Fox News."

Cryptome

"In March 2001, an alert was issued by the National Counterintelligence Executive, a branch of the CIA, warning federal employees to be aware of "suspicious visitors to federal facilities." There had been reports of Middle Eastern persons showing up at government buildings—many of them DEA offices—claiming to be Israeli art students. At first it was thought the Israeli art students might be Arab terrorists planning an attack. However, it later turned out the art students were indeed Israelis.

"The Israelis would appear unannounced at various government offices or at the homes of federal officials. They would falsely identify themselves as art students from the University of Jerusalem or Bazala Academy in Israel and attempt to sell their artwork on canvas. Astute government employees soon discovered the Israelis were more interested in obtaining information than in selling artwork. The students, in the course of their conversations, would ask for business cards and inquire about the officials' work activities and those of their associates. At times, the Israelis were found breaching government entrances through back doors and parking garages. Others appeared at government offices that were hidden or undisclosed to the local community. Some were found with diagrams of government buildings showing entrances and offices of various employees—indicating prior surveillance. Others were found with photographs of government agents. One Israeli 'art student' had a computer printout with the heading 'DEA groups.'

"The DEA, with the help of the FBI, began to compile a report on the Israeli art students. The report, prepared in June 2001, listed over one hundred Israelis by name along with their personal identifying information. After the Israelis were arrested, the government, for sensitive political reasons, was reluctant to prosecute any of them for espionage, so they let them go.

"One DEA agent, in an apparent attempt to prevent a government cover-up, had the report posted on the Internet in March 2002. The report provides information obtained from the Israelis during their interrogations. In a general assessment of the Israelis, the report states, 'Most admit to having served in the Israeli military. This is not surprising given the mandatory military service require [sic] in Israel, however, a majority of those questioned has [sic] stated they served in military intelligence, electronic signal intercept, or explosive ordnance units.'

"Within the various agencies of the US government, there was a debate regarding the entire Israeli art student phenomenon. Most were convinced this was an intelligence operation, but at the time, its purpose was unclear. The best clue in understanding the mystery was their main target: the Drug Enforcement Agency. Although the Israelis penetrated other federal facilities, such as military bases, the spies seemed focused on the DEA.

"During this period, the DEA was investigating the activities of Israeli organized crime. Israeli mobsters, along with the Russian Mafia, control the distribution of the drug Ecstasy in America. It should be noted there is no real difference between these two criminal organizations. It has been known for a long time that the Russian Mafia is made up of Russian Jews from the former Soviet Union. Questions still remain: Why were Israeli spies posing as art students interested in the activities of the DEA? What connection does the Mossad have with the Russian Mafia? The conclusion that best fits the known facts is that Israeli intelligence launched an operation against the DEA to protect their new intelligence asset, the Russian Mafia, from prosecution.

"After September 11, the activities of Israeli art students were seen in a new light. The FBI began to investigate the trail left by the Arab hijackers and found many of them had residences in Florida. Interestingly, one third of the art student spies were also based in Florida. It was discovered that some of the Israeli art students had addresses in the same locations as the hijackers. One commentator said that, at times, they were just yards apart.

"Carl Cameron with Fox News was the first major reporter to break this story, in a four-part series that aired in December 2001 and was subsequently pulled by Fox. In the series, Cameron gives several examples of Israeli espionage activities in America. In his first report, Cameron focuses on the Israeli surveillance of the Arab hijackers. Cameron reported, 'There is no indication that the Israelis were involved in the 9/11 attacks, but investigators suspect that the Israelis may have gathered intelligence about the attacks in advance and not shared it.'

"Cameron based his reporting on information he obtained from investigators in the FBI, DEA, and the INS. In his report, one investigator acknowledged there were 'tie-ins' between the Israelis and the Arab hijackers.

"Writer Alan Simpson appears to have obtained the unaired portions of Carl Cameron's report concerning the Israelis' monitoring of the hijackers:

> According to the FBI list, the Arab terrorist and suspect cells lived in the same neighborhoods as the Israeli cells in Irving, Texas and Hollywood and Miami, Florida, from December 2000 to April 2001. In the case of Irving, the Israeli cell used a rental mailbox in a shopping center just one block away from an Arab suspect's apartment. In Hollywood, the terrorists, including lead hijacker Mohammad Atta, the Egyptian who piloted American Airlines Flight 11 into

the North Tower of the World Trade Center, used a rental mailbox drop two blocks from an apartment rented by an Israeli "art student" team leader.

It is not the only case where the Israelis were found to be in the same location as the Saudi cells. According to the DEA report, another Israeli team operating out of Hollywood, Florida, led by team leader Hanan Serfaty lived at 4220 Sheridan Street, #303, Hollywood, Florida 33021 (Emerald Greens Apartments) while the Saudi hijackers Khalid Al Midhar, Abdulaziz al Omari, Walid Al Shehri, and UAE national Marwan al Shehri, operated from a mail drop at Mailbox Rentals, 3389 Sheridan St. #256, Hollywood, Florida 33021-3608. Another Serfaty residence at 701 S. 21st Avenue, Hollywood was located near the homes of Atta and Al Shehri, including a residence on Jackson Street, just a few blocks away, and the Bimini Motel Apartments, Apartment 8, at 1600 North Ocean Drive. On September 7, just days before their terrorist attack, Atta and Al Shehri spent several hours at Shuckums Oyster Bar and Grill at 1814 Harrison St., just blocks away from Serfaty's 21st Ave. residence. A Miami-based Israeli unit, led by Legum Yochai, operated from 13753 SW 90th Ave., Miami while hijacker Al Shehri lived nearby at Horizons Apartments, 8025 SW 107th Avenue.

nucNews

"There appears to be little doubt that Israeli intelligence knew exactly what Atta and company were doing in the weeks leading up to September 11th. We'll continue to explore the Israelis' means, motive, and opportunity—their disinformation and hoax campaigns—and the likely chronology of the anthrax murders—on the next program in this series."

Part 3

"Carl Cameron's reporting of the Israeli spy ring appears in part to be based upon a secret FBI document that shows the 'tie-ins' between the Israeli spies and the Arab hijackers. The fact that a secret FBI document exists is also evident in the *Die Zeit* article 'Next Door to Mohammed Atta.' *Die Zeit*, a German paper, based their article on information obtained from the French intelligence agency. The FBI apparently shared their report on Mossad activity with the French. The following portions of the article 'Next Door to Mohammed Atta,' closely parallels Carl Cameron's unaired report.

"Not until after the attacks of September 11 did the consequences of the spy ring become clear. Apparently, the agents were not interested in military or industrial facilities [sic], but were shadowing a number of suspects, who were later involved in the terrorist attacks against the United States. According to a report of the French intelligence agency that Die Zeit examined, 'According to the FBI, Arab terrorists and suspected terror cells lived in Phoenix, Arizona, as well as in Miami and Hollywood, Florida from December 2000 to April 2001 in direct proximity to the Israeli spy cells.'

"According to the report, the Mossad agents were interested in the leader of the terrorists, Mohammed Atta, and his key accomplice, Marwan al-Shehi. Both lived in Hamburg before they settled in Hollywood, Florida, in order to plan the attacks. A Mossad team was also operating in the same town. The leader, Hanan Serfati, had rented several dwellings. 'One of Serfati's apartments was located on the corner of 701st Street and 21st Avenue [sic] in Hollywood, right near the apartment of Atta and al-Shehi,' French intelligence reported later. Everything indicates that the terrorists were constantly observed by the Israelis. The chief Israeli agent was staying right near the post office where the terrorists had a mailbox.

"*Le Monde*, the French paper of record, in the article 'An Enigma: Vast Israeli Spy Network Dismantled in the US,' also appears to have had access to the secret FBI document or at least the French intelligence agency's version of it. The French paper provided a new detail and reported that six of the Israeli spies had cellular telephones bought by an Israeli ex-vice-consul. Another source reported some of the phones had a special walkie-talkie feature which made them difficult to intercept. This would indicate the spying was not some rogue operation-but was instead directed by Israel.

"The evidence is overwhelming that Israel, in the first half of 2001, launched an extensive intelligence-gathering operation within the United States. One part of their assignment was to learn as much as possible concerning the DEA investigations of the Russian Mafia and Israeli organized crime. Their other task was to monitor the al-Qaeda terrorists.

"Through electronic surveillance of the hijackers, the Israelis would have been able to learn the time and place for the September 11 attack. If the spies were monitoring the hijackers' Internet activities, they would have known the date of the flights and airlines involved since the hijacker's tickets were bought on-line.

"A newspaper article that appeared in Haaretz, an Israeli paper, further indicates prior knowledge of the coming attack. Haaretz reported two Israeli employees of Odigo—an instant messaging company with offices near the World Trade Center and also in Israel-received a warning two hours before the attack. This, roughly, would have been when the hijackers were seen boarding their planes. The Mossad, in order to minimize Jewish losses around the World Trade Center area, could have easily issued the warning via the instant message service. The *Washington Post* reported, "The Odigo service includes a feature called People Finder that allows users to seek out and contact others based on certain interests or demographics." Those whose interests relate to Israel or Jewish topics could have received the message—even if the persons were unknown to the sender. On that day, the Odigo warning may have saved many Jewish lives.

"Another mystery surrounding September 11 concerns insider trading of 'put' options days before the attacks. Put options, a variation on short selling of a stock, are investments that constitute a bet that a stock will decline in the near future. A few Israelis would have been in a position to make a great deal of money before the al-Qaeda attacks. An unknown number of insider traders made millions of dollars by buying puts during the three business days prior to the World Trade Center attack. United and American airline stocks had highly significant numbers of put options placed upon them, while other airline stocks were not affected in a major way. Only United and American planes were hijacked. A number of insurance and investment companies also had unusual put options placed on their shares. The names of the investors who profited from the tragedy of September 11 have never been released.

"The US administration has refused to disclose those who knew about 9/11 in advance and profited from it. This implies the administration and those people are in cahoots.

"Obviously, Israel's overarching objective in the anthrax mailings was to terrorize America. Once the people realized they were again under attack, panic and shock spread throughout the land. But Israel had a special reason for this type of bio-terrorism. For Israel the anthrax attacks had an important strategic purpose, namely shifting the new war away from al-Qaeda in Afghanistan and toward Saddam Hussein's Iraq.

"Shortly thereafter, the cry went out concerning Iraq's alleged weapons of mass destruction and her supposed ties to terrorists. With the help of Israel's neo-conservative allies within the Office of the Vice President, the Pentagon, think tanks (such as the American Enterprise Institute), and some media outlets (like the *Wall Street Journal*), the campaign for invading Iraq was launched. The campaign, for the most part, was based upon lies. Some of these lies came directly from Israel.

"Within the office of Israel's Prime Minister Ariel Sharon, a unit was established to prepare 'intelligence' reports in English for a new group within the Pentagon known as the Office of Special Plans (OSP). In addition to the Israeli input, some of the OSP's questionable intelligence came from Iraqi exiles. The Office of Special Plans bypassed the CIA and took the cooked intelligence directly to the Oval Office. The CIA, for the most part, tried to be professional in their analysis, but in the end, the neocons and the Israelis got their war against Iraq.

"There was no massive intelligence failure that led America to go to war in Iraq. Instead, it was a massive intelligence fraud. Some suspect the forged Niger documents, concerning the allegation that Iraq tried to obtain 'yellow cake' uranium oxide from that African country, may have originated with the Israelis. Also, the unconfirmed report on the alleged meeting of Mohammed Atta and an Iraqi agent in Prague was most likely disinformation on the part of Israel. In one bizarre aspect of the story, the *London Times* reported the Iraqi agent was seen giving Atta a vile of anthrax. The *Times* reported this as if it actually occurred—and said Israeli security sources had observed the transfer.

"Israel's objective was to bring America into a new war against Iraq. When the al-Qaeda plot was discovered, Israel let the terrorists proceed, thereby insuring America would go to war. The anthrax attack that followed was the bio-terror event needed to focus America's attention upon Iraq and its alleged weapons of mass destruction. However, Israel had planned the anthrax attacks upon America years before the discovery of the al-Qaeda plot. The anthrax hoaxes that preceded the anthrax attacks were an integral part of the conspiracy.

"The planning for the anthrax attacks of 2001 goes back to at least 1997. In April of that year, the national headquarters of the Jewish organization B'nai B'rith in Washington, DC, received a package that contained a petri dish labeled *Anthracis yersinia*, implying the dish contained bacteria that could cause anthrax infections or plague. The dish had been broken and was leaking a red fluid. Tests later determined the petri dish to be relatively harmless, and it did not contain the bacteria *Anthracis* or *Yersinia*. However, it did contain *Bacillus cereus*, which is less dangerous and is sometimes used as an anthrax simulant.

"A two-page typed letter accompanied the petri dish. The letter was largely incoherent and contained comments on Jews, Nazis, and the 'Holocaust.' The letter was signed, 'The Counter Holocaust Lobbyists of Hillel.' Months prior to the B'nai B'rith hoax, a movement was forming on college campuses calling for a debate to question some assertions concerning the 'Holocaust.' Those responsible for the mailing chose to blame historical revisionists or so-called "Holocaust deniers."

"The B'nai B'rith hoax received a great deal of media attention. Television outlets like CNN and other networks broadcast the incident live to a national audience. The nearby area was evacuated, and for a period, office personnel were quarantined. The case has never been solved, and the cost to the government was two million dollars.

"Israel's Mossad most likely was responsible for the mailing. The hoax benefited Israel and the Jews in several ways. First, national publicity was generated in this first major anthrax scare. Second, sympathy was elicited for the Jewish organization that was attacked. Third, the persons supposedly responsible—namely, those who have questions concerning the 'Holocaust'—were demonized. However, on another level, something more important was achieved: This would be the first anthrax hoax used to implicate Dr. Steven Hatfill.

"Dr. Hatfill was attending a terrorism seminar in Washington, DC, the day the B'nai B'rith incident occurred. At the time, Hatfill was employed as a researcher at the National Institutes of Health where he likely had access to petri dishes containing bacteria. This, in all probability, was the reason a petri dish from a bioresearch lab was used this time, instead of a suspicious powder. This anthrax hoax, along with others that followed, would help to make a circumstantial case against Dr. Hatfill if a real anthrax attack ever occurred.

"Dr. Hatfill likely came to the attention of the Mossad when he first appeared in a photo with the pro-White Afrikaner Resistance Movement leader Eugene Terre'Blanche and members of its paramilitary unit Aquila. The Mossad's front organization, the South African Board of Jewish Deputies, would have taken notice of the newspaper photo. As an organization, they keep track of individuals and groups they consider hostile to Jews and their interests. The Afrikaner Resistance Movement would be the type of organization they would want to monitor. The information they obtained on Dr. Hatfill could very well have been passed onto the Mossad. In America, the sister organization of the South African Board of Jewish Deputies is the Anti-Defamation League (ADL).

"Don Foster, an English professor at Vassar and at times a forensic linguistic analyst for the FBI, reviewed several of the anthrax hoaxes in an article he wrote for Vanity Fair. Foster believes Hatfill is a good candidate for the anthrax perpetrator and is impressed by the apparent relationship between Hatfill and the anthrax hoaxes. Foster said, "When I line up Hatfill's known movements with the postmark locations of reported biothreats, those hoax anthrax attacks appeared to trail him like a vapor cloud." In his article, Foster implies Hatfill was responsible for the B'nai B'rith hoax and suggests he may have been responsible for others that followed.

"Another hoax, that Foster thinks 'trails' Hatfill, occurred in August 1998. In this incident, a white powder was dispersed throughout several floors of the Finney State Office Building in Wichita, Kansas. Foster suggests this was a reenactment of a bio-terror scenario that Hatfill developed as a part of his responsibilities while employed at USAMRIID. Foster also implies Hatfill and his new mentor, anthrax expert William Patrick, were in the area of Wichita the day of the incident and later arrived together in San Diego to attend an anti-terrorism conference.

"An anti-government Christian Identity group claimed responsibility for the office building incident in a rambling eleven-page letter. Christian Identity is an unusual religious sect that looks upon Jews in less than flattering terms. A basic tenet of Christian Identity (though there are of course some splinter groups which differ, as with any religion) is the claim that the 'chosen people' of the Old Testament are the peoples of Europe and their descendants, with the Jews of today are considered to be the offspring of Satan.

"The Wichita incident is similar to the B'nai B'rith anthrax hoax. Both were designed to implicate Dr. Hatfill solely by his presence in the areas where they took place. In both cases, the Mossad wanted the public to know that groups thought to be hostile to Jewish interests had claimed responsibility for the terrorist acts. Also, the same type of rambling disjointed letters accompanied the attacks, probably written in an effort to mislead the FBI and other investigators.

"Several other anthrax hoaxes were designed to implicate Dr. Hatfill. The most important one was the anthrax hoax letter mailed from London and addressed to Senator Tom Daschle. Hatfill, at this time, was in England training with the United Nations weapons inspectors. The Mossad used the anthrax hoaxes to misdirect the authorities. By following these false leads the FBI and other law enforcement agencies wasted valuable time and resources investigating and shadowing Dr. Hatfill.

"Israel is perhaps the only country in the world that could have succeeded in the anthrax attack upon America. With the help of Jewish scientists from the former Soviet Union, Israel's bio-weapons research has probably surpassed that of all other nations. The Soviet Union's bio-weapons program had thirty-two thousand scientists and staff working in forty different research and production facilities. Two thousand of these scientists worked exclusively on the Soviet anthrax program. A significant number of these scientists may have immigrated to Israel and become employed in her bio-weapons programs.

"Anthony Cordesman with the Center for Strategic and International Studies wrote a report, 'National Developments of Biological Weapons in the Middle East: An Analytic Overview,' assessing Israel's bio-weapons programs. Cordesman reports Israel has stockpiled anthrax at her bio-warfare center and, at times, provides Israeli intelligence with deadly pathogens to be used for assassinations. Anthony Cordesman unknowingly has given us the 'smoking gun,' pointing to Israel's responsibility in the anthrax attacks.

"On the day of September 11, 2001, the Mossad was waiting for al-Qaeda to strike. Soon the greatest bio-terror event in history would follow. Different grades of anthrax were prepared at Israel's bio-warfare center at Ness Ziona. Coarse brown granules that would cause only skin infections were prepared for the New York media letters. The deadlier 'weapons-grade' anthrax was reserved for senators Daschle and Leahy.

"The envelopes were pre-addressed and waiting for the letters and the anthrax material to be placed in them. The letters were written with only the date at the top to be added later. In his analysis, Ed Lake has suggested the '09-11-01' top portion of the letter seems to have been printed at a different time and perhaps by a different hand. This would be a necessary precaution if the terror flights were changed or delayed by a few days.

"On the day of September 11, or perhaps shortly thereafter, copies of the original letter were made at a publicly accessible copier in New Jersey. Through analysis of scratches on the glass, the FBI is certain they have found the copier used to produce the letters. The original letter used to make the copies may have been destroyed. The Mossad officer could have taken the copies to Israel the next day. The anthrax letters were likely prepared, taped, and brought back to America days later via Israeli diplomatic pouch into New York City or Washington, DC. This speculative scenario could have all occurred within the week that followed September 11. The first batch of anthrax letters was mailed in Trenton, New Jersey, exactly one week after the devastating airplane attacks.

"Israel took a huge gamble when she attacked America, but this was not the first time. In June 1967, at the height of the Six Day Arab-Israeli War, Israel deliberately attacked an American intelligence ship, the USS *Liberty*, in an attempt to destroy the vessel and to lay blame on the Arabs. They failed to sink the ship, but 34 Navy crewmen were killed and 171 were wounded. A cover-up was ordered at the highest levels by the US government.

"Israel must not be allowed to continue in her attacks upon America or in her misdirection of our foreign policy. Israel must be disarmed of all weapons of mass destruction. If not stopped, she may strike again, perhaps this time by exploding a radioactive 'dirty bomb' in a major American city. Fake signal intelligence could be generated by Israel to indicate that a country such as Iran was responsible. Jewish neo-conservatives in America could then argue that since we were attacked by Iran with a radioactive weapon, our response against Iran should also be nuclear. If President acceded to this advice, Israel would have destroyed yet another Middle Eastern country and brought us another step closer to global war. Israel is an enemy, not a friend. America and her political leadership must finally realize this important fact.

"Americans are preposterously generous to Israel, giving them the lion's share of America's foreign aid, which amounts to about per

Israeli citizen per year. This is odd, since Israel is not even a third-world country. That America would put up with such ungrateful treatment in return is a measure of how tightly Israel is holding the balls of American politicians."

As I listened to this presentation and to the proliferation of information, I decided that my contacts in Utah were correct. There is a triangle of power with a dot in the South, one in the Midwest, and the culmination of this power and strength in the Pacific Northwest. This particular group will be my key to getting on Mitch's trail—that is, if there is a trail. I feel a deep regret for having sent him into harm's way. I never intended for this to happen. I picked up a small leaflet on my way out and later read it in my motel room as I plotted my next move, always remembering that my name is now John Mays, a natural-born citizen of the state of Florida—Tampa, to be exact.

Is blind patriotism a good thing? That is patriotism as defined by the establishment!

Read this and decide for yourself!

Dissent is the highest form of patriotism.
                    —Thomas Jefferson

The spirit of resistance to government is so valuable on certain occasions that I wish it to be
always kept alive.
                    —Thomas Jefferson

War does not determine who is right—only who
is left.
                    —Anonymous

A sea of red coats and white trousers, in perfect
step, the airs of the Republic blasted with particular gusto, the kind of sing-along oom pah of
which patriotism is made.
                    —Anonymous

I love America more than any other country in
this world, and, exactly for this reason, I insist on
the right to criticize her perpetually.
                    —James Baldwin

Patriotism is fierce as a fever, pitiless as the grave,
blind as a stone, and as irrational as a headless
hen.
                    —Ambrose Bierce

Patriotism: combustible rubbish ready to the
torch of any one ambitious to illuminate his
name.
                    —Ambrose Bierce

God and Country are an unbeatable team; they
break all records for oppression and bloodshed.
                    —Louis Buñuel

Patriotism is the religion of hell.
—James Branch Cabell

I found out why war is hell—army authority is absolute. You are defended and judged by the same kind of people who accuse and prosecute you.
—Michael Caine, *Playboy*

"My country, right or wrong" is a thing no patriot would ever think of saying except in a desperate case. It is like saying "My mother, drunk or sober."
—G. K. Chesterton

Many a bum show has been saved by the flag.
—George M. Cohan

Men in authority will always think that criticism of their policies is dangerous. They will always equate their policies with patriotism, and find criticism subversive.
—Henry Steele Commager

Restriction of free thought and free speech is the most dangerous of all subversions. It is the one un-American act that could most easily defeat us.
—William O. Douglas

Never was patriot yet, but was a fool.
—John Dryden

Heroism on command, senseless violence, and all the loathsome nonsense that goes by the name of patriotism—how passionately I hate them!
—Albert Einstein

I find it difficult to believe that I belong to such an idiotic, rotten species—the species that actually boasts of its freedom of will, heroism on command, senseless violence, and all of the loathsome nonsense that goes by the name of patriotism.

—Albert Einstein

No matter that patriotism is too often the refuge of scoundrels. Dissent, rebellion, and all-around hell-raising remain the true duty of patriots.

—Barbara Ehrenreich

When a whole nation is roaring Patriotism at the top of its voice, I am fain to explore the cleanness of its hands and the purity of its heart.

—Ralph Waldo Emerson, *Journals*, 1824

Freedom of speech and freedom of action are meaningless without freedom to think. And there is no freedom of thought without doubt.

—Bergen Evans

That kind of patriotism which consists in hating all other nations.

—Elizabeth Gaskell

Patriotism is when love of your own people comes first; nationalism, when hate for people other than your own comes first.

—General Charles de Gaulle

Naturally the common people don't want war: Neither in Russia, nor in England, nor for that matter in Germany. That is understood. But, after all, it is the leaders of the country who determine the policy and it is always a simple matter to drag the people along, whether it is a democracy, or a fascist dictatorship, or a parliament, or a communist dictatorship. Voice or no voice, the people can always be brought to the bidding of the leaders. That is easy. All you have to do is tell them they are being attacked, and denounce the peacemakers for lack of patriotism and exposing the country to danger. It works the same in any country.

—Hermann Goering, President of the Reichstag, Nazi Party, and Luftwaffe Commander-in-Chief

Patriotism ruins history.

—Goethe

Patriotism…is a superstition artificially created and maintained through a network of lies and falsehoods; a superstition that robs man of his self-respect and dignity, and increases his arrogance and conceit.

—Emma Goldman

Patriotism: noun, a nationalistic cheerleading that causes a peculiar form of blindness that magnifies the faults of your rivals and makes your own country's faults invisible.

—Roedy Green

Patriotism tugs at the heartstrings. It is matter of loyalty. This goes right back to our hunter-gatherer past. You must support your chief no matter what a bastard he is. The alternative is being clobbered by the neighboring tribe. My tribe right or wrong.

—Roedy Green

Patriotism is like the ring in the nose of a pig. It lets somebody else lead you around by the nose. If you are super patriotic, most of your critical faculties are turned off. You are a patsy.

—Roedy Green

I am a citizen of planet Earth first, Canada second.

—Roedy Green

Patriotism is proud of a country's virtues and eager to correct its deficiencies; it also acknowledges the legitimate patriotism of other countries, with their own specific virtues. The pride of nationalism, however, trumpets its country's virtues and denies its deficiencies, while it is contemptuous toward the virtues of other countries. It wants to be, and proclaims itself to be, "the greatest," but greatness is not required of a country; only goodness is.

—Sydney J. Harris

Treason doth never prosper. What's the reason? Why, when it prospers, none dare call it treason.

—Sir John Harrington

A politician will do anything to keep his job even become a patriot.

—William Randolph Hearst (1863–1951), US newspaper publisher, recalled on his death, August 14, 1951

The US public is depoliticized, poorly informed on foreign affairs…and strongly patriotic in the face of a struggle with "another Hitler." Even though the public is normally averse to war, even with modest propaganda efforts…the public can be quickly transformed into enthusiastic supporters of war.

—Edward S. Herman

The heights of popularity and patriotism are still the beaten road to power and tyranny; flattery to treachery; standing armies to arbitrary government; and the glory of God to the temporal interest of the clergy.

—David Hume

One of the great attractions of patriotism—it fulfills our worst wishes. In the person of our nation we are able, vicariously, to bully and cheat. Bully and cheat, what's more, with a feeling that we are profoundly virtuous.

—Aldous Huxley

At least two thirds of our miseries spring from human stupidity, human malice and those great motivators and justifiers of malice and stupidity, idealism, dogmatism and proselytizing zeal on behalf of religious or political idols.

—Aldous Huxley

The tree of liberty must be refreshed from time to time with the blood of patriots and tyrants. It is its natural manure.

—Thomas Jefferson

Patriotism is the last refuge of scoundrels.

—Samuel Johnson

When a dog barks at the moon, then it is religion;
but when he barks at strangers, it is patriotism!
—David Starr Jordan

Patriotism does not oblige us to acquiesce in the
destruction of liberty. Patriotism obliges us to
question it, at least.
—Wendy Kaminer

Patriotism is a kind of religion; it is the egg from
which wars are hatched.
—Guy de Maupassant

The highest patriotism is not a blind acceptance
of official policy, but a love of one's country deep
enough to call her to a higher plain.
—George McGovern

In the United States, doing good has come to be,
like patriotism, a favorite device of persons with
something to sell.
—H. L. Mencken

Whenever you hear a man speak of his love for his
country, it is a sign that he expects to be paid for it.
—H. L. Mencken

The notion that a radical is one who hates his
country is naïve and usually idiotic. He is, more
likely, one who likes his country more than the
rest of us, and is thus more disturbed than the
rest of us when he sees it debauched. He is not a
bad citizen turning to crime; he is a good citizen
driven to despair.
—H. L. Mencken

We must not confuse dissent with disloyalty.
When the loyal opposition dies, I think the soul
of America dies with it.

—Edward R. Murrow

Patriotism is often an arbitrary veneration of real
estate above principles.

—George Jean Nathan

Patriotism is usually stronger than class hatred,
and always stronger than internationalism.

—George Orwell

Political language is designed to make lies sound
truthful and murder respectable, and to give an
appearance of solidity to pure wind.

—George Orwell

The nationalist not only does not disapprove of
atrocities committed by his own side, but he has
a remarkable capacity for not even hearing about
them.

—George Orwell

Sometimes the first duty of intelligent men is the
restatement of the obvious.

—George Orwell

The nationalist not only does not disapprove of
atrocities committed by his own side, but he has
a remarkable capacity for not even hearing about
them.

—George Orwell

If patriotism is "the last refuge of a scoundrel,"
it is not merely because evil deeds may be per-

formed in the name of patriotism, but because patriotic fervor can obliterate moral distinctions altogether.

—Ralph B. Perry

Socrates said he was not an Athenian or a Greek, but a citizen of the world.

—Plutarch, *On Banishment*

To me, it seems a dreadful indignity to have a soul controlled by geography.

—George Santayana

A man's feet must be planted in his country, but his eyes should survey the world.

—George Santayana

Men love their country, not because it is great, but because it is their own.

—Lucius Annaeus Seneca

The peace and welfare of this and coming generations of Americans will be secure only as we cling to the watchword of true patriotism: "Our country—when right to be kept right; when wrong to be put right.'

—Carl Schurz

You'll never have a quiet world till you knock the patriotism out of the human race.

—George Bernard Shaw

Patriotism is a pernicious, psychopathic form of idiocy.

—George Bernard Shaw

A healthy nation is as unconscious of its nationality as a healthy man of his bones. But if you break
a nation's nationality it will think of nothing else
but getting it set again.
—George Bernard Shaw

I can train a monkey to wave an American flag.
That does not make the monkey patriotic.
—Scott Ritter

To announce that there must be no criticism
of the president, or that we are to stand by the
president right or wrong, is not only unpatriotic and servile, but is morally treasonable to the
American public.
—Theodore Roosevelt

Patriotism means to stand by the country. It does
not mean to stand by the president or any other
public official, save exactly to the degree in which
he himself stands by the country. It is patriotic to
support him insofar as he efficiently serves the
country. It is unpatriotic not to oppose him to
the exact extent that by inefficiency or otherwise
he fails in his duty to stand by the country. In
either event, it is unpatriotic not to tell the truth,
whether about the president or anyone else.
—Theodore Roosevelt

Patriots always talk of dying for their country
and never of killing for their country.
—Bertrand Russell

Patriotism is the willingness to kill and be killed
for trivial reasons.
—Bertrand Russell

Patriotism is your conviction that this country is superior to all other countries because you were born in it.

—George Bernard Shaw

Moral cowardice that keeps us from speaking our minds is as dangerous to this country as irresponsible talk. The right way is not always the popular and easy way. Standing for right when it is unpopular is a true test of moral character.

—Margaret Chase Smith

Patriotism means unqualified and unwavering love for the nation, which implies not uncritical eagerness to serve, not support for unjust claims, but frank assessment of its vices and sins, and penitence for them.

—Alexander Solzhenitsyn

Patriotism is not short, frenzied outbursts of emotion, but the tranquil and steady dedication of a lifetime.

—Adlai Stevenson

During times of war, hatred becomes quite respectable, even though it has to masquerade often under the guise of patriotism.

—Howard Thurman

The time is fast approaching when to call a man a patriot will be the deepest insult you can offer him. Patriotism now means advocating plunder in the interest of the privileged classes of the particular State system into which we have happened to be born.

—Leo Tolstoy

Each man must for himself alone decide what is right and what is wrong, which course is patriotic and which isn't. You cannot shirk this and be a man.

—Thomas Tusser

The government is merely a servant—merely a temporary servant; it cannot be its prerogative to determine what is right and what is wrong, and decide who is a patriot and who isn't. Its function is to obey orders, not originate them.

—Mark Twain

Each man must for himself alone decide what is right and what is wrong, which course is patriotic and which isn't. You cannot shirk this and be a man. To decide against your conviction is to be an unqualified and excusable traitor, both to yourself and to your country, let me label you as they may.

—Mark Twain

Man is the only Patriot. He sets himself apart in his own country, under his own flag, and sneers at the other nations, and keeps multitudinous uniformed assassins on hand at heavy expense to grab slices of other people's countries, and keep them from grabbing slices of his. And in the intervals between campaigns he washes the blood of his hands and works for "the universal brotherhood of man"—with his mouth.

—Mark Twain

Born in iniquity and conceived in sin, the spirit of nationalism has never ceased to bend human institutions to the service of dissension and distress.

—Thorstein Veblen

It is lamentable, that to be a good patriot one must become the enemy of the rest of mankind.

—Voltaire

Guard against the impostures of pretended patriotism.

—George Washington

Beer commercials are so patriotic: "Made the American Way." What does that have to do with America? Is that what America stands for? Feeling sluggish and urinating frequently?

—Evelyn Waugh

Patriotism has become a mere national self-assertion, a sentimentality of flag-cheering with no constructive duties.

—H. G. Wells

Our true nationality is mankind.

—H. G. Wells

Patriotism is the virtue of the vicious.

—Oscar Wilde

There are two visions of America. One precedes our founding fathers and finds its roots in the harshness of our puritan past. It is very suspicious of freedom, uncomfortable with diversity, hostile to science, unfriendly to reason, contemptuous of personal autonomy. It sees America as a religious nation. It views patriotism as allegiance

to God. It secretly adores coercion and conformity. Despite our constitution, despite the legacy
of the Enlightenment, it appeals to millions of
Americans and threatens our freedom.

The other vision finds its roots in the spirit
of our founding revolution and in the leaders of
this nation who embraced the age of reason. It
loves freedom, encourages diversity, embraces science and affirms the dignity and rights of every
individual. It sees America as a moral nation, neither completely religious nor completely secular.
It defines patriotism as love of country and of the
people who make it strong. It defends all citizens
against unjust coercion and irrational conformity.

This second vision is our vision. It is the
vision of a free society. We must be bold enough
to proclaim it and strong enough to defend it
against all its enemies.

—Rabbi Sherwin Wine

You're not to be so blind with patriotism that you
can't face reality. Wrong is wrong, no matter who
does it or says it.

—Malcolm X

I wonder who compiled this list, I thought. *They do not sound like your typical White Supremacist.* I looked for the signature. Yes, there it was: "Joseph Whitaker, Americans for America," with an attached motto that read, "God Bless America, No Exceptions!" That was strange. What was Joseph doing at this "I hate everyone" meeting? *I think that I will give the ole boy a call...*

I dialed the number just below the motto, and a very young-sounding girl answered, "God bless America! How may I help you?"

"Is Mr. Whitaker in?"

"No, he is attending a rally in Michigan."

"When will he be available?"

"I don't expect him to be back here in Spokane until Friday."

"Spokane?"

"Yes, we have membership all over America—in every state, to be exact. However, we're headquartered here in Spokane. Well, we're not in Spokane—we're actually just outside of Spokane."

"I have never heard of your group, and I have been looking for some real involvement in something to help fight this so-called War on Terrorism at home. I just cannot stand to look at all of the Arabs and other olive-skinned people here managing and running our businesses while sending money to their home country or to their home country allegiance to help them kill our young men and women in the Middle East. I think that it is time to send them all back home!"

"You sound just like the type of individual that finds our activities patriotic and just. Where do you live?"

"Knoxville, Tennessee."

"Let's see…no, we do not have an affiliate there. However, we do have one in Atlanta."

"I might go there this week. Do you have a phone number?"

"Yes, the leader there is Wayne Simpson, and his number is 770-345-7898!"

"Great! How can I get up with Mr. Simpson?"

"If you will give me your phone number, I will have him call you. We are very hesitant and careful about our communications. The number that I gave you for Wayne in Atlanta is not really the number for our organization. It is the number for Wayne's personnel business, 'Debt Consultants of America.' In fact, the number that you just dialed is the phone number for my beauty salon that is in downtown Spokane. We will need to know you better before you can move any further into our organization."

"Okay, give him my number." I gave her the number to my personal cell and then hung up the phone and immediately called the airport to book a flight to Spokane. I knew that I must keep up my fight; however, I must also try to locate Mitch.

CHAPTER 12

Back at the Bureau in Atlanta

"What have you got, Beth?

"Nothing! However, you just as well give up on getting up with Jonathan until he contacts you. I know that he is undercover by now!"

"He can't go under alone! Who the fuck is helping him?"

"Jonathan knows a lot of people in this business and has many covert contacts. Help will not be a problem for him in this endeavor."

"He had better not be getting help from within the bureau or from any of our outside people or heads will be falling, and that includes you, little girl!"

"Speaking of heads falling, sir, your secretary left a message that DC had called and that you should return their call immediately."

"I'll return their call in my office! Now get Jonathan, dammit!"

"Beth?"

"Yes!"

"Jonathan here, I need your help!"

"Goddamn you, Jonathan. Oh, holy shit! I never say that but you have got all of us and yourself on the hot seat now! David is about to have a cow because we cannot get up with you. You have got to talk with him now!"

"No!"

"But!"

"No fucking buts about it, Beth. You and Rodney have got to get some old pictures—you know, the Wanted type stuff out on me—ah, I mean out on who I am right now. That is, John Mays from Tampa, Florida. Make it quick and real, and get it out to our operatives and others in the Spokane area. I have got to look real, and I have got to do it fast if I stand a snowball's chance in hell of finding Mitch."

"Do you want to be on the wanted list now?"

"No! It needs to be some really old stuff, like maybe I could have already served time for, just something to back up the fact that I am a real anti-government and racist freak. I need to be believed and trusted by the Neo-Nazi/Christian/White Supremacist crowd!"

"Where are you?"

"You don't need to know that!"

"Well, I will not be able to keep this publicity shit from David, and even he will be able to surmise that you are either in Spokane or will be in that area soon."

"I know that, and I will deal with David in due time, but right now I am trying to save Mitch!"

"Do you have a line on him?"

"No! I do know how things work when an informant is discovered by this type of organization, and my experience tells me that if that is indeed what has happened, then he is most likely already dead and his body will never be found. Either way, Beth I have got to try to either save him or to get revenge against the bastard or bastards that may have killed him."

"It will not help anyone, Jonathan, if you get yourself killed—the investigation will most likely die, you will have lost your life, and your children will be without a father."

"You left one thing out. Beth, my ex-wife, will be happy as hell!"

"Jonathan!'

"Forget what I just said, Beth. However, they had better be good if they plan on getting me for I am *just a little bit* more experienced than Mitch. I should have never sent him into the eye of this thing! I did not know just how widespread and complex this thing was at the time. I heard where Congress, just today, is trying to stop the prosecution of our soldiers for war crimes in the Middle East, and as far as I am concerned, it is about fucking time."

"How fast do you need this done?"

"No rush. Tomorrow will be just fine!"

"Fuck you, Jonathan! You know that is an impossibility!"

"Do you think that we have time?"

"Go to hell! You know what I mean!"

"Just think of it this way, Beth. Take as long as you need to, remembering all the time that without it, I cannot be safe undercover, and the longer it takes, the longer it will be for me to try to either save Mitch or to waste his killer or killers. If I don't find Mitch alive, I will not let it be. I must now solve this case!"

"We will get on it immediately! Please be careful!"

Beth almost ran to Rodney's office and quickly explained the urgency of what they had to do for Jonathan!

"We had better get it done, Beth, because I expect David to be on us quickly to do something to help him after his teleconference with DC."

"You think?"

"I know there are some major changes coming down. I just do not know what or when. Every person that has been involved with this thing from day one is now under extreme pressure and facing the possibility of losing their jobs from the director down to us lowlings. Hell, Beth, even the president and the director of homeland security are getting hourly criticism from all types of special interest groups and the liberal press. I truly think that David will be removed and that Jonathan, and maybe even you and I could be fired."

"Why us, Rodney?"

"Somebody has got to take the blame, and I can guarantee you that it will not be the higher ups!"

"Why can't they see that this is not an easy solve?"

"They can, Beth. However, it is also as plain as the nose on your face that the bureau sat on this thing way too long. I believe that we failed to act early on because we thought that we could justify the murders. Just think about that for a minute—we had 9/11 and its aftermath, the war in the Middle East, and the publicity given to any and all crimes committed by Muslims in the United States. The stage was set, it appeared, for us to let the killings go unfettered because the hate and the hurt after 9/11 ran deep and continues to grow as we speak. Here are just a few entries on a long list of individual criminal acts over the last few years by Muslims here in the United States, some of whom were self-described Islamic warriors.

- On January 31, Ismail Yassin Mohamed, 22, stole a car in Minneapolis. He went on a rampage, ramming the stolen car into other cars and then stealing a van and continuing to ram other cars, injuring one person. His father told officials that Mohamed was suffering from mental problems; his mother added he had been depressed and hadn't been taking his medication. During his rampage, Mohamed repeatedly yelled, "Die, die, die, kill, kill, kill," and when asked why he did all this, he replied, "Allah made me do it."
- Omeed Aziz Popal, a Muslim from Afghanistan, who killed one person and injured fourteen during a murderous drive through San Francisco city streets in August, during which he targeted people on crosswalks and sidewalks, identified himself as a terrorist after his rampage, according to Rob Roth of San Francisco's KTVU. Later the murders were ascribed to Popal's mental problems and to stress arising from his impending arranged marriage.
- On July 28, a Muslim named Naveed Afzal Haq forced his way into the Jewish Federation of Greater Seattle. Once inside, Haq announced, "I'm a Muslim American. I'm angry at Israel," and then began shooting, killing one woman and injuring five more. FBI assistant special agent David Gomez stated: "We believe…it's a lone individual acting out his antagonism. There's nothing to indicate that it's terrorism-related. But we're monitoring the entire situation."
- In March, a twenty-two-year-old Iranian student named Mohammed Reza Taheri-azar drove an SUV onto the campus of the University of North Carolina at Chapel Hill, deliberately trying to kill people and succeeding in injuring nine. After the incident, he seemed singularly pleased

with himself, smiling and waving to crowds after a court appearance on Monday, at which he explained that he was "thankful for the opportunity to spread the will of Allah." Officials here again dismissed the possibility of terrorism, even after Taheri-azar wrote a series of letters to the UNC campus newspaper detailing the Qur'anic justification for warfare against unbelievers, and explaining why he believed his attacks were justified from an Islamic perspective.

"Are you trying to say that the FBI justified the murders?"

"Not as a bureau, Beth. However, I do believe that we turned our heads and choose to work on other problems and issues relating to terrorism and not to trying to solve the murders early on."

Later that day

"Beth?"

"Yes! Where are you, Jonathan?"

"On a flight to Utah—Salt Lake City, to be exact. Have you and Rodney got things going there?"

"Yes, the information you needed should be circulating everywhere west of the Mississippi in Patriot and FBI circles. Rodney has even sent it out to many of the sheriff departments in the state of Washington. John Mays is a questionable dude out on parole and feared to be dangerous and a threat to government policy. He was never convicted of murder—however, many within the bureau believe that he has committed violent acts against Muslims here in the United States and against other minorities, especially in the Hispanic community."

"Great! That should send the message I need out there and help me to be believable and seen to be a part of their cause!"

"Rodney?"

"Yes," Rodney responded as he looked up into David's face.

"Call Beth in!"

"Sure! What's up?"

"We're no longer the lead on this thing. Washington has brought it under their auspice. In fact, we are being informed after the fact. I believe that they already have covert operations underway and have undercover agents in the field."

"So what does this mean as far as we are concerned?"

"I don't know right now. However, I do know that this thing is getting a lot more complicated now. Have you or Beth gotten up with Jonathan?"

A denoted "No!" came from the doorway to Rodney's office as Beth walked in. "I haven't heard from him at all I just know that he is undercover somewhere."

"Well, he is not by himself. Washington just informed me that we are no longer the lead on this, and I believe that they informed me after the fact and that they already had a plan in place and undercover agents in the field. I do not know for how long either."

"What about our jobs?"

"No change yet, Beth. However, this will be day to day, I guess." You could sense a sigh of relief in David's voice and yet a blush to his face that told you that he was very worried and upset at the same time. "We are to keep on keeping on until further notice working our routes to resolution. However, we will just not be informed as to what Washington or any other office is doing for that matter, at least not in a timely fashion."

"What about Jonathan?"

"There has been nothing said. However, I just cannot believe that they will leave him in charge of anything."

"They won't have to. He is already in charge and will not relinquish it until this thing is resolved."

"What about his money?"

"There have been no steps taken in that regard either, so I guess all that I can say is that for right now, all of us, including Jonathan, are still employed."

"What they're doing in Washington will not work. They need us and they need our files and research, especially the compilation of data that has been gathered after we joined up with Jonathan on this thing. Have they requested any of this?"

"Nope!"

"What message is that sending?"

"I am not sure it is sending anything other than the fact that they need to look active and busy on this thing."

"David, Rodney seems to think that there is a hidden agenda somewhere within the bureau. What is your thinking?"

"So you're going down that road again? Well, I know that there are a lot of indictors that we dragged our feet on this. However, you must remember that we had so much going on with this anti-terrorism and homeland security thing not to mention all of the emphasis on border security and air traffic security. What I am trying to say, Beth, is that I am not sure that the delays had any sinister motives. The post 9/11 syndrome is still with us and will most likely be with us forever. What worries me is that we are all, from the president down, continually questioning our every decision and every act, and we are always looking over our own shoulders so much that I am afraid that we might not see danger standing right in front of us. That type of thinking is what has led Washington to usurp our prerogatives in this case. I fear for Jonathan and anyone else out there now undercover—hell, we might be chasing and shooting our own people for Christ's sake."

CHAPTER 13

Somewhere in the western skies

"Would you like another drink, sir?"

"Yes, and make it a double scotch this time!"

"I will give you one glass of water and two bottles of Scotch."

"Forget the water. The guy that made it knew how much water to put in it. Just give me a glass of ice please."

I drank it down and then reached into my travel bag for two more that I had stashed away from some previous flights for I knew that she could not serve me anymore. My mind was a little blurred after two doubles; however, the buzz felt good and was needed. After I landed in Salt Lake, I would get some rest and then proceed to search for my best avenue to get to wherever it was Mitch was just prior to his disappearance. Fuck Washington. Those dumb bastards could not hit a bull in the ass with a base fiddle. How in the hell did they expect to solve this thing? *They can't solve shit without me! I am the alpha and the omega, and they will soon know this to be factual. I will get Mitch's killer and/or captors and the rag head slayer too! Ha ha! Or at least I will give them one of the slayers for everyone except the press knows that there have been killings in almost every state. No way that this is the work of just one perp. The president knows this, the director knows this, and David knows this; however, they all also know that the press and all of the special interest groups want one arrestable perp, so by God I will give them just what they want.*

Somewhere at an undisclosed location in the Pacific Northwest

The news of the increased infiltration of protest groups by the government around the country and abroad is not good. I strongly condemn this infiltration and warn you that we have also been infiltrated and this action will not be tolerated by our organization and affiliates. We are in the right on this one; these covert police operations set a dangerous precedent and represent a direct attack on the entire movement for social justice. The police have zeroed in on our movement because they know that we have figured it out and that we know on whom we are waging war. Please send out immediately a warning to everyone, including our direct and indirect affiliates nationwide and worldwide. We must stop this infiltration now! Let them know that this is a direct attack, so this is all out-war. We cannot allow our organization nor our goals of protecting the rights and the lives of our people and of our white Anglo-Saxon/Christian heritage.

My sources tell me that we are being targeted also by the FBI and possibly others as I talk with you these infiltrators must be discovered and dealt with permanently as we have regretfully done in the past.

Two days later at the Double Dribble Bar in Spokane

"John Mays, huh? Where are you from?"

"Knoxville, Tennessee!"

"What brings you to this part of the world?"

"I have a friend that came out here several weeks ago, and I am looking forward to hooking up with him soon. His name is Allen."

"Pardon me for interrupting," a cute barmaid said as she leaned onto the bar. "Did you say that you were from the South?"

"Yes!"

"Well, again, I ask for your forgiveness for not only interrupting—I was also listening to your conversation mainly because of your accent—but did you also ask about someone named Allen?"

"No, not really. I said that I had a friend out here from Memphis, Tennessee, named Allen that I was planning on hooking up with soon."

"Is he in the furniture business?"

"Yes, a traveling salesman to be exact. Why do you ask? Do you know him?"

"Well, you might say so. However, I have not seen him in weeks, maybe even longer. He asked me out one weekend then canceled, and after that, I have never seen him again."

"Really? That does not sound like Allen! However, I have tried to reach him by phone without success. I do have an address on him and I plan to go there in the morning."

"Can I go with you? I do not go to work until two p.m.? Excuse me. I know that you don't even know who I am, but I have a special interest in Allen and I would like to know that he is all right, if you know what I mean."

"Sure. I plan on going there about nine a.m."

"Where is Allen's apartment?"

"I tell you what, ah…"

"My name is Rachel!"

"Nice to meet you, Rachel, and I am John Mays. Let's meet for breakfast about eight-thirty at the Waffle House just down the street from here for breakfast, my treat!"

"Great, I must get back to my other customers, but I will be there and I will be prompt."

"Good, see you, hun. Oh yes, bring me another beer and get one for my friend here."

I stayed there another couple of hours planting anti-government seeds and speaking often of my hatred of all of the immigrants that our government love so dearly and that are spoiling the heritage of our Christian ancestors. In the back of my mind, the entire time, I was wondering about what this Rachel might know about Allen, what kind of a relationship they might have had. It did seem to be obvious that she was genuinely worried for him. She just might know of some reason that he might come up missing. She seemed to have a sparkle in her eye when she heard of information that he might not be missing, so I doubt if she had anything to do with it. However, she might know of something of Allen's actions and whereabouts in the hours and days prior to his disappearance. I was also wondering if anyone else had been around asking about Allen.

Rachel and I spoke with an increasing amount of volume in order to be heard over the crowd. "Bring me the tab and I would like to ask you something."

"Sure," she exclaimed as she retrieved the tab from the register and starting walking in my direction.

"You stated that Allen had not been around here for a long time. Has anyone else showed up here of late looking for or asking about him?"

"Yes, one normal-looking dude and one official-looking man with a nasty attitude."

"How long ago?"

"The normal guy was here just a couple of days ago, and the other guy a couple of weeks back, I think."

"Interesting. We'll talk more tomorrow. See you then! Bye!"

"Okay, and I will see you at the Waffle House."

Back at the FBI offices in Atlanta

"David!"

"Yes, this is Sam Smart in DC. I want your guy retrieved from the field immediately."

"That might be easier said than done, sir. I do not know of his whereabouts at the present time."

"What? Who in the hell is in charge down there anyway? Look, David, I have a plan in place for you to have a respectable retirement after this thing is completed. However, all bets are off if your guy fucks this up. Do you understand?"

"Yes!"

"We're close to having something, and we all need the good press on this without complications. Off the record, I can tell you that we have top people undercover and we believe that an arrest is imminent."

"Where are they, sir?"

"That is confidential at the present, and if I break the confidence, it could jeopardize the safety of my people."

"So what about my guy? He is FBI. What about his safety?"

"Pull his ass in, and he will be safe. In fact, if you can get him out of our way, I will double his money that you promised and I will up the money on your retirement pay."

"So my guy must be close to something too or you would not be so concerned."

"I am not saying anything of the sort. I am just saying that I don't want any fuck-ups here."

After getting off the phone with the head of the FBI in Washington, DC, David went down to the office of Beth Lewinski.

"Beth?"

"Yes, sir!"

"If you hear from Jonathan, tell him to get his ass back to Atlanta!"

"I doubt seriously if I hear from him for a while."

"Well, I know that, or I at least think that, sometimes, if not oftentimes, you don't always tell me everything when it comes to Jonathan. However, he needs to know that if he quits now and comes back to Atlanta and totally off the case, Sam Smart will double his so-called *guaranteed* money."

"He ain't coming in, David, until he at least gets Mitch or Mitch's killer or killers, you know that as well as I. At this point in time, he is not thinking about the money nor is he thinking about the case. If he gets anything on the case, it will be a byproduct of finding Mitch."

"Shit! I was afraid that is what you would say. I don't understand why he needs to be a damn hero. I know that he is good. However, he is too fucking old to be out there playing Rambo or John Fucking Wayne. He is going to screw this up, get himself killed, and ruin my retirement all in one fell swoop. Can we use his children to get to him?"

"What is wrong with you, David? You had better leave his kids out of this. They have enough problems of their own."

'Well, think about it for a minute. If they could help get him in, they would not have as many worries, with twice as much money, at their disposal."

"No, dammit! And I do mean no!"

"Okay, it was just a thought."

Back in Spokane at the Waffle House down the street from the Double Dribble Sports Bar

"What do you want to eat, Rachel?" I said as we took a booth at the Waffle House after running in from a pouring rain. "Does it always rain here?"

"No, it just seems that way because it is always overcast. The average rainfall is under twenty inches a year."

I looked around the restaurant to see if anyone looked suspicious, almost hoping that they did. However, everyone looked just like normal Waffle House folks.

"Tell me first about you and Mitch?"

"Who?"

"Ah? I'm sorry, I ah—"

"Coffee, guys?" came a voice from behind the side of the booth.

"Yes," I said. "Make it black with cream on the side please."

"I'll have a Coke," Rachel said to my amazement.

"A Coke?"

"Yes, I detest coffee!"

"And what will you have with your Coke for breakfast?"

"Two poached eggs on toast and sausage."

"Hell, I bet the Waffle House doesn't know how to poach an egg."

"Yes, they do. I eat here a lot, and as a matter of fact, they're really good."

"Okay, order up!"

After she placed her order, I requested a pecan waffle with bacon and then went back to sipping my coffee, hoping she had forgotten about my slip of the tongue."

"Who is Mitch?" she asked.

"My brother who lives in Atlanta. I have been thinking about him all morning because my sister called last night and said that he had been sick. I am sorry. So tell me about you and Allen?"

Without hesitation, she accepted my reasoning of saying Mitch and immediately started talking about a relationship that really never was but of one she hoped to have had with Allen.

She went on for about fifteen minutes before asking just why I and the others were looking for Allen.

I then started to ask her a series of questions to try to evaluate both her intent and her value in the search. In my line of work, you can never totally trust anyone and you never ever really know anyone either. It was apparent to me after a while that her intent was honorable; however, I began to doubt her value except for the fact that she knew the people of this region and sincerely wanted to find Allen.

I then started the final test by stating that I felt that she was of no value to me in this endeavor and that I was enjoying the breakfast; however, we should go our separate ways afterward.

"*Of no value*? Who do you think you are mister? You come to me and ask me a bunch of random questions revealing fully that you haven't a clue at this point of his whereabouts, and then you drag me here and buy me a cheap breakfast and then tell me that I am no value. You must have balls as big as bowling balls! And furthermore, you have still not stated as to why you are looking for him. Are you a relative or what?"

"No, I am not a relative!"

"Then what brings you all the way across the country?"

"I tell you what—let's finish our meal and then go by Allen's place, and then we can talk more."

"I don't know. If it were not for my curiosity, I might just go back home. I am tired of being talked down to."

"Okay, I promise that I will not do that anymore and that I will tell you more after we visit Allen's motel."

"Motel?"

"Finish your meal and I will get a coffee to go and I will explain on the way."

FBI headquarters, The J. Edgar Hoover Building, Washington, DC

"Mr. Smart, have you forgotten about our GPS mobile phone tracking system?"

"No! Why, Gary?"

"I can locate this Jonathan Beck for you in a matter of minutes. In fact, I took the liberty of checking it before calling you over here."

"What do you have?"

"I have a location near Interstate 15 and the lake near Logan it appears."

"Great, call our nearest field office and get someone up there immediately."

Back in Spokane

"Here we are, Spokane's finest."

"Surely not? Why would he stay here? He drove a nice car and seemed to have plenty of money and he even rented one of the most expensive bed-and-breakfasts in the mountains the weekend that he stood me up."

"I will explain later. Right now, let's go in and see what we find."

"Do you have a key?"

"I won't need a key!"

Allen's efficiency was on the second floor of the "Pay by the Week" motel, the first being filled with mostly Hispanic migrant workers. We walked around a game of soccer and a pyramid of beer cans then up the spiral staircase, took and immediately left and walked up to room 219, and then with one swift twist and a turn, the door opened.

"How did you do that?" Rachel asked as I put a small tool back into my front trousers pocket.

"It's easy once you learn how!"

As we entered the front room, it was obviously that someone had been there before us for every single item had been tossed or thrown everywhere and every single piece of furniture had been torn to shreds, and every place where there had been a drawer or compartment had been removed and tossed out of the way.

"What the hell is this?" Rachel asked, and then she sat down and started to cry.

"What the hell is wrong now?" I asked as I laid my hand on her shoulder.

"Don't touch me, you bastard! I can't believe that I have been so stupid!"

"What?"

"You son of bitches are drug dealers!"

"No! No!" I exclaimed, as I reached for her again.

This time, she slapped my hand and said, "Get the fuck away from me and take me back to my car now!"

She then went into a state of near hysteria as she started to yell! I then thought, *I hate the way women always get so damn emotional!* She was beginning to get so loud I knew that I must get control because I just did not want any attention drawn to us and Mitch's—ah shit, I mean Allen's—demolished apartment.

I reached again for her shoulders; however, she ducked and slapped me in the face. That was it—my natural instincts took over and I slapped her back—a little too hard, maybe—for her skull hit the wall and then bounced back into my grasp, and I then held my hand over her mouth and repeated to her, "Please shut the fuck up!" After several minutes of sobbing and wiggling around in my arms on the floor, she finally began to get quiet and still.

"Look, Rachel," I said. "This isn't what it seems. Just get control, and in a bit, I will explain. However, for the moment we must think of Allen."

She just lay there and looked up into my face with her tearful eyes. In a way, I thought, as I looked at her, she was now more attractive than before. Her blue eyes now seemed to be the color of the ocean, and her T-shirt was torn, revealing her small but perky breasts tanned all the way to her bubble-gum nipples. Thank God for tanning beds! There is no way a girl could get that type of tan in the Pacific Northwest without help. I don't know why I thought she was more beautiful now because I really had not found her all that attractive at the bar. Maybe it was her lying on the floor with her clothes in disarray, her hair in her face, and me on top now, in control, with my body against hers, and for just a brief moment, the thought of having sex with this young thing drifted gently across my mind. My thoughts were in slow motion, and I could feel a youthful Jonathan, many moons ago, in some girl's apartment making passionate love to her on floors very similar to these, and just the thought caused me to become aroused, and at that point, I think Rachel could sense what was happening, so she got control quickly and adjusted her shirt, flipped back her hair, and began to apologize about her emotions. This brought me quickly back to the present reality and to my senses, and I too started to apologize for having hit her as I got back to my feet.

"What is going on, John?" she said as she got to her feet and started to walk over to the kitchen area.

"You have got to trust me for now. After we leave here, I will explain everything."

"Okay," she said as she opened the refrigerator door.

"It's empty!"

FBI offices, Washington, DC

"Have you heard anything from Logan?"

"They are calling in now, sir. Just a minute!"

"Au! Hu! Okay! Well, I don't know. I'll get right back to you… just hold please."

"What is it?"

"We have a problem, sir. Ah, it appears the phone…must have been thrown over a bridge and into the water."

"Water?"

"Yes, sir! Our locator is only accurate to about twenty-six meters, and in this case, that is all it took to throw us off. I had no way of knowing without getting someone on the scene."

"Okay, so much for that!"

"There is another avenue we can take here, sir."

"And what is that?"

"Jonathan's auto should have had a tracking device on it too?"

"Okay, check that out and get back to me as soon as possible!"

Back in Atlanta

"David, Beth and I called you into our office because of some underground chatter that we have been picking up the past few hours."

"What is it?"

"Someone or some groups are now offering a ten-thousand-dollar bounty, if you will, for the—and I quote—*ruthless murder* of any undercover FBI agents and/or operatives."

"Oh no! Now we have a real miss starting to heat up. I don't believe that they really knew about our covert activities. However, there are snitches all over DC. I tried to get them to stay out or at least not to jump in the way that they have."

"It is worse than you might think. They are naming names on this so-called hit list, and both Jonathan's and Mitch's names are on this infamous listing."

"This is going to be even worse than I thought. Now we have Jonathan, agents known and unknown from Washington, and God only knows from how many other offices, possibly the CIA, the groups that Allen was tracking, and most likely now the entire Neo-Nazi/Christian/White-Supremacist movement and their hitmen and hitmen from all other facets of the underworld, all in this massive and confusing melting pot in the Pacific Northwest area looking to kill someone."

"You left out Allen."

"I know, my basic instincts tell me that there is no Mitch or Allen if you will."

"There's more, David! Turn Fox News on, Beth. Watch the tape rolling at the bottom of the screen."

"How is that connected, Rodney? An Arab dyke is murdered by her Jewish dyke lover. I don't see the connection."

"The Jewish lover is just a person of interest at this point, David. However, I have got information that the Jewish girl was involved with a man on the side."

"An affair? Where and when did this murder occur?"

"They have not given a time of death as of yet, but the location is a small suburb of Salt Lake called Draper, I think?"

"Do you see a connection to our murders?"

"I don't know at this point. However, it is worth watching. The location seems odd to me, considering the fact that Salt Lake and this general region seems to be connected to Spokane."

Chapter 14

Back in Spokane

"Rachel, I don't know about you, but I could use a drink!"

"You damn straight. There is a small hole-in-the-wall place about a mile down the road here that serves a shitting breakfast, an awful lunch, and a pissy dinner. However, the beer is cold."

"That'll work!"

"Tell me what's going on, John Mays."

I hesitated for several minutes as I evaluated the wisdom of what I was about to reveal to this almost-perfect stranger. The fact is, however, I did need help, and to be most honest with myself, Rachel was my best bet. I was worried about the possibility of getting another almost innocent person killed or harmed, but I was out of options, so I told her the entire story as best I could without notes or preparation from my first meeting with Marty to the time I decided to send Mitch into harm's way. I closed the story by saying that if she revealed this information to anyone, anytime, anyplace now or in the future, she would most likely be killed—not necessarily by me but she would be killed.

Several more minutes went by before she killed her beer and ordered another before she looked me dead in the eyes and said, "Why me?"

"You just would not go away, Rachel, and besides that, you do seem to care, and on the selfish side, I need your help."

"I thought that you said that I was of no value?"

"That was just my way of determining if you were of value. Are you in or out?"

"It appears that I have no choice in this thing. If I opt out, I die. If I stay in, I will probably die. I have no good option here."

"I can't make any promises. However, I can say that I will do my dead-level best to protect you as much as possible. However, there is no discounting the risk. We will be investigating and messing with ruthless, determined, desperate, and dangerous individuals and groups as we try to find Allen—or I guess, now I can say Mitch to you—and try to find the FBI's scapegoat so the government and the press can have their lynching and their closure of sorts."

Both of us decided that we needed a day off, so we drank too many beers for too long. I lost count at fifteen, and Rachel passed out in a corner booth after her tenth. The owner lets us bunk in his back room on a couple of cots, and somewhere around nine p.m., I woke up and got Rachel back to consciousness, and then we got into my car—if you use *my* loosely—and headed back to Rachel's to get her things. To her chagrin, I decided that would pose too much risk now that she was part of the action, so I decided it best for us to stop somewhere to get her a new wardrobe. Beth was still feeding money into a private ATM account that only she and I knew about so money would not be an issue.

"Where do we go from here, Jonathan?"

"You have got to call me John. Even though you know the truth, we must keep up the facade. You are now officially undercover."

"What is our story? Are we lovers?"

"I don't know, to be exact. Let me think about it a while."

"Is Allen or, I mean, Mitch alive?"

"I don't know that either! Hey, there we go—you can be Allen's sister who is concerned about his disappearance, and by being his sister, it will be easy to sell the fact that you are a racist, a bigot, or whatever."

"Was Allen really all of those things?"

"No! It was all part of his undercover disguise. Mitch was—or is—a really decent human being, a much better person, citizen, and patriot than I. He was—or is—all God and country, biscuits and apple pie."

"Good!"

"You liked him very much, didn't you?"

"Yes, and I think he liked me? If that was not part of the undercover disguise? But I may never know that answer, will I?"

"You might! Let's try to find him!"

Back in Washington

"Sam, I have got a location on him now. He is mobile in Montana."

"Montana?"

"Yes, he is traveling out of Helena toward Bozeman."

"Daniel, get Bozeman on the phone immediately. We have got to get him this time."

"Yes, sir!"

"Keep someone on the line there and keep them up to date on his location at all times, and have someone on a cell phone at all times on the scene as we try to intercept him. Do not fail!"

Back in Spokane

"Where do we start, John?"

"I have got a lead on a group near here that I think might be a good place to start. The group's leader is Joe Whitaker, and the name of the group is Americans for America."

"That's innocent-sounding enough!"

"Most of the hate groups in this country have very innocent-sounding names. That is how they lure potential members to their cause. Right now, we are potential members, and I have a phone number for Joe that I got after a rally in Michigan. Mitch was getting close to a group near here that he described as being 'involved.'"

"Do you think that these groups are one in the same?"

"I don't know, but maybe? However, if not, I think there must be a connection between the two. It was just after Mitch made me aware of his involvement in or suspicions of this group that he disappeared. He believed that it was very well financed and organized, and he mentioned something about a twenty-acre compound."

"Now that should not be hard to find!"

"A twenty-acre compound in a large city would not difficult to find. However, in this part of the world, twenty acres is not very big. Our best bet is to start with Joe Whitaker and then see where he leads us."

Somewhere at an undisclosed location in Spokane

"I have picked up some FBI communications, and this Beck guy appears to be traveling through Montana. What is up with that? I thought we were to track him down somewhere around here. Hell, you are not paying me enough money to chase him all over the fucking country."

"Listen, pencil dick, you will go wherever I need you. However, right now, we need to sit tight until we verify his location."

In a corner booth in the Peacock Lounge at the Davenport Hotel in Spokane

"What's the plan here, sir?"

"We are to find this Jonathan Beck and then bring him in."

"Why? Isn't he one of us sir?"

"In a way, I guess. Hell, I don't know. The bureau is like the Marine Corps—*it is not our place to ask why, just do or die or some shit like that.* I can't remember—it has been a while since my days in the Corps. I think this guy is some sort of renegade type that was brought back after having been fired or forced to retire to work on some special assignment. However, he went postal again or something, and now they want him back."

"Do we have a plan?"

"Yes, he is expected to make contact with a group near here anytime now. And when he does, you and I are to move in on him. However, until he does, we are to just stay here."

"How will we know that he has made this contact?"

"We have sources embedded there that will call us on this private cell phone. Look, just sit back and relax for now. This is one hell of a nice place, and there are some real lookers in the lobby, and I am sure they will be coming in here sooner or later. This ain't no bad gig, son. Just sit back and enjoy."

On a luxury yacht off the coast of British Columbia

"I am getting nervous. There are just too many feds in the area."

"Relax, boss. There is no way to make a connection back to you. I have taken care of everything."

"That sounds good. However, there is always a way to make a connection if enough of the right people work on it and at it long enough. There is no perfect crime, James! My sources are telling me that there are several groups of feds in or near Spokane. However, it is unclear at this point just what they are all doing."

"I am hearing that they are looking for one of their own that has gone astray or something."

"I know that. However, why do they think that he is out here?"

"I have some of my guys looking into it now, boss."

"I need some answers, James, and I need them quickly."

"I would have already had them, boss. However, it is scary out there right now. We not only have the feds snooping around, there are others out there snooping around, and it is hard to tell just who is who. I am hearing rumors of hired guns and of a ten-thousand-dollar bounty on this guy's head. We have to move carefully!"

"Bounty? Find out who is willing to pay this kind of money to have this guy killed and why!"

"Okay, boss. I will get on it first thing in the morning."

"Good, James. Go on to your quarters. It is time for us all to turn in for the night."

After James left, the boss went by the bar and picked up a couple of young maidens and then went on to his suite.

"Wait a minute, girls. Have a joint first on me while I make a phone call and then get undressed and give me a little show before coming to bed." They immediately started to kiss each other and undressed in the floor as a young butler came into the room wearing an open robe, revealing his endowment as he bent over and gave both of the young maidens a joint that, unknown to them, was laced with angel dust. In a few moments, they were melting in his arms as they loved on him and each other.

"Listen, Jake, up the bounty on this guy if they can get him in twenty-four hours."

"What?"

"Just double the fucking bounty and don't ask any questions. If this guy stays alive, he will sooner or later take us all down. He is on a mission. Bye!"

"Okay, son, get the fuck out of here and send the whores over here. You can go fuck my wife now! Ha ha! Ha! Don't stand there looking dumb, you faggot. I know everything that goes on—and I mean everything. It doesn't matter—I can't get it up for her anymore anyway. Ha ha ha!"

"Ohhh! Now that's nice, bitch! Keep it up, sweetie, and you might even get a raise."

CHAPTER 15

At a truck stop near Bozeman, Montana

"Sam?"

"Yes, have you got him?"

"Uh, not really. We do, however, have his car!"

"Uh?"

"The tracking device in the vehicle evidently was damaged when the vehicle was crushed and stopped working for a period. It seems now that it evidently started back to working after being loaded on a flatbed with umpteen other vehicles on the way to the scrap metal processors in Bozeman."

"How in the hell did his vehicle get...uh, shit! I don't think it matters now! I guess he must have ditched it somehow and then stole or bought another, so I guess we go back to Spokane."

"I am sorry, sir."

"That's all right, it sounded too good to be true anyway."

Back in Atlanta

"Beth, I am beginning to get worried. I first thought that this was going to turn into a three-ring circus out there, but you know, I think it will be more like a Wild West show with a huge shoot-out somewhere. It seems that everyone on all sides in this thing are over-reacting, and I think that the feds—and that includes all of us—have forgotten about our original objective of *finding the killer or killers*."

"Well, you can bet your ass that our boy is trying to solve this thing, if it is related, in any way to the death or disappearance of Mitch."

"But, Beth, Jonathan didn't know Mitch all that well."

"I know, but I also know Jonathan, and you do too. He put Mitch in harm's way, and he feels the obligation to get him out of harm's way or to get revenge—whichever works or is needed."

"I am thinking about going out there too, Jonathan is going to need a friend and some help."

Back in Spokane

"Rachel, where were you and Allen going for the weekend the time that you say he stood you up?"

"Somewhere in or near Hayden Lake."

"Then let's start there. You never saw him again after that, did you?"

"No! He just dropped off the face of the earth as far as I was concerned. I first thought that he just went back home, and then people started to ask questions about him, and that is when I got nervous and afraid for his safety."

"Do you remember anything suspicious happening anytime close to his disappearance?"

"No, not really! You do realize that everything that happens in a bar can and does look suspicious."

"Well, you know what I mean. Was there a fight, an abnormal confrontation with anyone? Maybe Allen's mood changed? Could he have had a reason for you not going with him up there?"

"I am sure he had a reason. However, I am not sure what it was. I don't remember anything close to a fight or even and argument of any significance."

"Do you know where you and he were going to stay up there?"

"Yes, I will have to think a minute, but it was a really nice bed and breakfast, uh…the Clark House, yes that's it, the Clark House! I had always wanted to go there and never had the opportunity. That was one of the main reasons I had decided to go with him. That place is really nice and has a ton of history connected to it too. I believe that it was built by a shipping tycoon named Clark."

"I thought maybe it was named after Lewis and Clarke?"

"No, this guy was a shipping magnate."

"Well, let's start there!"

"What about this Joe Whitaker?"

"We will get up with him too!"

"You call on your cell and make the reservations, and I will call Joe."

"For when?"

"Tonight!"

"Tonight! Dammit, Jonathan, that is a busy and very popular bed and breakfast. You can't just call and get a room like that!"

"The hell you can't! Pay them twice or even three times the going rate if you have to. I want to be there tonight, and by the way, put the room in your name."

"My name...hell, I don't have that kind of money unless you give me your credit card."

"Nope! That is not an option now. My credit card charges, Internet access, and cell phone usage can be traced and traced quickly. Everything from here on in has to be in your name."

"Fuck that! Where am I going to get that kind of money or credit?"

"Call your credit card company, and we will make a deposit to cover whatever we need."

"How and when?"

"Tonight!"

"Okay, now what about the how?"

"Don't worry about that. I will take care of it from our next stop."

"Why?"

"Right now, I don't believe that anyone can connect the dots to get us together—at least not for now! Do you have family that might start looking for you?"

"Not anytime soon. My dad is dead, and my mom is who knows where. I hear from her about twice a year, my birthday, that is sometimes, and Christmas, ah, about every other year."

"Good, then we have no worries on your end."

"Good? You know sometimes I hate your ass!"

"Join the fun, hun! Hating me is popular these days!"

I tuned her out as she made the necessary calls and arrangements, including our late-arrival reservations at the Clarke House.

Back in Atlanta

"Beth, how long have you known Jonathan?"

"I don't know. He was about to retire when I was transferred to the Atlanta Office."

Rodney then asked her, "You do know of his Vietnam background?"

"No! Not really! Why?"

"He was a POW, in what is most commonly referred to, as the Hanoi Hilton. That background is what got him into the most sensitive and most volatile FBI situations. That is also why his name was one of the first to come up when the bureau decided to increase the manpower on this project."

"Why was he forced out? I know that the proper story is that he retired. However, I also know better than that. What happened?"

"Jonathan can go ballistic at times when faced with certain situations, and he can make an enemy out of someone that just looks like an enemy."

"I don't understand?"

"He still hates anyone of Vietnamese or Southeast Asian descent. His view of the Vietnam war and of our current conflicts are a little bizarre. He is old school and believes that war is war and not politics! Don't ever tell him, but I was actually against the feds bringing him back!"

"But, Rodney, he picked you to help him!"

"I know that, Beth, and I am here helping. However, I never believed him to be right for this task."

"Why have you never said this before?"

"Well, he was working and acting within the lines. However, now I think that the real Jonathan has surfaced, and who knows what he might do next? There is more to my thinking!"

"What might that be?"

Ring! Ring! Ring!

"Hello!"

"Beth?"

"How did you know that we were working late?"

"Listen, Beth, I don't have much time here. I need money moved to an account for me ASAP—no, a Western Union wire. That would be better."

"Jonathan, I don't have any money to move. David is pulling everything in the morning."

"That's in the morning. Send it tonight."

"Jonathan—"

"Do it Beth," Rodney whispered. "That will at least let me know where he is right now."

"Dammit, Rodney."

"*Just do it,* Beth!"

"Okay, where do I send it?"

"I will pick it up at a 7-Eleven in Spokane on 1317, South Grand Boulevard."

"Jonathan, there is only about fifty thousand left in that fund."

"Send it!"

"Jonathan?"

Click!

"He hung up!"

"Let's go and wire the money! No, you do that. I am going home and getting ready to fly to Spokane."

"What do I tell David?"

"Tell him that I am on a leave of absence."

"Not that, Rodney! What do I tell him about the money?"

"Tell him that I had you send it. That way, it might save your job. At this point, I don't care about mine. Oh yes, see what number

Jonathan called us on and call me on my cell later. If it was his cell, track it immediately and see if you can trace his movements."

Offices of Magnum Shipping in Los Angeles

"What do you have, Jake?"

"Not much. I have raised the bounty as you asked. However, this guy seems to have become invisible all of a sudden. My moles inside the bureau say that the feds have not been able to find his exact whereabouts either."

"What do your moles say that he is up to?"

"They say that he is on an unsanctioned hunt for one of their own named Mitch Blaylock. It appears that this Mitch disappeared while working undercover in the Spokane area. Could this be our guy?"

"Yes, he was using an alias."

"We had better circle the wagons and eliminate as many people in our involvement as fast as we can before someone says something to someone else that gets to someone else and then eventually to us! How good is this guy?"

"I don't know! Find out!"

"You know that he is the guy in charge—or that was in charge—of the hunt for the rag head murders!"

"Yes, so he must be good. However, he does have faults and everyone makes mistakes."

CHAPTER 16

At the Clarke House, Hayden Lake, Washington

"Now this is nice, Rachel. How did you register us?"

"I used my former married name of Jacobs. I still have a driver's license in that name, so we are Mr. and Mrs. John Jacobs."

"Were you married?"

"Yes, twice before I was twenty-one, and I married again about a year ago, a marriage that lasted nine days."

"So you are from Spokane, Washington, and you married a Jew?"

"He was not Jewish. His wing of the family had converted to Catholicism a couple of generations back."

"Okay, so you are comfortable with sleeping with a total stranger then?"

"Well, it isn't like I haven't done it before. However, I hate your ass, so don't get any funky ideas."

"That's good. However, all women hate me at first. But, that will change."

"I don't really hate you, Jonathan. Your cause is noble, and I need to know what happened to Allen or Mitch or whomever. However, I just hate that you got me involved."

"I didn't. You did when you got attached to our boy wonder."

"Let's go register. They should not have any trouble believing that we are married. Both of the girls have been watching us fuss."

After registering with no hassle, we went to the elevators and took one to the second floor. As I opened the door, I was amazed at the beauty and the elegance of the room.

"Well, honey, we have a king bed, I see. How much did this cost us for tonight?"

"Two hundred fifty dollars, and I had to register and pay in advance for three nights, and I gave the girl named Marla a two-hundred-dollar tip."

"I am glad that I don't travel with you often!"

"I was only being the good wife and obeying orders. I am going to take a hot bath. Why don't you call that Joe guy and make our plans for tomorrow?"

FBI offices, Washington, DC

"What do we know?"

"The first thing is that we don't have a clue where this guy is other than the fact that he is somewhere in the Spokane and Pacific Northwest region. He is not using any of his former cell phones, either bureau or personal, nor any of his personal or bureau credit cards. Here is what we do know—a former FBI agent named Rodney Fischer sent him a large sum of cash via Western Union to a 7-Eleven in Spokane just yesterday. He thinks that he is on a self-assigned leave of absence. However, David in Atlanta fired him, and another person that actually sent the wire as soon as it was discovered. This Rodney guy is now on his way to the region for God only knows what."

"So at this point in time, who is working on the murders?"

"You tell me, Sam?"

"I have got to give a news conference on it tomorrow. Get the word out to the press that our efforts are now being concentrated in the Pacific Northwest and that an arrest is coming soon. I do believe that we are on the right track here and that the solution is intermingled somehow in all of what is happening out there."

"That is a big promise and a large area."

"Don't be specific, and I did not make a promise. I just need to buy more time. I do think that Mitch and Jonathan are close to the perp or perps and we might get lucky."

After leaving the Clarke House

After we both got a great night's sleep—with our bodies never touching, I might add—we had a great breakfast and then traveled back to Spokane to meet Joe Whitaker.

"Why are we meeting him back in Spokane?"

"I do not want him or anyone else to put us together here or in Hayden Lake, so we are not meeting him. I will drop you off at the mall with a couple of hundred dollars to spend while I meet with this with Joe."

I spent a good three hours convincing Joe that I was no threat and that I was a real patriot and that I wanted to become more involved with their movement. I started the conversation off with a five-hundred-dollar donation that made all my tales and stories more believable because Joe's organization was beginning to run low on funds. Slowly but surely, I got to my real reason for meeting with him, and I popped the question about the twenty-acre compound. He did know of it; however, it became crystal clear that Joe was not connected and that he was not militant enough to be involved with any group of murders or even a murder, so he quickly fell off my radar screen after he gave me the location of the compound. I did promise to attend some meetings and to donate more to his illustrious cause, and I congratulated him for being the great patriot that he was and told him of how motivated I was after hearing him speak in Michigan. I knew when we shook hands and parted company that I would most likely not see him again.

I then drove back to the mall to retrieve a bewildered Rachel.

"What took you so long?"

"Just talking and trying to be believable enough to get some information, and it went very well. He gave me the location of the compound and some very valuable information. We should drive by there this evening."

"That was easy! I thought that it would take days to find, if we ever did. What do you know of this Joe Whitaker?"

"I have told you everything I know. Why do you ask?"

"I don't know—it just seems strange that he gave you this information so easily. Remember when you said that finding it would be difficult?"

"Yes, but, uh…maybe I see now what you are saying. However, I think we should still just find it for now."

"Okay, but this guy might have motives of his own here. We need more information before we approach this compound or any of its members."

Back in Atlanta

"Beth?"

"Yes."

"I am sorry that you were fired. However, it was important for us to get the money moved so that I could have a starting point in my hunt for Jonathan."

"I hope that it is worth something. This thing has gotten so crazy now."

"Beth, watch the news closely for a few days for any suspicious activity near Spokane."

"What type of thing are you referring to?"

"I don't know. It is just strange that Jonathan is so invisible right now. I believe that he may not be working alone. What did you find when you tracked his call for the money transfer?"

"Nothing. He called from the payphone at that convenience store."

"Dammit! He is just too good sometimes. I was hoping that he might have used someone else's cell phone."

"You are acting funny right now. Are you trying to help Jonathan, or are you—I don't know—you seem, ah…!"

"What are you asking, Beth?"

"Well, at first, I thought that you were going out there to help Jonathan, but somehow, I am getting a funny subliminal message that you might be trying to stop him or something. I really don't know what you would be stopping him from. However, it just seems that way."

"I don't know either, Beth. All of this is strange to me too. You do remember me saying that I was against Jonathan being put in charge of the investigations."

"Yes, but you did not say why."

"I thought it would be too much like putting the fox to guard the hen house. His Vietnam background and post-traumatic stress, along with his earlier difficulties at the bureau, should have been reviewed more closely. This syndrome or mental disorder can be very unpredictable and deadly to its sufferers and to others."

"I don't understand what you are saying? Is it that you somehow suspect Jonathan of something?"

"Not suspect, just capable. Yes, that's the word, *capable*."

"Of what?"

"I don't know. Just keep your cell by your side at all times and let me know if something suspicious happens out there—anything!"

"Okay!"

"Again, Beth, I am truly sorry!"

"Bye."

Back in Spokane

"Let's go back to the room and think through this for a bit before we act, John."

"Okay, that is probably a good idea. However, we need to get some gas on the way."

"Okay, there is a Conoco near the Clark House. We can stop there."

For the next thirty minutes or so, neither one of us said much. However, I was beginning to notice that Rachel was wearing a very mini miniskirt today, revealing her young legs and an occasional view of her satin panties. I knew that she had no ulterior motives; it is just the way of the younger generation today.

"Rachel, if you will go inside and pay, I will pump."

"Why don't we put it on my card?"

"No way, it might eventually get traced back to us!"

"You said just this morning that no one can put us together!"

"Yes, that is right, and I intend to keep it that way."

"Okay, how much?"

"I think that forty should get it close to full, so just prepay forty bucks and I will be in there shortly."

I pumped in the forty bucks' worth and then went in to meet up with Rachel, who had picked us both up a cup of black coffee. I then looked behind the counter at this Iraqi or Indian-looking bastard, and I thought I would just let Rachel handle everything and I would just get my coffee and then wait on her outside, so that is what I did. However, after a few minutes, I began to realize that she had not followed, so I looked inside only to see her in what appeared to be an argument with the rag head.

"What's wrong, Rachel?" I said after I opened the door and walked up to the counter.

"He says that you pumped forty dollars' worth of gas and that I had only prepaid for thirty!"

"What? The fucking pump would have shut off at thirty if that were true. Shut the fuck up, you bastard. She gave you forty dollars, and the pump shut off at forty even."

"No, sir," he replied in the damnable accent that the sand niggers speak and then reached for the phone like he was going to call the cops or something. A light went on in my brain, and then for the next little while, I don't remember exactly what happened. However, he did not make his phone call, and we were gone in a flash without further ado and without any witnesses. When I came to my senses, I was dragging Rachel by the hair across the parking lot of the motel with my hand over her mouth and blood was all over my hands and her face. I stopped as soon as I was cognizant of my current state and begged her to settle down so that I could talk with her and ask a question or two for I was afraid that I had hit her. She and I both got control, and we walked out back of the Clark House. "What happened back there, Rachel?"

"You don't know."

"Not exactly. I sort of lost it when that bastard went for the phone."

"You beat the holy shit out of him before I could pull you away. I am afraid that you seriously hurt that man, John."

"Did I hurt you?"

"No! You just all of a sudden got an incredible amount of strength and physically removed me from the premises and threw me into the car. That man had no chance against you in that state of mind. Where did that come from?"

"I don't know. Flashbacks maybe. Or maybe I just did not want to have to face any cops right now and the bastard was wrong—we had paid him properly! Did anyone see what happened?"

"I don't think so. However, I can't be sure. Everything happened so quickly. Let's just get into the motel and back to our room and think all of this out! You have been so careful as to not to let anyone know of our whereabouts and whatever and then you do this shit! I just don't understand you sometimes."

"Rachel, this shit is bigger that you and me, and it is bigger than the FBI or the fucking CIA. This country is heading full speed into another civil war if we are not careful. Just ask the Native Americans what can happen if you don't control the borders. You tell me what an American will look like fifty years from now? It will be a 'high yellow,' living on welfare and worshiping some fucking idol or some sort of shit like that! The average white man or woman for that matter will be a slave to their wishes and whims!"

"I don't know—let's just go to the room and think this out!"

Back in Atlanta

"Rodney!"

"Yes!"

"I just noticed something over the wire about a man of Middle Eastern descent being beaten up at a convenience store just out of Spokane! There may not be anything to it, however, you wanted me to inform you of anything strange that happened in that region."

"Thanks, that is just the sort of thing that may lead me to our boy. I still don't understand how he has been able to operate out there completely under the radar. He has got to have help of some variety for he is leaving no footprints or tracks—however, someone is—and that is my task at the present. I have got to determine who is helping him and how. That person is leaving tracks, and we are just not seeing them right now because we do not know what to look for or where. You have just given me the where, and now I have got to determine the why and the how!"

"I don't know, Rodney. I think that you are making this more difficult than it is when all I think Jonathan is doing is trying to catch the murderers and in the process find out what happened to Mitch!"

"I hope and pray that you are right, Beth!"

"Where are you?"

"I am moving rapidly through the airport in Spokane. I plan to get a cab and then visit that convenience store clerk. Well, not a cab—I think that I will rent a car instead. Check with DC and see if they have anything on Jonathan or any group or groups that he might be trying to target!"

"Hey, asshole, you seem to forget that you got me fired! The feds will not give me any information!"

"Check with David. His ass is on the line here too!"

Finally, Rachel and Jonathan Are Back in Their Room at the Clarke House

"I will pour us a drink. Jonathan, why don't you get a bath and that will give us both a little time to think through all of this?"

"That is a good idea. Make mine on the rocks."

As I was showering, I began to wonder how I had gotten myself into this situation! Prior to getting the call from Marty several months back, my life had become rather simple and mundane. My main worries were of keeping up with the slot limits and other regulations on the lakes. I loved to fish, and there were all the complicated hunting seasons in place now just to hunt whitetail deer. Now I may have just killed a man. However, he would not be my first. In Vietnam, I was paid to kill and to destroy, and the FBI loved me for that so they had recruited me through the military and the CIA to come to work stateside. It makes one wonder just what is murder? We kill every day somewhere somehow! If you get approval, I guess, then it is not murder. However, someone still dies. Some mother loses a son or a daughter. Some child loses a father or a mother.

John Calley Jr. was a hero to me and a murderer to others. I wondered what Vietnam was—a war, a political contest, or a place to destroy just so we could help build it back so that they could now make my Rockport shoes and fun of our disabled vets. All of a sudden, the shower curtain opened and Rachel handed me my drink. I did not know what to think or say at first for there I stood in all of my nakedness and she in just a bra and a pair of panties. We both just stared at each other for what seemed like forever, and then she broke the silence by saying, "Get out of the fucking tub so that I can take a bath too." Well, so much for what I thought might be a romantic moment of sorts!

Rachel followed me into the tub without even thinking twice about being half naked and I was now just wrapped in a towel. She was a really good-looking girl, probably twenty years or more my junior, but not exactly beautiful. Some girls, I have always thought, were built to look at and others for fun, and that would be Rachel!

She must have stayed in the shower for at least an hour before walking through the room with only a towel half wrapped around her body. I had them other kind of motives for a minute; however, I knew that I must now send her on her way before I got her hurt or, even worse, jailed at some point for helping me.

She eventually came over to the sleeper sofa in our suite dressed only in a pair of loose-fitting shorts and a T-shirt with no bra, revealing a shapelier pair of tits than I had imagined.

"Okay, Jonathan," she said, "what's next?"

"You need to pack your shit and get out!"

"What?"

"You heard me, Rachel. I appreciate your help, and I would not be this far along had it not been for you. However, I am now getting worried about your safety."

"Fuck you, Jonathan. I am not going to back out now, and you can't make me either."

"Oh yes, I can!"

"You can? What if I call the authorities after I leave and tell them the whereabouts of the infamous Jonathan Beck? Where would that put your ass?"

"Look, Rachel, I don't want a fight with you. I am just trying to protect you. This is going to get dangerous, and I might not even get through this alive. I am not living under any false pretenses. Mitch is dead, and I don't want you to fall victim to the same fate. At this point, I am only trying to find his killer or killers, and I really don't give a rat's ass about who might be killing the resident rag head motherfuckers in this country."

"Look, dumb ass, you think that I don't already know all of that? You only signed back on with the feds for the money for your kids. A blind man or woman can see that you are not after the mass murderers."

"Well, that is not entirely true. I would like to solve this thing in the process of getting revenge for what happened to Mitch."

"Why? I don't think that you even knew Mitch that well."

"Maybe not. However, he got killed doing what I had asked him to do! I was thinking in the shower that it might be a good idea if we changed motels after what happened back there. We're just too close."

"On that I agree. Why don't you pack our things while I check us out?"

"Sure, and I will look in the phonebook for an alternate place to stay!"

While Rachel was gone, I decided that I needed her too much to worry about her life—or mine for that matter—for without her help, I stood no chance to get this thing finished dead or alive. Besides that, the bitch would most likely turn on me if I ran her off anyway. This high-stakes poker game of such seemed to turn her on anyway. I guess her life had been pretty ho-hum until Mitch and I came into her life. If I made it through this shit, I had to remember to never become a bartender!

"Okay, big guy. Let's hit the road. We are no longer residents of the Clarke House. Where are we off to?"

"I think that we need to go back to Spokane. This Hayden Lake place is just too small. I found a Super 8 that should work and they have vacancies."

"Okay, let's go!"

We then loaded the car and drove past the now infamous convenience store, and then we came to a sign that read "Spokane." However, I went the other direction!

"What's up with this shit, Jonathan? I thought that we were going to Spokane?"

I thought that we might do a drive by on the compound just to get our bearings and directions straight.

Back in Hayden Lake at the convenience store

"My name is Rodney Fischer. Is the gentleman in that was hurt the other evening?"

"No!"

"Does he still work here?"

"Yes! However, he is out on leave right now!"

"Where might I go to see him?"

"You might start at the hospital. I don't think that he has gone home as of yet?"

Rodney was at the convenience store at the same time as Jonathan and Rachel drove by, leaving the area. At this particular point, while Rachel and Jonathan drove to who knows where Jonathan is being sought out by the feds, Rodney, Magnum Shipping, and an untold number of bounty hunters and possibly paid assassins. The hunter was now the hunted! The murders that plagued the Middle Eastern communities nationwide were now just a national headline, a political pawn, a reason to fund, but not the concentration of all our efforts to solve.

Jonathan and Rachel found themselves near Mt. Spokane State Park on what was most likely at some point in history, a logging trail on the backside of a heavily fenced and fortified compound. It appeared to be more than twenty acres. However, now was not the time to split hairs on some small details.

"How much does a fence like that cost, Jonathan?"

"Don't ask me, Rachel. However, I can tell you that the number of people in the Pacific Northwest that could afford this type of setup is on a very short list. I am going to climb the fence or find some other way over. In the interim, why don't you access the tax records for the county? This bastard must be at the top of the list of payees in the county."

"Jonathan, you do not even know if this is the compound or not?"

"Yes, I do, and I am going to find out more. Just stay here and work on the computer."

My military training pays off every now and then, so I quickly determined that the fortification was not very sophisticated to say the least. I disarmed a couple of low-tech cameras and an alarm and was moving toward this huge house on a ridge overlooking a lake. I quietly approached a large Japanese garden near an area encasing an Olympic-size pool and then approached a series of sliding glass doors cautiously. My intuition told me that I was near something, something of significance to my search. My sniper experience and my other military training along with my CIA and FBI training led me quietly and stealthily around a small portion of the outside of the house to a large five-car garage. I looked in and discovered that it was only housing one Porsche 911 Carrera, indicating to me that I might only have to worry about one person in the house. That did not make sense. A house, compound, or whatever of this size could never, at any time, be maintained by just one individual. I had to be missing something. Finally, I decided to enter the house to see what else I might discover there. To my surprise, one of the sliding glass doors was unlocked, so I took advantage of that and moved carefully and cautiously into the house and down a hallway to a double set of stairs one going up and the other down. I quickly decided to look upstairs instead of down since if I got discovered, I knew that I could run faster downstairs than upstairs, and it was at that point that I realized that I did not have a gun on my person. At the top of the stairs, I came across what appeared to be a library with a large empty sitting area that contained a podium that appeared to be used for lectures and such.

My sense slowly started to tell me that someone or something was approaching, so I jumped into the room and closed the door, leaving just a small crack. A few minutes later, I heard footsteps coming down the hall and then almost out of nowhere, there appeared a scantily clad middle-aged lady moving nonchalantly in the direction from which I had come. After she disappeared around the corner with no indication in her movement or actions that she might return soon I began to look around the library. A library can tell a lot about a person or group of persons, so I spent the next hour looking through a vast array of books and magazines, quickly confirming my suspicions that I was on to something here. However, the only resident that I had come across so far did not appeared to be worried, concerned, or anything of that nature. In fact, I would have bet on her preparing to meet some young guy to get laid. All of this was too confusing to confront or to try to figure out tonight, so I eased back out of the house and returned the way that I had come, and I reset the alarms and the cameras as I exited the compound.

Rachel was nearly hysterical when I returned to the car and went off on me for a good ten minutes before calming down and then asking what had I discovered.

"This is our infamous compound, my dear. There is an entire library on governmental issues or, should I say, anti-government issues. This guy is a—quote, unquote—patriot of some description. However, tonight all I saw was a very good looking middle-age woman looking to get laid, most likely by some young pool boy or such! The library also housed an array of anti-Muslim publications and an unbelievable collection of books on the shipping industry with special emphasis on the history of some West Coast shipping tycoon."

"Who is the tycoon?"

"You know, for the life of me, I cannot remember the name. It was a name, however, that I have heard before."

"I will get on the computer when we get to the motel and see if I can Google it up for you. If there are books written about this person or persons, then we can find them out without too much difficulty. Will you recognize the name when you hear it or see it?"

"Yes!"

We then returned to Spokane and checked into the Super 8 after having a quick pass through the local McDonalds for a quickie supper. The thought of a quickie got me to thinking about maybe leaving Rachel at the motel for a few hours while I either breeze through a local bar and check the traps or maybe even visit a local massage salon. I was now in much need of relief. In the male species, fast adrenaline rushes, danger, and even challenges have the mystical effect of increasing the sex drive even in a middle-aged guy like myself. That has always been my reasoning for why athletes, high-profile executives, and most men in positions of power seem to always have fidelity issues.

I mentioned this to Rachel, and she did not like the idea, so I reluctantly changed my thinking back to the task at hand. I had come up with an idea while driving from Hayden Lake to Spokane, so I thought that I would run it by her.

"Rachel, I have an idea that might just work."

"What's that?"

"I am going to try to get up with Rodney and/or Beth tomorrow. Why don't you rent a car and go back to Hayden Lake and stake out our sex queen in the mansion on the compound. I would like to know what her day consists of, where she goes, whom she sees, and every little detail of even what she buys at the grocery."

"Why do you need to talk with them? They have most likely turned on you by now after having lost their jobs and all."

"I have thought of that. However, I don't think that is the case. I will still drive out of town and find a convenience store somewhere to make the call from just in case. I would like to know what they know about what all is going on at the bureau now and if I am on the most wanted list as of yet."

"As John Mays or as Jonathan Beck?"

"Both!"

"Okay. However, I don't trust you at a convenience store. Why don't you use a payphone at a mall or something?"

"Yeah, that may not be a bad idea."

"You are still a secret, Rachel, so you should make a good tail on this broad. Come to think of it, she already has a good tail…uh, ah, excuse the pun!"

"I may not be. You must remember that I just walked out of the bar and never returned. Someone may get to thinking and may have even gone by my apartment by now. You were not the first to come in there looking for Mitch, and I doubt if you were the last. They may have put the possibility of us having got together by now. If they connect the dots between me, Mitch, and then you, my cover may also be blown."

"There is only one person in Atlanta that is that smart, and that would be Rodney, and he is not employed now or at least not by the bureau."

"Jonathan, think about it a minute. We have got to have everyone suspicious by now in all circles."

"Okay, I thought about it. However, we have still got to move forward. Will you tail the broad?"

"Yes. However, let's get on the computer like you first mentioned and see if we can determine who she is? Let's see if I Google 'West Coast shipping companies—gee, there must be hundreds. However, the first one is a company called 'Magnum Shipping.' They have offices in, ah, in almost every port on the West Coast with their home offices in San Francisco."

"You are getting the cart in front of the horse, Rachel. We must first identify the woman and then see where that leads us."

"I bet she is the estranged wife of the president of this company or of some other huge shipping company. Remember, you saw all of the books on shipping in the library in the mansion."

"Well, you are probably right, and it is plain as day that she is not hurting for money. What is the name of the guy at the top of Magnum?"

"Clarke B. Goldman."

"Okay, let's get some rest tonight and then get a fresh start in the morning. You can drive to Hayden Lake early and I will see what I can find out. Wait a minute—the name in the library was Clarke, you know, Clarke like the Clarke House. That's strange, Goldman makes sense, you know, by being Jew and all like our famous Yankee owner Steinbrenner. However, Clarke is not a normal-sounding Jewish given name, and why is it the same as the surname referred to in the books in the library and in the brochures of the Clarke House? That will be worth looking into also. However, for now, we will just stick to our immediate plans."

The next day, Rachel got up about 5:00 a.m. only to find me already gone. *Now why in hell would he have gone this early?* she thought. However, she knew very well not to try to ever predict his thoughts or actions. *Oh well, Hayden Lake, Miss Whomever, here I come!*

CHAPTER 17

Late that night at the "Double Dribble Salon"

"Yeah, thanks, lady. I'll take a double shot of your house brandy on the rocks please."

"Sure," the cute barmaid replied and then left and quickly returned with the brandy. "You are new to these parts, aren't you, cowboy?" Rodney occasionally dressed in urban cowboy-type garb.

"Just traveling through from Georgia!"

"Georgia!"

"Yes! You look shocked!"

"No, I, ah, ah…oh, never mind. I have got to get some more drinks. Enjoy."

Rodney quickly determined from her expression and from her actions that something concerned her about him being from Georgia. For the rest of the evening, the girl stayed on the other end of the bar and had a guy serve Rodney and the folks on his end. Finally, at about 2:00 a.m., the place was beginning to clear out, and the girl still seemed to be purposely avoiding Rodney. It was time for Rodney to make his move, so he walked down the bar and motioned directly to her. "Hey, what's your name?"

"Why?"

"I would like to know the name of the person I'm about to leave a twenty-dollar tip with if that is not asking too much?"

"No! I am sorry. It's Karen!"

"Does Karen have a surname?"

"Weekly."

"What time does Karen get off tonight?"

"I'll be leaving to go home shortly after two a.m. I don't have to clean up tonight."

"Would Karen Weekly like to have an early breakfast somewhere?"

"Not really," she said as she walked around the bar and then whispered lightly, "meet me at the Corner Bar down the street in fifteen minutes, but for right now, get out of here!"

"Okay, Karen. Thanks for the advice," I coolly replied. "Have a good life. Maybe I'll pass through here again sometime." and then I laid a twenty on the bar and walked out slowly without ever looking back.

Thirty minutes later

Rodney knew not to order anything now but beer, so he had ordered a Heineken Light and was drinking it slowly and was still about to have an empty bottle. *Where is the bitch?* Rodney thought as he looked toward the door about the time Karen walked through the swinging doors. She gave the bar a once over then saw Rodney standing at the edge of the bar near the restroom signs.

"Sorry I am late. However, the bastards still made me clean a little even though it was my night not to. I don't have a lot of time. I have a live-in boyfriend that is already at home, and he would not take kindly to me meeting a stranger here."

"Why did you do it then?"

"Well, number one, this would be the last place he would look for me. He knows that I hate this bar, and number two, he always expects for me to be late."

"That is not all, is it?"

"No! Who are you, and how did you just pop up at the Double Dribble?"

"Why?"

"Answer my questions first. I hate people that answer a question with a question."

"Rodney Fischer!"

"Why are you here? I know that you are not just traveling through!"

"How do you know that?"

"Because, wise ass, you are not the first person from Georgia to just happen to turn up here of late."

"Don't get so upset, Karen Weekly! I am not here to do you or anyone else harm."

"Oh yeah, well, a waitress that worked here got involved with a young man from your area, and then mysteriously, he turned up missing and then later, after several visits from other people from down there, she too turned up missing."

"Maybe they just ran off together."

"No way. She just vanished, left her apartment untouched. She did not pack. She left her family pictures and fresh food in the fridge and newspapers stacked sky high in front of her door by the time Mel checked on her."

"Mel?"

"He is the guy that runs the bar, and he got suspicious after several weeks and decided to go by there. Something happened to her. However, we cannot get the police to look into it because all of her bills are being paid, including her rent from mysterious places all over the northwest. The police seem to think that she just ran away too. However, I am not buying it. I knew her some, and that is totally out of character for her."

"Okay, now may I ask a few questions?"

"Yes."

"After the young guy became missing and before the girl, she... ah, what is her name by the way?"

"Rachel, Rachel Jacobs, I believe."

"Jewish girl?"

"Hell, I don't know I did not know her all that well."

"Yet you think her running away would be out of character, and you didn't know her all that well."

"Not exactly, there was another guy that came through here just before she became missing, and I think there is a link. He was an older guy, maybe mid-fifties or so. However, he really did not look or act that age most of the time, and he was you know in good shape for his age."

"Describe him to me!"

"Six foot two maybe about two hundred pounds thinning brownish gray hair."

"What did he drink?"

"I don't know. He kept Rachel occupied every time he was here, and she was very secretive about him and their relationship."

"Do you think that they were seeing each other?"

"Not in the way you might be thinking. He was old enough to be her father. However, she did at times date older guys, but I don't think that is what was going on. At the time, I did not think much about it, but when I look back, there was something…something suspicious about them and him in particular. But that is not all. After they turned up gone, others have come through looking for the older guy and the younger guy, but none of them ask about Rachel."

"Who were these other people that came through? I don't know their names. However, two came right out and said that they were FBI, and two others looked like gangsters, and then strange as it may sound, the right-hand man for Clarke B. Goldman and then later Mr. Goldman came through looking for the older guy and never asked the first fucking question about the younger guy, and that was just too fucking weird."

"Why?"

"Goldman's slut wife hangs in here a lot, and one night, maybe more, I know that one night, she picked up the younger guy and took him home with her. Goldman never comes in here. In fact, he never comes anywhere around here. He, for the most part, stays held up on his gigantic yacht or private island hideaway with his horde of young things. When he is working, he is at one of his offices up and down the coast but never in Spokane, so we were all shocked the night he came through."

"Okay, let me see if I can get this straight…ah, no…I can't what do you think happened?"

"I don't know, but even if I did, I would not tell you!"

"Why!"

"Because you are no different than all of the others. You are looking, I presume, for the younger guy and the older guy, and you did not even know—or I don't think you knew—of Rachel. So if you want anything else, then you must answer in complete detail and with proof. Just who the fuck are you?"

At this point, Rodney knew that this was his best shot at finding Jonathan and at piecing this puzzle of bizarre behavior together that might just lead to the whereabouts of both Mitch and Jonathan. It was also clear to him that this Rachel bitch might just be traveling with Jonathan, and that may be why Jonathan has been moving so stealthily through the region. No one including Rodney had tried to come up with a paper and/or an electronic trail on this Rachel Jacobs. He could be using her car, her ID, and her credit cards and her cell phone. Knowing it was a long shot, Rodney told this almost complete stranger the whole story of what had happened from Jonathan's return to the bureau to track a serial killer to the assignment of Mitch to the Pacific Northwest, specifically, the Spokane area, to get an inside track on the Nazi/Christian/White Supremacist movement with a special interest in one in particular.

"Holy shit, Sherlock. Just about everyone in this part of the world falls into that broad-ass category. I can't believe that the FBI could be that fucking stupid. I guarantee you that if Goldman and his goons found out that your boy was FBI, he became shark food that same day, and then she began to cry."

"What's wrong now?"

"You bastards have not only got two of your own killed, and that is why no one seems concerned about Rachel. You are trying to find the killers of your guys."

"Now wait a minute. I'll give you the likelihood that Mitch is no longer with us. However, I will not concede the death of Jonathan or your Rachel. I have proof that Jonathan is alive and operating in the region to try to find the killer and or killers of Mitch and who knows on what other agendas of his own. Furthermore, I believe that this Rachel Jacobs is not only traveling with him. She is now helping him in his endeavors. Jonathan is a highly skilled operative with Vietnam sniper and undercover experience that in part got him recruited by the FBI through this CIA work. This Goldman cat may have met his match in Jonathan Beck. There are other things about Jonathan that I will not go into right now because I have probably told you too much already, Karen."

"Will you look for Rachel as you try to find this Jonathan?"

"Yes, but not just because it is the right thing to do for I know that by now, she is in this thing over her head. Will you get me some pictures of Rachel, recent ones, so that I may use them to help locate her?"

"Yes!"

"Does she have family that may be looking for her by now?"

"Not likely. Rachel was estranged from them for years and pretty much lived on her own."

"Good! That means that I won't have to worry about running into them somewhere along the way. There are too many players in this thing already. May I drop by tomorrow and pick up some pictures?"

"Yes!"

The next day, Rodney got the pictures and then headed back to the convenience store in Hayden Lake.

Another day passed by, and Rachel had returned late the night before and readied her report of the travels of the now infamous Mrs. Goldman. However, Jonathan did not return during the night. Rachel was not too much concerned for Jonathan was always erratic in his travels and never left or returned to or from anywhere in an exact pattern or on exact time. The next morning, she awoke and still no Jonathan, so she got partially dressed and went to the lobby for coffee.

After pouring her coffee, she noticed that most of the patrons' eyes were glued on the television watching a CNN report of some description. She then walked over to the desk and asked the lady behind the counter what was up, and she replied that a man had been killed at or near a convenience store just south of Salt Lake. With that news, Rachel's hands started to quiver, quiver to the point that the lady asked what was wrong.

"Oh, nothing, I am just nervous for some reason today." Rachel was afraid to ask the lady about the race of the dead person since she was of some Middle Eastern descent. After her hands began to settle down and her nerves along with it, she got to thinking that south of Salt Lake was just too far away for Jonathan to have been involved in any way.

Somewhere between Spokane and Hayden Lake

"Beth, this is Rodney!"

"Rodney, have you heard?"

"Heard what?"

"A man was killed sometime yesterday at a convenience store near Salt Lake."

"Let me guess…an Indian or some other Middle Eastern?"

"You got it!"

"Well, don't rush to any conclusions. Jonathan is not in that area. I have got a solid line on him and a name I need for you to trace, a Rachel Jacobs of Spokane. I need anything and everything you can get—social, recent credit card, and bank account history—the type of car she drives and all. Oh yes, her cell phone records of late."

"Oh great, Rodney. You must have forgotten that I am not FBI anymore thanks to you, and I guess you have forgotten about the new privacy laws or do you give a damn?"

"Nope! Please trust me on this. I am on to something, something really big. Armed with that information, I think that I can pinpoint Jonathan's location within twenty-four hours, if not sooner. I have reason to believe that she is traveling with Jonathan, and that is why we nor anyone else has been able to establish a paper or electronic trail. Jonathan is using her for this, knowing that we have not made the connection."

"Well, there is something else you need to know, Rodney!"

"What?"

"Jonathan called me yesterday!"

"And?"

"He was in Salt Lake."

"What?"

"You heard me. He was in Salt Lake. He called from a payphone in a mall."

"What did he want?"

"He was picking me to see what if anything we had on Mitch and on the suspect groups in the region. We talked for about an hour, but if you ask me, he was mainly trying to find out just what, if anything, we know about his whereabouts. He was particularly interested in the publicity we were supposed to get out on John Mays. He also asked about what the feds and you had on him—him, as in Jonathan Beck."

"What did you tell him about me?"

"I told him that you had left on vacation somewhere and that you were fed up with this whole thing."

"Great!"

"There is only one thing wrong."

"What?"

"I don't think he bought it."

"Why?"

"Well, he just laughed and said, 'Yeah right. I bet you next year's wages that I will see him soon.' And then he laughed louder and said, 'Oh yes, what fucking wages?' and then he hung up the phone."

"It is good that you traced the call, thanks."

"I did not trace the call."

"Well, how did you know that he was in Salt Lake? Wait a minute, no, he did not tell you, did he?"

"Yes, first thing. He just got that information right off the bat, as if he wanted to make sure I understood."

"Did you verify?"

"Yes, after that. Oh, about an hour. I then traced the call as a precaution, and yes, he was at a mall near Salt Lake."

"Okay, thanks. I have got to go for now. Call me as soon as you have something. Here is my new cell phone number. I am changing them daily with prepaid phones."

"Rodney!"

"Yes?"

"You don't really think that Jonathan could, ah, you know?"

"I am not sure of anything right now, but I don't think so. I think that he must be getting close to something or someone, and if he was involved—and I don't think he is—it would be his way of getting even with those that took Mitch out."

"How would a convenience store clerk come into play here?"

"Listen, Beth, I said that I don't know anything, but we are getting close to Jonathan, so we should have some answers soon."

After Rodney hung up, he decided that a drink was in order, so he pulled into a small pub.

CHAPTER 18

Headquarters of Magnum Shipping, San Francisco

Clarke Goldman was busy cleaning out his desk and offices of any material that related to his work for a freer America and of any of his affiliations with any and all Christian/White Supremacist organizations. He had just finished calling all his associates and contacts not only in the region but all over the country and abroad to make sure that they understood that if they ever wanted or needed any funding from his empire now or in the future, they had better make damn sure his present and past affiliations were expunged from their rolls and records.

Clarke then looked at his head goon. "I want a meeting tomorrow night of the inner sanctum on my yacht in San Francisco. That is all of them except two, and you know who they are, and I expect them to turn up permanently and mysteriously missing, not to be found forever."

"Yes, boss, just like that FBI fellow, right?"

"Shut up, you fool, and get out of here!"

"Yes, sir, and by the way, boss, you can notify their next of kin by daybreak."

Clark then moved over to the window of his suite and gazed into the magnificent California sky in deep thought, knowing that one by one and day by day, he did not need them anymore. All of his supposedly trusted associates had to meet the same fate if he and his empire were to survive. He could no longer think about the good of the movement or of the restoration of America. He now had to work to save himself and his financial empire.

Just down the road from the Super 8 in Spokane

It was raining, not hard, just a typical Spokane rain complete with fog and a cold wind. Rachel seemed to be walking around in a dream after having waited again all day for Jonathan's return...or was it John's return? It had been two complete days now without a word. Had he left the area, or had something happened to him? Would this be like Allen or Mitch? Would she ever see him again? After all, he was now one of, if not *the*, Most Wanted Man in America. However, he would never be a feature on America's Most Wanted like the serial killer. His situation was like his job of late and those of his past of a more secretive nature, but he was just as wanted, wanted not only by the FBI and the FEDS but also by the people he was chasing and pursuing.

Beep! Beep! Beep!

A man driving a Mercedes again sat down on the horn and then shot her the bird for stepping off the curb in front of him.

This brought her back to the reality of the moment and of the fact that she had walked way too far from the motel. She then turned back walking in the direction of the Super 8, realizing that she had much needed information for Jonathan after having tailed Lady Goldman for a day. Her actions seem to indicate that her home was the compound in question, but with no Jonathan, she thought what would she do with the information? Whom would she contact, if anyone, or would she just get up in the morning, pay the motel bill, and then disappear into the mainstream of America in some other bar in some other town?

"You are soaking wet," said a nice lady behind the registration desk. "Can I get you a towel?"

"No thanks, ma'am. I'll dry off in the room."

"Oh, you are the lady in room 106, right?"

"Yes!"

"Well, he's back!"

"Who's back?"

"Your dad! Oh, I am so sorry," she said as she noticed a strange look on Rachel's face. "I should not have made that assumption!"

For a brief moment, Rachel wanted to get mad with her. However, her instant anger for Jonathan took over, and she ran to the room, dropping the key card twice while en route and then using the Lord's name in vain as she struggled to open the fucking door!

"Hey, Rach!" Jonathan said as he sat at the table near the window sipping on a drink. "Damn girl, you sure are wet!"

Back at the convenience store in Spokane

Rodney walked in the store, carrying the picture of Rachel Jacobs and hope of finding someone that could recognize her on duty. However, he was quickly informed that a guy named Aamir was the only person on duty that night, so he was the only one that should have been able to identify the people that hurt him.

"What do you mean by 'should have'?"

In the young lady's broken accent and with a small tear in her eye, she said he had lost his memory of that day.

"Is he all right other than that?"

"Yes, but the doctors say that he may never ever recover his memory of that night."

Rodney thanked the ladies and then left fully armed with what might now be a worthless picture. However, somebody somewhere in this area had seen them together eating breakfast, lunch, shopping, or something. Rodney thought, *I have just got to think and work harder now*.

FBI offices, Washington, DC

Sam had just left a three-hour teleconference with all the heads of the FBI offices in a five-state area of the Pacific Northwest. His direct orders were that the finding of Jonathan Beck was mission number one. Now it was to take precedence over anything and everything else on the agenda.

Sam then went on national television detailing in broad, vague terms the progress being made on the serial killer case and ensuring the American Muslim population and others that these criminals would be brought to justice soon and that the FBI was dedicated to protecting them and their families.

Back at the Super 8

Rachel had just finished calling Jonathan everything but a decent human being and had run into the bathroom to settle down and to take a nerve pill.

Jonathan, for one of the few times in his fifty-five years, found himself speechless, realizing that he had just totally pissed off the one and only person on the planet right now that could help him. His ability to operate under the radar was getting more unlikely by the hour; however, without Rachel, it would disappear immediately. He must act and act quickly and successfully when she returned from the restroom to keep her on board.

Again, he got lucky when she finally returned to the room. She had settled down and simply asked, "Would you like to hear about our infamous lady of the compound?"

"Yes," he replied and then smartly shut up and listened.

"Well, to begin with, she never left the compound until afternoon. What a life! Her first stop was the hairdresser, a young man she is obviously either having an affair with or would like to have an affair with, and that took the better part of two hours. She then got her nails done at a small Japanese shop and then stopped at a bar for a couple of martinis before paying a visit to a lawyer around four o'clock. I found that to be strange until about four thirty, when they both left the offices in her Mercedes and then checked into the Family Inn on the outskirts of town for a two-hour tryst. They both then returned to his offices for a brief time, and then she left and went to another bar for drinks with yet another guy that appeared a little angry because he had been waiting there for her for over an hour. However, after a few flirtatious flips of her hair, a few rubs of her miniskirt-clad legs on his crotch, and a couple of kisses on the check, he seemed to recover like any hormone-filled male would do.

"After that, she made an odd visit to an old Army and Navy supply store, and that is when things really got confusing. Jonathan, she met a guy there and they fussed, yelled, and screamed at each other for at least an hour in front of all of the employees and several customers. I stopped one of the customers as he ran out and asked him who they were, and he just rushed by saying, 'You must not be from around here.' He then jumped into his truck and sped away. I then entered the store and got a picture of them on my cell phone, pulled across the street, and did a Google on our Mr. Goldman, and bingo, there he was in all his shipping magnate glory, and there he was screaming at his wife in an Army and Navy store." She handed Jonathan her cell phone. "And there he is on my cell. So, my dear, all the dots are now connected—from our slut to our shipping magnate and to the compound."

"Good job, Rachel. Now we must get back inside the compound. I just know that Clarke Goldman knows what happened to Mitch, and he may know more."

"What do you mean, more?"

"Don't forget we are still trying to find the mass killer or killers."

CHAPTER 19

Back at Beth's home in Atlanta

"Yes, Rodney," Beth said just after he had asked her if she had any information on the Jacobs girl.

"You're right. She must be traveling with Jonathan. However, I don't have a current location, and my last-case scenario of her credit card was payment at a bed-and-breakfast called the Clarke House in Hayden Lake."

"Dammit, they must now be making only cash transactions. What about her car?"

"It is an old Honda. However, I do not have a location on it as of yet. I am guessing that they have probably changed vehicles by now. Do you want me to get a photo of her to David and the others at the bureau?"

"No! I want to find him first. However, they already have that information anyway. I know that there are at least two agents in the area and probably more. The two I know of paid a visit to the same person that I got my information from days before I was there. So who knows who or where they may be at this point? I need to get up with Jonathan before they do for by now, he may be on some sort of elimination list."

Back in Spokane

It was now morning, and time was running out on my ability to move undetected, so I now had to make some risky moves to get this Goldman guy. My brain was rushing in nine directions, trying to figure out how to get back into the compound while he drank coffee. Rachel was scanning the newspaper when something caught her eye.

"Jonathan, look, the Goldmans are having a fundraiser at the mansion tonight for the Sierra Foundation, a five-hundred-dollar-a-plate dinner around the pool. Do you think he will be there?"

"I don't know, but it does not matter. You must go there tonight."

"Why just me?"

"Okay, we will both go! Do we have enough cash?"

"Yes, cash is not a problem since I closed out the account and stopped using debit and credit cards!"

"All right, let's get dressed and go to town and pay a visit to the folks at the Sierra Foundation as soon as they open."

On the way to the infamous Goldman Compound

"Look, Rachel, we must appear to be married and guests from out of town with a lot of money."

"Well, with our age difference and penchant for spending money, that should not be difficult. Let's stop by a clothing store and I will doll up—or should I say slut up—like the typical young thing with the older guy syndrome, and you can buy a conservative business suit to fit the sugar daddy look. Oh yes, it would help if we doubled the per-plate fee so that everyone is happy and overlooks asking too many questions."

"Okay, Rachel. However, that gets us in, then we must look to get information. I guess that we will just play it by ear and then shoot from the hip. It is nearly six-thirty, and we need to be in the large group of folks going in on time so that we don't look too suspicious, so let's hurry!"

At the compound, 7:00 PM

"Damn, Jonathan," Rachel whispered. "I did not think that this many people could afford five-hundred-dollar-a-plate dinners or even gave a shit about the Sierra Foundation."

"Money turns up in odd pockets sometimes," I said as I leaned over and gave her a big juicy and sex-starved kiss.

Rachel almost moved away, then she thought of their ruse and she too laid on the sex appeal, which was not difficult for the others to see with her partially see-through top and micro-mini skirt. She had not looked nor had she felt any sexier in years. This was beginning to be fun, she thought just before realizing that this was all an act. *Oh well,* she thought again. *I might as well enjoy the feeling and the evening while I can.*

I enjoyed it too and held onto her hands as we went through the welcoming line and then moved onto a gigantic reception area near the pool where everyone was given a first-class second greeting, and each couple received a complimentary bottle of two-hundred-dollar French-imported wine.

"Let's separate a minute, and you see if you can find our infamous Mrs. Goldman, and I will see if I can locate Mr. Goldman or get a chance to get back into the library area to snoop around some."

"Okay, but don't get too far away. I am not as good a liar as you."

I then proceeded to a short line in front of a bar to look around and get a scotch and water; I had left the high-priced wine with Rachel.

A short, portly man in his sixties just in front of me turned and asked, "And may I ask what chapter of the Sierra Club do you belong?"

"Ah, ah, not any. My wife and I are just here to support the cause. We spend most of our time in Europe and abroad. We love to travel."

"Well, it is certainly great to have you and your donation. I sincerely hope that you both enjoy the evening."

"Thank you, sir, and might I ask a question?"

"Yes!"

"Are you a friend of the Goldmans?"

"Yes, I am. I am proud to say an excellent family and a real credit to the region…and to this country for that matter."

"I bet he has a really interesting study and reading area here."

"Oh yes, and he is very well read and truly a great American too!"

"Do you have access to that room?"

"Normally, yes. However, it might be difficult tonight!" The elderly guy then handed me a business card that read, "James T. Kronnan, Magnum Shipping, Portland, Oregon."

With that dead end, I moved on in the line and got my drink and then decided to look around on my own. The door leading out to the pool was open, so I walked through, looking up at a long, winding staircase, the one I had exited by before on his previous trip there. However, tonight, there were just too many people that would see me and wonder why I and I alone was ascending them. I then looked for an elevator, and sure enough, there it was just around the corner, near some restrooms. I walked up and discreetly pushed the Up button. However, nothing happened, no light nor sound of a descending elevator or of the doors opening. A gray-haired black man in a tux then walked and asked if he could be of assistance.

"Yes," I replied. "I would love a tour of this magnificent place?"

"Not tonight, sir. All the guests are being asked to stay only on the bottom floor."

"That's good! Oh, by the way, is Mr. Goldman with us tonight?"

"I am not sure, sir. Mr. Goldman pretty much comes and goes as he pleases, but now, Mrs. Goldman is by the pool."

Oh well, that did not work, I thought as I walked back toward the pool, and then I noticed a young guy talking with Rachel. It was easy to see that she was not comfortable and that she was looking around for me to save her; however, I moved over out of view to collect my thoughts for a moment. Then it hit me. Rachel might be able to get upstairs if she played her cards right. *Or maybe I should say play her ass right,* I thought. She did look hot and slutty tonight, and it did appear that this young man might be ripe for the taking if he had access. I then asked a waitress as she walked by, "Excuse me, ma'am, but who is the young man near the pool talking with the girl in the short skirt right down from Mrs. Goldman?"

"Oh, the young blond guy?"

"Yes!"

"That is Mrs. Goldman's son. He attends Harvard Law School and is just in for the weekend."

Bingo, I thought. *I bet he has not had a good piece of ass in a while with all those stuck-up bitches in the Ivy League.* Now the problem would be to get Rachel to play along. It was plain to see that he was awestruck with her body and with her willingness to show it off. I then walked quickly to where they were standing, and I could see a sigh of relief come over her face as she saw me approaching. She then reached for my hand and said, "Hi, baby. Where have you been?" as she kissed me on the cheek.

"Excuse me, young man," I said as if not even noticing Rachel. "Who are you?"

At first, he looked a little nervous but eased up as he noticed the friendly look on my face.

"Jacob Goldman and you?"

"Wilson Smith, and this is my lovely young wife, Rachel. I am going to be busy for a bit. Do you mind showing her around a while?"

"No, sir, but—"

"But nothing, young man. She enjoys the company of young men, and I have business to conduct here and with you being a Goldman and all, I bet you could show her this magnificent place."

"Yes, sir, not a problem, sir!"

All this time, Rachel looked confused and somewhat mad; however, she was quickly understanding my motives. She then reached for the young man's hand and whispered something in his ear as they walked away back towards the interior of the house. Her sudden eagerness bothered me somewhat; however, this was no time to be jealous, and I really was not sure what I would be jealous of. However, the feeling was still there in the back of my throat for some strange reason.

In no time, they were out of sight, and then I noticed a group of strange-looking characters near Mrs. Goldman by the pool. Drawing from my experience with goon types, they fit the mold perfectly, and they seemed to be on a mission and suspicious of something.

It became more and more apparent that I could not personally get to any room upstairs via any normal access. That would have to be left up to Rachel and her youthful sex appeal. My best chance might come later in the night after everyone was wasted on booze, wine, or whatever.

The last time I had noticed Rachel, she seemed to be making progress with young Goldman, and again, I was experiencing strange feelings deep within my heart or something, feelings that resembled jealousy or some similar emotion of the soul. Our brief time together had generated a bond of some description. I could not determine just exactly what it was; however, maybe it was some type of twisted love or something as simple as just a deep sexual desire even though I was old enough to be her father.

I had tried to drop the thoughts as I had watched them together in the shadows just south of the pool before they had disappeared. I then moved up a small knoll unnoticed in the direction of the upper level of the split foyer second floor. A house this large must have vulnerabilities of entrance. I then noticed a row of small buildings about one hundred yards from the pool area. They were storage buildings of some sort so I thought that I might just investigate.

I picked the lock to the first building in seconds and then entered the dark area only to discover a mostly emptied room. I should say *emptied room* instead of *empty room* because there were skid marks on the floor and portions of the walls indicating something had been moved recently and in a hasty manner. Interestingly enough, there was also a faint smell of gunpowder or something in the now empty small backroom. I was not sure what had been stored here; however, it was easily to see that whatever it was it had been removed recently and quickly.

I then exited out of the rear window and then walked over to the second unit, finding much of the same, except there was no smell of gunpowder.

I then exited the same as the first and then entered the third building through a rear window the same way as the second. Only this time, the inside area was totally empty with no sign of any recent movement within.

I then exited the third on my way to the fourth building when I heard something moving in my direction from the upper level of the house and around the back of the fourth building. All of a sudden, two gigantic Doberman Pincers appeared moving slowly toward me. My first thoughts were to run away; however, on second thought, I knew that I could not outrun them, and drawing from my past experiences, most guard dogs are trained to corner their foes not to attack, so I thought that if I did not move, they would not attack and I was right. I then noticed a small group of men coming toward me from a point of departure from the rear of the house. This must be the people that had released the dogs or something. As they got closer, I recognized them to be the goon types that were by the pool earlier talking with Mrs. Goldman. My credentials as John Mays were in order, so I hoped to continue the ruse of being the anti-government type and pro Neo-Nazi, Christian/White Supremacist type. The lead goon had a flashlight in one hand and a handgun in the other. "Hey, buddy!" he yelled. "What the hell do you think you are doing?"

"Ah, ah…just stumbled over her to take a piss and then these monster-ass dogs came running."

"Why didn't you use the fucking bathroom by the pool?"

"Oh, I don't know—I had to go quickly and I just did not want to deal with the crowd there."

"Hey, Shorty?" the lead goon shouted over his shoulder. "Check the buildings out. Let's see if any of the doors are open."

While Shorty checked out the buildings, the third goon took control of the dogs and started back up the ridge with them in tow.

"What's your name, buddy?"

"John Mays!"

"Are you here by yourself?"

"No, sir," I replied. "My wife and I are donating guests of this fine establishment."

He then pulled a cell phone from his pocket, dialed a number, and then walked a short distance away to where I could hear his conversation. He looked back at me and said, "Stay put, friend." His pronunciation of the word *friend* did not sound very friendly. About the time he got off the phone and returned to where I was standing, the goon that had been checking out the buildings returned and said, "Everything is locked up tight, boss."

"Okay, Mr. Mays, you are free to return to the party, but don't be straying away from the others tonight. I will be keeping an eye on you."

I did not hesitate and quickly turned and started walking back to the crowd. It appeared that they had bought my story; however, the lead goon's expression told another tale as he said, "I will be keeping an eye on you."

Back at the gathering, everything seemed to be normal except I did not see Mrs. Goldman around. I walked over to an open bar, got another scotch, and then I did notice one of the goons from the buildings walking up the long staircase inside. *Oh shit*, Jonathan thought. *What is he up to, and where is Rachel?*

Inside the compound's control room

"What is that?" a young man asked as he watched one of about ten monitors on a huge wall.

"What is what?" another asked.

"Look, young Goldman is walking down the hall of the second floor, holding hands with some hottie."

"Don't worry about that. He is probably just trying to find a good place to fuck the bitch away from the others."

"Okay, but Larry said no one absolutely no one from the party was to be allowed upstairs."

"Look, Henry, he did not mean young Goldman. Hell, the rich bastard lives here. Mrs. Goldman went by earlier toward her bedroom with one of the black pool boys, so what the hell, do you want to run her out too?"

Back by the Pool

I was getting nervous, and then I saw a familiar face near the entrance. It was Rodney! *Holy shit*, I thought. *What else and who else is going to show up here tonight?* It was time to leave. I would worry about getting into the other parts of the compound at another time, but then I thought, *Hell, I can't leave Rachel here. I must think of something. I will not be able to hide from Rodney for long if he comes into the party.* In the meantime, I raced to the bathroom, jumped in one of the stalls, quickly closed the door, and stood on one of the toilets so I could look out a small window. From there, I could see the gate, the people administering to guests' needs, and a couple of normal-looking, maybe even guest types, talking to Rodney. However, I soon began to breathe easier when it became clear that he was not going to be admitted. Just as I started to step off the toilet, I looked over the next stall, and a guy was standing there with everything exposed and a big smile on his face as he said, "Come on over here, you can see better. I have been looking to hook up all evening."

I told him to fuck off and then exited the bathroom at almost a run. When I pushed the door open, it hit another guy in the arms, and I apologized profusely. As I walked away, I heard the guy say, "That's okay, Mr. Smith," just about the time I was face-to-face with the lead goon from the buildings.

"Mr. Smith, huh?"

'I don't know what he is talking about. He must have me confused with someone else here."

The goon didn't say a word; he just walked quickly into the bathroom behind the guy I had hit with the door.

It was crystal clear now that I had a multiplicity of problems on my hands now, not the least of which would be locating Rachel. The only thing on my side was that even though a line of dots were forming around my presence there, I did not think that anyone had yet started to draw the lines together to connect them, so I still had a small window of time to fix this thing. *I must get to young Goldman*, I thought, *but how?* If I could just get him paged back to the pool area, Rachel would be with him. *That's it—I have got to report Rachel as missing and tell them that the last time I saw her she was inside with Jacob Goldman.*

I then remembered that I also had the Rodney problem, then I thought, *That might not be a problem. I might be able to get his help.*

Back at Control Central

"Young Jacob can pick them, can't he?"

"You damn right. If I had his family's money, I could get pussy like that too!"

While they were watching Jacob get it on with Rachel, I was creeping up the stairs so far undetected.

Control Central was continuing to watch Jacob make out with Rachel in the library with little to no interest in the other monitoring screens.

Rachel found Jacob somewhat attractive. However, she was also worried about me, and it was already clear to her that the library she was now seeing was not the same library that I had seen days ago. There was not a trace of any information on any subversive groups of any sort—just a litany of books on the Goldman shipping empire. With her bra already loose and young Goldman's pants half off, she thought it time to work her way free from this situation. However, Jacob had other ideas, and he started to force himself on her. It suddenly became apparent to Rachel that her quickest way out of the situation that she was in was to go ahead and let him have his way, and she did. As soon as he got relief and started to relax, Rachel bolted for the door, and in a flash, she was out of the library, down the hall, and on the elevator before Jacob could even get his pants on.

When the elevator hit the bottom floor and opened, two armed guards met her and genuinely seemed concerned when they asked, "Mrs. Smith, are you all right?"

"Yes," she said as she tried to regain her composer. "Where is my husband?"

"He is on his way here. He was concerned of your whereabouts. Is everything all right?"

"Yes!" she almost screamed as she jumped into my arms and whispered, "Get me the fuck out of here, you bastard!"

I quickly swept her out of the corridor, through the pool area, and then out of the entrance gate. Behind me, I could see the goons gathering by the pool in a confused state talking with Mrs. Goldman. "Move quickly," I said. "We have got to get the fuck out of here and now!"

Rachel was crying, and yet she was able to keep pace with me.

The two of us jumped into the car and raced down the knoll toward the main highway. As we approached a Stop sign at the intersection, a voice came from the back seat, saying, "Well, my friend, what's next?" It was Rodney! It was also no surprise to me but a complete fright from the night to Rachel, who screamed loudly at the exclamation.

Rachel then leaned toward the passenger's side door as if she was about to jump! She had an extreme expression on her face as if she had seen a ghost, but she was totally silent.

In fact, silence was all that was heard for what seemed like forever, then I spoke. "Well, Rodney, what took you so long?"

"Long? I thought that I found you rather quickly!"

"Okay, buddy. Let's go to our motel and discuss what you know about all of this, including the bureau stuff and David!"

I then started to drive away when Rodney said, "Hey, we have got to get my car."

"Where is it?"

Down a road across from the parking area, I had to park there because the lot was full.

"Your car is history, Rodney, because I am not about to go back there. The goons and Mrs. Goldman have got to be on to us by now. Let's go to your place. I am not sure that they are on to you as of yet."

"Well, let me tell you something, Sherlock, they may not be on to me here, but the feds have got to be all over my ass by now."

"All right, let's just drive the fuck around and talk. I have got to know what you know, and you most likely need to know what I know, and then two and two will probably not get us four but it may save our lives."

By this time, Rachel was totally confused, hurt, and in a state of shock when she exclaimed, "Would you heartless bastards please tell me what the fuck is going on here?"

I then pulled over to the side of the road and gave Rachel a brief history of my and Rodney's relationship and history.

She was quiet as I spoke, but when I finished, she laid into me and laid into me good. "Look, Jonathan—or is it John, I don't know, and I don't really give a shit who you really are. However, over the past several days, I have given up my job, my life, and now my ass to a young rich thug that I did not even know just because you asked me to. I deserve to know more and I will know more!"

Rodney and I both agreed that it was time for a three-way partnership, and we all agreed that it was not a good idea to go to either my or Rodney's room. Whatever any of them had left there was now gone, and it was probably a good idea now to get all three of us new identities all over again, and that would require a trip back to Spokane. On the way there, I explained everything to Rachel as to what he was doing and how Rodney and Beth fit into the mix.

A now calm Rachel looked at Rodney and asked, "Then you are not our enemy?"

"No! I am here to help Jonathan."

She then looked curiously at me.

"Look, Rachel," I stated. "Rodney is here to help. I am sure of it."

"Then why did he not call or something?"

'He knew that I would say no!"

"Why would you say no if you trusted him?"

"I did not want to get anyone else involved or killed. You do know that it is now too late for all three of us now, don't you, girl."

"I don't understand?"

"Let me explain. The Goldmans have figured us out by now. They may not know our motives in totality, but they know enough to know that we are the enemy. It has been nearly an hour since we left the compound, so I will bet my ass that both motel rooms have been seized by now and that Rodney's car is also in their possession. Mr. Goldman is en route to the compound if he is not already there and orders have been given to shoot and ask questions later. I predict that a total meltdown is taking place in the Goldman empire."

"Why?"

"Rachel, he knows that we know, and he knows that too many people are alive in his organization that know so he will change that immediately. Blood is being let all up and down the west coast as we speak, and if they have anything to do with it, ours will be next."

"Why?"

"Come on, Rachel. You have heard of white-collar crime where the perps left no paper trail?"

"Yes."

"Well, these bastards want no trail of any kind—paper, personal, or whatever—that could incriminate them in any of this."

"While I was upstairs with the young bastard, I did see that the library had been changed."

"I suspected so. The proper terminology would be *sanitized*, and that is what is happening in his empire right now—it is being sanitized. Anyone and everyone that knows anything is being exterminated. Trust is not an issue, nor does it exist in Goldman's mind. Within twenty-four hours, he will have only three problems, and the three are all in this car right now. Welcome, Rodney, to the Goldman death list!"

"Jonathan, I did not realize that it could come to this."

"I know, Rachel, but it is too late to reconsider right now. We have got to concentrate on advancing in our investigation and in surviving. It can be done. We are not dead yet!"

"Rodney, I think that you should get up with Beth right now to see what she knows."

"Jonathan, I would like to know more about what you know before I get too much further along."

"Look, Rodney, you evidently don't understand your situation here. Once you decided to find me, you got further along automatically. You are in this now as deep as you can get. There is no turning back, no going away, no, just saying I am sorry and going home to live happily ever after. So call Beth and let's start trying to get ahead of them."

"Them?"

"Yes, Rodney. We not only have to worry about the Goldman clan, we have also got the feds after us and only God knows who else. I am the most wanted man in the Pacific Northwest! Oh, by the way, ask Beth how the serial killer investigation is going too. While you are talking to Beth, I will come up with a plan to deal with the imminent Goldman threat!"

Rodney knew all of that but was just trying to pretend something else. It gets that way in survival mode.

Back at the compound

The goons had been sent on their missions.

CHAPTER 20

Rodney stayed on the phone with Beth for just a short while and then quickly informed Jonathan that all was quiet on that end. Beth said that no one was saying anything to anybody anywhere that she could determine. Rodney then looked at Jonathan and said, "You do know what that means, don't you?"

"Yes! Something is coming down and coming down soon. I doubt if Beth will be of any use to us from here on in."

"What have you come up with, Jonathan?"

"Do you know of anywhere that we can go to have more time to think and to plan? We also have to get some information from somewhere about what is happening with the feds and the others."

"No, but let's think about it a minute. There is something else."

"What's that?"

"I don't think that wasting time on new identities at this point will help us any. They already have picture identification of us from the compound."

"Pictures?" Rachel asked.

"Yes, you do not think for a minute that place was not wired and loaded with cameras."

"Great! Then all of those bastards have pictures of me fucking that son of a bitch!"

Rodney finally spoke as Jonathan remained quiet. "Most likely. However, right now, that is a minor issue."

"I am sure it is to the both of you, but it is no minor issue to me!"

"Rodney," Jonathan asked, "do you think they have identified you and put you with us as of yet?"

"I don't know, but they will as soon as they find my car."

"Yeah, I guess you are right."

"Okay, the trip to get new identities is off, so where do we go from here? Goldman is king in this part of the world, and I suspect that he will have the local police force after us soon. We have got to do something quickly. We just need a place to think and to plan so we can turn the cards on them."

Rachel then spoke up. "If we go ahead back to Spokane, the population is larger and so is the area, so we can get lost easier."

"Good idea, Rachel," Jonathan exclaimed. "And do you know of anyone there that we can trust?"

"Karen Weekly!"

With that statement, Rodney got a cold chill. Then he spoke up and told both of them about his encounter with Karen and how that helped to lead him to them.

"Well, so much for that idea. I do know a priest at a small Catholic church on the south side. He will put us up and he will not tell a soul."

"I am not worried about fucking souls, Rachel. It is the bastards that still have bodies that are after us. This priest had better be trustworthy!"

"You got a better idea, asshole."

"No! So let's go to evening mass, I guess."

Later, at the church!

The three of them were greeted by a small man who fit the bill for a small-time Catholic priest even though he did have the look of a man needing a drink. *But,* I thought as Rachel started to make her introductions, *hell, Catholics drink anyway, so maybe this one has some beer.*

"Thanks for taking my call, Father. We had nowhere to go."

"That's fine, my dear, and who are these fine gentlemen with you tonight?"

224

Rachel thought to herself before she answered, "Gentlemen my ass!"

"This is Jonathan Beck." And then again she thought, *Or is it John Fucking Mays?*

"And this is Rodney Fischer."

"Fischer? Are you from these parts, young man?"

"No, sir," Rodney replied.

"Well, strange as it may seem, my surname is also Fischer—Father Mark Fischer, to be exact."

"Okay, Father," Jonathan said rather abruptly. "Do you have three beds for us in a private area?"

"Not exactly so, but I do have a double bed in my study and a couch that pulls out into a bed, and you three are welcome to stay there for the evening—that is, unless ah…some of you…ah…"

"Don't worry, Father, we will all be keeping our clothes on. We do not have a change, so privacy will not be an issue."

"You are welcome here, my dear, but all of you must remember that you are in the house of the Lord."

"Yes, Father, and I do appreciate your hospitality."

"Rachel, do you remember where the study is located?"

"Yes!"

"Then make yourselves at home, and oh yes, there is a small bathroom with a shower next to the study."

"Great!" Jonathan replied. "Oh yes, Father. Do you have a place we can hide—ah, put—the car?"

"Yes, you may pull it into the garage after I pull out."

"Thanks again, Father."

"Oh yes, Rachel. There is some beer in the small fridge in there."

"Great!" I exclaimed as I followed the father out. "You are not only a friend in need but a friend indeed!"

"Okay, guys. Let's get with it," I said as I closed the door to the study after my return. After noticing that Rachel and Rodney had already made themselves at home with the beer, I walked over to the fridge and got one for myself. As I popped the top, I looked at them and said, "Okay, guys, we have all night, so let's come up with something good. Rachel, you did pick up three new prepaid cell phones while I got gas earlier?"

"Yes, and I am still paying with cash and a false ID."

"Then we should be able to communicate for a while without being traced. However, we need to change them every day or so from here on in, maybe even daily. We will just have to make that decision based on how each day goes, I guess. Rodney, what do you think the feds are doing?"

"Right now, they are trying to find you! No doubt about it! You do know that the wackos have a bounty on you too?"

"Yeah, I guess? So that means that the first thing we need to do is to get them off me and on to Goldman."

"I am sure by now, Jonathan, they are also after me and Rachel, and I am sure that they know by now that we are together."

"I am positive, Rodney, that Goldman is our guy. There has been too much coverup going on at the compound. He is not the trigger guy, but he is the one financing this entire operation."

"You may be right, but do you realize what you are saying? Hell, that will be like going after George Steinbrenner. Goldman is king out here, and he not only controls the shipping industry, he controls the cops, the courts, and every damn thing else. I recommend that we back off, give the feds what we have, and then let them fuck with him."

"That ain't happening, and you know it. We are going to take that son of a bitch down. Besides that, Rodney I don't trust the feds, and I am not real sure that I trust you either."

"Trust? Did you say trust with your background, and you want to talk about trust? You don't even want me to go there! I thought you were brought back to help solve the racist killings, and now here we are in a Catholic church all the way across the fucking country chasing or running from something—something that I...that I... hell, I am not sure what we are doing other than pissing a whole bunch of rich bastards off! A bunch of rich bastards that are probably going to kill us in the end, and you want to talk about trust?"

"Okay, I know. Well, I did not mean for it to come down like this, but hell, we cannot quite know. What about Mitch?"

"Mitch? The poor bastard is dead, Jonathan, and you know it, and if Goldman catches us, we will all three be shark food too."

"I have got a plan!"

"What is it?" Rachel asked after having been quiet for a while.

"We will have to separate."

"What?" Rodney replied.

"Just give me a few minutes to explain my thinking. First of all, we cannot turn this over to the feds for I am afraid they are in this more than we know."

Rodney did not say anything, but he thought, *Yeah! And what about you?*

"We should all be in agreement that Goldman is a crook."

Yeah again, Rodney thought. *But is he…oh, never mind, Rodney, just listen.*

"I don't think there is any doubt that he killed Mitch and that he is the financier of a worldwide Nazi/Christian/White Supremacist movement that is working to rid the planet of blacks, Mexicans, Muslims, Hindus, and anything and everything that is not white. Therefore, it is no great leap to say that he is most likely, at least, financing the killing of Muslims in this country after 9/11."

"Jonathan—"

"Wait, Rodney, let me finish. So if we make that assumption coupled with the other evidence that we have, then we can go after him for the murder of Mitch, racketeering, interstate transportation of firearms, and for the serial killing of Muslims. Now that does not even mention the fact that the bastard is trying to find us to kill us as we speak. So I got no problem with taking him out, and just like with a snake when you cut the head off, the rest will die, although sometimes, it may take a while. In this case, it will die quicker because he is killing them off too because he does not want anyone left that can finger him."

"Now, Rodney, do you have a problem with that analysis?"

"Look, Jonathan, you may be right, but hell, you do not have any proof of any of that other than the fact that you have got him so mad that he is trying to kill you."

"He was trying to kill me, Rodney, before I let him know who I was. That is why Mitch is dead, and why he was getting so nervous before I even came out here. He knew that Mitch was just a pawn in this giant chess game. Now he knows who—at least he thinks he knows—who is the king."

"Okay, Jonathan, you are going to do whatever it is that you are going to do, so keep talking. What's the plan?"

"I will go after him alone. You and Rachel will be my diversions and my information source. He will not harm you nor Rachel until he gets me. However, I got a feeling that you two can stay a step or two ahead of him, especially if I draw his interest in another direction. Just give me two days, and you two will have no worries for he will be concentrating all his manpower and resources on me, and that is when I have my best chance of getting him. I do better on the attack. Counter-punching is just not my style. You know that, Rodney!"

"What?"

"Come on, Rodney. I know that you have seen my FBI bio and dossier. You know me, the real me. You know the Vietnam vet decorated to the hilt, recruited by the CIA, and hired by the FBI. They did not recruit nor hire me because I was a wuss. You know, Jonathan the sniper, Jonathan the jungle rat, Jonathan the survivor, Jonathan the one-man army. I have lived since then under false pretenses. I have been a family man, a husband—a piss-poor one at that—a hunter, and a fisherman. The FBI fired me because the real me would creep out every now and then, but you know that too. This is war now. I am back in the jungle. It may look a little different, but it is still a jungle, and there are rats too, but these just have two feet instead of four. I have appeared for several years now to be the Great White Hunter and/or the Old Man and the Sea, but I am not. I will show you, the FBI, and everyone else what it takes to catch a gook—ah, and I don't really give a rat's ass about the rag heads. The bastard killed Mitch, and now he thinks that he can kill me. *Fuck him!*

Rachel and Rodney were in total silence, a silence brought on by how intense I had become.

"I need for you two to get out all of the bad publicity you can on Goldman. Rodney, I am going back into the compound, and I will retrieve any pictures that I can of Mrs. Goldman fucking around on her husband. As soon as I get them to you, I want them to be leaked to the media. You can also get word to Beth so she can feed some information to the feds so they start to target him too. That will help to open his defenses up for me to get him. Tell Beth that this information should give David enough to save his ass. He can have his much needed and much wanted press conference."

"Jonathan, do you realize that you are asking us to help you commit murder?"

"This is not murder. If you want to see murder, just go out there tonight in the car we came in and drive around downtown for a couple of hours, and then you will see murder when they blow your ass away."

After several hours of listening to more and more details of my plan, Rodney and Rachel both agreed that it was time to get some rest and that they would let me know in the morning if they were in or not.

The next morning, Rodney and Rachel awoke only to find me gone.

"Rodney?" Rachel said in a questioning sort of way. "Has he already left us?"

"Who knows, Rachel? However, I don't think so even though Jonathan is totally unpredictable."

"If that is true, Rodney, then how did you find us?"

"I know him better than most. However, I really do not know him at all."

"Now what sense does that make?"

"Not much, but that is how it is with Jonathan. You like him very much, right?"

"I guess."

"But why? He is much older. In many ways he is old school and washed up. You are young, beautiful, and you have a whole life ahead of you, and Jonathan has most likely already lived most of his."

"I have never met anyone in my life like him, Rodney. He is like—I don't know—maybe like the man I always wanted but never found. I realize that he could be my daddy, but I never had much of a daddy either. Jonathan is stern, mean, demanding, and in a way insane, but he is also a very loving and caring person. Now I want you to understand one thing: this has and still is all business with Jonathan and me. I have never slept with him or anything like that. I just cannot leave him even though I know that I should. In fact, I did consider ending our relationship here and now, but like I said, I cannot now. I originally signed on to find out what happened to Mitch, but now I don't think I want to know. I still might back out."

"Were you and Mitch involved?"

"In a way, it was just a fling, maybe just a passing piece of ass to him, but he was a nice guy. By the way, I think that Ms. Goldman was somehow involved in his death."

"Why?"

"She picked him up in the bar one night, and I never saw him again after that."

"Have you mentioned this to Jonathan?"

"No!"

"Why?"

"It has taken me a while to figure it out. After all, I am not a fucking FBI agent like you guys. I am just a simple barmaid that got caught up in this mess and cannot find a way out."

About that time, the door to the room opened and in walked Jonathan.

"Here is the morning paper, guys. Look at the front page!"

"Local Barmaid Found Murdered in Apartment! Karen Weekly, a barmaid at the popular Double Dribble lounge in town was found—"

"That's enough," Rachel said as she threw the paper across the room. "Count me in, motherfucker. Karen died because she talked with you, Rodney, and the only reason she talked with you is because she was concerned with my safety, and now she is dead. I am in this thing, whatever it is, to the brutal end, whether I live or die in the process does not matter."

"But, Rachel," Rodney said.

"But nothing, Rodney. You may leave now, but as for me, the fight has just begun."

"Okay, guys, you can count me in too! It is probably a mistake, and I cannot imagine any of us getting out of this thing alive, but count me in!"

"Come on, Rodney," I said. "It is us against them, and we are gonna win."

I then walked over to the fridge and got out a beer and then smiled to the others and said, "Breakfast, anyone?" They had a big laugh, and then Rachel and Rodney joined in by opening a beer each.

"Listen," Rachel said to me in a serious voice, "and hear me out before you start shouting. I want to go with you, and we can let Rodney work any communication or diversion tactics. I can work my own magic in keeping you alive as long as possible."

"No! I must work alone! I do appreciate your concern, and in many ways, you are right. At some point, I may need you, but initially, I can move better alone. I do not want either one of you to think that this is a one-man show. I need you both to make this operation a success. I am thrilled that you both are staying with me on this, even though if you had not, I would have gone on alone. By staying with me, it increases our chances of getting this bastard and of all of us living to tell about it."

"What is next, Jonathan? We cannot stay here much longer."

"No! It is time. The first thing that I am going to do is to get back into the compound, pick up a few pictures, show the goons that they are not dealing with any amateur, and then kill me two dogs. I could have killed them last night, but then that would have given them too much information about their foe. I will be back here before dark, so keep the priest happy for that length of time, and then we will thank him and be on our way."

"Be careful," Rachel replied as she walked over to me and gave me a big kiss. It was not the kind of kiss that one gives their father either. It had emotion and attachment all tangled up in the warmth of the touch.

I was speechless for a minute or two, then I just reached out and gently touched her on the arm and said, "I will return, dear," and then I walked out the door.

"Will he be all right, Rodney?"

"Yes, at least for now. They will not take him out easily. Jonathan is a formidable foe—to put it lightly. Goldman's goons have not seen anyone like Jonathan. I failed to tell you everything about his Vietnam experience. He was not only a sniper, an infiltrator, and one of the best scouts of the war—he was also a POW."

"POW!"

"Yes, but that's not all. He escaped from the prison, and then he returned and rescued some of the other prisoners. Some accounts of the rescue have him killing over one hundred singlehandedly. However, that is probably overexaggerated, but it was one hell of a raid. That raid is what got the attention of the CIA because it was not an organized raid, at least not one organized by our military. It was Jonathan on his own. From there, they used him on many postwar missions all over the world. He worked with Oliver North and many others. It is rumored that he worked with Nixon on preparations of Nixon's now famous China trip. Most of what I am telling you is classified, and I don't even know details of any of this, and if you ask the CIA, they have no knowledge. You see, this is what is now driving him to get this Goldman guy because Goldman has set himself up as the enemy. From here on in, Jonathan will not stop until he either gets Goldman or Goldman gets him—it is as simple as that now."

"Will he try to take Goldman alive?"

"No, Jonathan does not take prisoners, and that worries me too. After Vietnam and after his other CIA experiences, he was brought stateside and used in the FBI. However, that did not work out very well in the long run."

"Why? If he is all that good?"

"Oh, Rachel. Being good enough was not the problem. You see when you do CIA missions, you have more of a free hand, and if someone dies...well, so be it. If the mission gets accomplished, the dictator gets taken out or whatever. However, back home in the FBI, there are more rules and regulations and killing the suspect is out of the question unless he or she or it shoots first. Therein was Jonathan's downfall—he shot first and asked questions later, especially if they were of foreign descent, and more especially if they were of Middle Eastern decent or Asian."

"Is that why he was fired?"

"That and many other reasons. Jonathan is a free spirit in many ways. That is why his marriage did not work and why he has trouble making and maintaining friends and relationships. He has hated the war on terror because it is being fought with concerns for being politically correct and without collateral damage. According to Jonathan, that is bullshit, and he thinks that we should have leveled that part of the world and then exported all the Muslims in this country. That is why I opposed the FBI bringing him back out of retirement to lead a team to capture the so-called rag head murders. Now it is not called that in the press. It is approached there as just a racist serial killer. But in private among old-time agents. It is the rag head murders. The bureau was criticized for having not acted more quickly in investigating the killings. However, in the post 9/11 climate, it just took a while to be a priority. In fact, if political pressure had not come on the White House and the bureau, I am not sure they would have ever acted. That is when the decision was made to get Jonathan involved, and again I opposed it."

"And, Rodney, again, I ask why?"

"I thought it was like hiring the fox to guard the hen house. It was the bureau's opinion that mentality or type of thinking that they knew Jonathan had would get this thing off their back more quickly. And in a way, I guess it has. We are within days now of bringing down Goldman. If Jonathan is successful, he will again be a national hero, and the racist serial killer will be dead, and all will be fine in the heartland again."

"Why do I get the feeling you do not buy into that? Jonathan has put all of this together so quickly, and I am not sure that I trust his conclusion."

"It is proven that Goldman is a racist, and he did, most likely, kill Mitch, and he was involved in international plots to support white supremacy, right?"

"Yes, but the key phrase is 'most likely.' I still do not see any hardcore proof, just Jonathan's opinion, that I am not sure is supported by facts. Goldman is like Saddam. He is a bad guy no doubt. However, I am not sure Saddam was an international terrorist, and I absolutely do not believe Goldman to be the racist serial killer. However, I do believe that Jonathan will bring it down that way and be successful in doing it, and the FBI needs this off their backs so badly they will accept it, buy into it, and publicize it and then bring closure to this thing quickly."

"Does Jonathan know your feelings about this?"

"Not really, but he does know me, and he looked at me in an odd way when I turned up in your car. He was not a bit surprised. He knew that I would be coming—it was just a matter of when."

"You're right. I got the same feeling in the car, and that is more of the reason I got so quiet, but then I thought, Well, he knew that you would come to help eventually."

"Maybe, but who knows what Jonathan is thinking?"

"So what are you going to do now?"

"I am like you. I am in it now to the bitter end."

"One more thing, Rodney. If it is not Goldman, then who?"

"Now that is the sixty-four-thousand-dollar question or, in today's lingo, the 'Who Wants to Be a Millionaire' question. In fact, I am not sure that it is any one person."

"Well, that would put an end to the serial killer theory, would it not?"

"Yes, the bureau put the 'serial killer' label on the murders, I believe, to make the case easier to solve or, I should say, easier to get it out of the headlines eventually. I believe that there is a mass hatred out there since 9/11 against everyone of Middle Eastern descent and that once a murder or two takes place, then I think we have tens, if not hundreds, of copycats. I have studied this thing along with Beth, and there are just too many examples of discrimination all across the heartland."

"There is a difference between discrimination and killing."

"I know, but the thoughts that create the acts have to be generated from somewhere, and it all starts with determined and malicious discrimination. I have to admit that I still today look at citizens of this country differently today if they have olive skin. The pictures of the hijackers are embedded in my brain forever, and I doubt if they will ever go away. One more thing—the acts of 9/11 gave credence to the hatred that has been propagated for years by the Nazi/Christian/ White Supremacist groups around the country and the globe and has helped justify the existence of the so-called 'Patriot Movement.'"

"Do we have to stay here all day and talk about this?"

"It would be risky to move about."

"What about a movie or something? I bet that I can borrow the father's car."

"Okay, but let's do it soon so Jonathan does not find out."

CHAPTER 21

Back at Hayden Lake Near the Compound

This looks too easy, I thought as I surveyed the premises from afar. *Goldman is many things, but he is not stupid. This looks like a trap. I had better wait for the cover of nightfall.* I then went over to the local boat dock across the bay from the compound and rented a small boat and some fishing tackle and then launched into the lake after some smallmouth and hopefully a walleye or two late. My cover was now set because I did not have to return the boat until noon the following day. This would have to be a catch-and-release day. I thought about calling Rachel or Rodney and then reconsidered, thinking it best that they not even know what I was up to at this point.

The fishing was decent, and for several hours, my life almost seemed to be back to normal—or maybe *mundane* would be a better term. Relaxation came so easily on the water that I even slept for an hour or so while just drifting.

Back at the Church

"Well, Rodney, here we go again. It is almost dark and no word from Jonathan."

"Don't worry, Rachel. This is normal for him. We may not see him until morning. Who knows? He may have decided for some reason to wait until dark to approach the compound."

"We must be out of here by morning, Rodney, no matter what."

"Hey, that brings up a question that I have been wanting to ask. How do you know Father Fischer?"

"AA."

"What?"

"We met at an AA meeting, and for a while, he had me attending mass on a regular basis, but then I sort of backslid and then I really began not to give a shit, so here we are. However, Father Fischer has remained a friend and confidant through it all. He is a good man."

"How did a priest become an alcoholic?"

"Drinking!"

"Huh! I guess that was a stupid question?"

"Are you an alcoholic?"

"I don't know? I know that I like to drink and I need to drink, so you make the call. Like I said before, I don't really give a shit one way or the other. We all have issues in life. I might drink too much and you might bitch too much or eat too much. We all do something too much, or hell, we would all live forever. I am not ready to die. However, I have never wanted to live too long."

"What age is too long?"

"Now that depends. I have seen people rather young that were disabled for some reason, stroke or something, and to me that was too long. If I cannot get out and make a mess of my life anymore, then I have lived too long. That is why I am so infatuated with Jonathan. I guess he is so full of life and is not afraid to die. A minute with him is like a year with most men I have met in life. I know that type of infatuation is not healthy and that it will not lead to anything positive in the future for me. However, it is one hell of a ride while it lasts."

"I think you have a Bonnie and Clyde type of an affair."

"Look, Rodney—and I have said it before—I have never slept with him, so there is no affair. I don't even think that he has thought about sex with me."

"Now that is stupid. Jonathan thinks about sex all the time. When he was younger, he would screw a snake if someone would hold its head still."

"Yeah, I have figured that out. However, I have purposely put myself around him in seductive positions, such as half-dressed and at times wearing no bra with a T-shirt, and he has never tried anything. Are you married, Rodney?"

"Divorced! Like almost everyone else in my line of work. When there is time for romance—well, you find out that you are not at home and you know where that leads. The wives go through hell too and find themselves looking for love where they should not, so there you go. By the way, does Jonathan ever talk about his children?"

"Yes, that is why he came out of retirement—to be in a better position financially to help them."

"I am not sure that is the only reason, but I will accept that conclusion for now."

"At what point do we go looking for Jonathan if he does not return?"

"Never? Yes, never. That would only get us killed, and after all, this is Jonathan's game anyway, is it not?"

On Hayden Lake Just after Dark

I slipped ashore after hiding my boat in some brush near an old fence line that ran about fifteen yards out into a small slough. I then slipped up the rusty fence line all covered in brush toward the house. *This would be easy this time*, I thought. However, I could feel the rush starting to build as I anticipated the coming encounter with Goldman. *That will not happen now, but it will come after I get through baiting him*, I thought.

Back at the Church

It was now after 2:00 a.m., and Rodney and Rachel had both fallen asleep when a noise was heard coming from outside the door to the study.

"What's that?" Rachel whispered to Rodney.

"I think it is Jonathan. However, let's make sure," Rodney said as he pulled a handgun from under his right pants leg and motioned for Rachel to hide behind the sofa bed.

The door then opened, and sure enough, it was me, so all breathed a sigh of relief as Rodney put away his weapon.

Rachel then revealed herself and quickly asked if I was all right.

"Sure, that was easy and it went well. I think that I dodged all of their detection devices and cameras. It is an elaborate system but simple from a technical standpoint. Nothing like getting into and then out of a foreign embassy without being detected."

"What about the dogs?" Rachel asked.

"What dogs?"

"Oh well," Rodney sighed with a little smile. "Look, it is late. What did you get?"

I then handed Rachel an envelope with several pictures of her and young Goldman and said, "I think that is all there was. However, I am not sure." I then handed Rodney one of Mrs. Goldman and the black pool boy walking down a hallway half naked and holding hands. "Now this one will look nice on the front page of the newspaper."

"I don't think that will fly, Jonathan. Goldman owns the paper."

"Not the offbeat paper called *The Radical Times*. That is where we go first, and then all the other surrounding papers that Goldman does not own will pick it up, and in time, Goldman will have to address the issue. Of course, the main objective is to draw him out."

"Was he at the compound?"

"Oh no! He is not stupid, at least not yet! Our next mission will be to make a visit to one of his local offices. Let's finish the night here and then be on our way."

The next morning, they all thanked the father, and then I informed Rodney and Rachel that their next stop would be the airport.

"Airport?"

"Yes, we can leave the car in long-term parking, and Goldman will most likely never look there—at least he will not look there for a car. We are going to Los Angeles to pay our friend Goldman a visit."

"Oh yes, I am sure that he will welcome us into his headquarters with open arms and then with loaded, soon-to-be-unloaded pistols. Not a good idea, Jonathan."

"Better than you think. Call Beth and tell her to get Rachel a full dossier as an FBI agent. Tell her to send it to the Fed-Ex office near the airport and that she has plenty of time, that we will not need it before tomorrow afternoon."

"Jonathan?"

"Just do it, Rodney. Remember you are now in this thing and there is no turning back."

"But what about Beth?"

"What are they going to do? Fire her?"

"I guess you are right. You have already got that done!"

"How are we on cash, Rachel?"

"Should be fine!"

"If we need credit cards, Jonathan, I have a scanner that was confiscated from a detainee in Atlanta and some blank cards in my briefcase."

"How did you get that?"

"I just never registered it and put it in FBI storage. David let me take it out to study, and I guess with all of what started coming down, he just forgot about me having it."

"I have heard about them. Do they really work?"

"Yes."

"Good, that might be handy in the future."

The trip from Spokane to Los Angeles was brief, less than nine hundred miles as the crow flies.

CHAPTER 22

The next day, after having spent the night
in a low-rent motel near the airport

I was up early as always! This night, I had slept in the chair near the window, and Rachel and Rodney slept in the two double beds, independent of each other of course. I was wide awake and alert even though Rodney was not sure I had slept a wink, when he asked me, "What's next?"

"Well, Goldman's docks are located on South Palos Verdes Street, and his offices are in a high rise downtown. Let's go to the docks first and look around."

Rachel and Rodney got dressed in a hurry for it was obvious that I was ready to go. Rachel paid cash to the clerk and gave him a hundred-dollar tip to forget we had ever slept there. We had registered under false names, so our trail should be clean, providing someone else did not offer him two hundred dollars to spill his guts. Our best hope was that Goldman's goons, who were already looking for us, did not place us there.

"Look, guys," I said, "this is just a fishing expedition. Goldman will be nowhere to be found as of yet. However, give us a little time and he will be running to us instead of away from us. I don't think that he expects us to show up at the docks here in Los Angeles as of yet, so we have the obvious advantage here. That will not always be the case."

In a very short period, we were pulling into a handicap parking spot just outside of the docks' offices.

"Rachel, go inside the offices and see if that is Goldman's yacht."

"You know that it is!"

"Probably, but make sure! Hey, I have got a better idea—you and Rodney go in there using your FBI credentials and do a mini search of the offices if they let you. Signal me if that is indeed Goldman's craft."

"What do we look for, Jonathan?" Rodney asked hurriedly as he shuffled through his wallet for his credentials.

"Anything interesting, but mostly just to get his people excited so they will alert Goldman of our actions."

In a matter of minutes, Rodney and Rachel rushed through the doors of the small office, flashing their credentials and then moving quickly to the filing cabinets.

A rather stately older gentleman came through a small opening in the back when he heard all the commotion. "What's going on?" he asked. Then he said the question we did not want to hear asked so quickly: "Where is your search warrant?"

"What are you looking for? All our papers are in order."

"That's it," Rachel said quickly. "Where are your papers?"

"What papers?"

"Ah...ah...the ones that you said are in order of course. Now hurry and get them—we do not have much time. Is Mr. Goldman on his yacht?"

"No," the gentleman replied. "He is not in town right now, but I must call him now!"

"Yeah," Rodney said as he dumped some papers on the floor. "Do that, sir!"

I had heard what was going on because I had wired them all before they left the motel and had now entered Goldman's personal craft. As I rounded the corner of the main cabin, I said, "No one inside." However, as I opened the door, a small furry dog came running out and grabbed me by the pants leg. Swiftly, I grabbed the pesky pet by the neck, snapped it, and then threw the lifeless carcass overboard. I then heard a female voice that sounded half asleep say, "Now calm down, baby, there is nothing out there but seagulls." I then stepped backward and returned from where I had come. I had done enough damage, and it was obvious that Goldman was most likely closer than the old man had said. As I exited the ship, I saw Rodney and Rachel exiting the small office and moving swiftly toward their car. We all met there about the same time, so we got into the car and then Rodney drove us quickly away.

After a few moments of silence, I asked Rodney and Rachel if they had found anything of interest.

"Not really," they replied. "However, I think the old man called Goldman while we were there so he knows something is up."

"Yes," I replied. "I think that he might really be in town."

"Why?"

"I discovered at least one female on the craft and maybe more, and there, uh, was…a small dog there too."

"Was?" Rachel asked

"Yes, the little bastard grabbed me by the pants, so I fed him, her, or it to the sharks. I may have accomplished two things with that—the world is short one pesky pet, and I bet it causes a real uproar there when Goldman finds his dog gone. It will take him a while to connect it to you guys being there, so he will give his whore or whores hell when they cannot produce the dog."

"How will he connect it to us? All the people in the office know there were just the two of us?"

"Well, I sort of accidentally dropped one of my old FBI business cards in the cabin. It will take them a while. He should have time to slap them around a little before he finds it on the sofa where I tossed it as I made my exit. After that, he will then start to put two and two together, and he will get mad as hell in the process."

"Where do we go from here?"

"Downtown?"

"Yes, I am betting that he was there and that he is about halfway to the port office by now, so let's pay them a quick visit."

"Shit, Jonathan, you are going to get us jailed or killed."

"Nah, we just need Goldman to be in a state of complete confusion right now. He will be mad, sad, and confused, and then he will start to make mistakes that will allow us to get the bastard."

"When?"

"Not now—the time is not right and I want to play with him a bit first. This needs to be fun too, you know."

Rodney and Rachel just looked at each other and said nothing. The look on their faces, however, said a bunch. This was it. I was in a zone, and I had on my game face ready for action. It would not be long now before I had this thing set up the way I wanted it to be. I was setting the stage—dealing the cards if you will and from the bottom of the deck to trap Goldman.

At Goldman's downtown office, we made our move again. This time, all three of us went in and we had to present our credentials to security on the first floor, and Goldman's offices were on the eleventh floor, so time would be of the essence. We rushed into the main office, flashed our credentials again, and then I asked for their shipping manifest for the past month. A very nervous young lady rushed to the files, pulled them out, and almost threw them at me; she was so nervous.

Rachel then saw another lady talking on her cellphone.

"Let's go, Jonathan. I bet that bitch has the bastard on her cell."

Back at the dock

"Turn this son of a bitch around. Go, you moron. The bastards are downtown."

The driver came to an almost stop, and then Goldman yelled out again, "Get us back to the offices now, you stupid shit!"

"Yes, sir boss, but I thought—"

"Don't think, you moron. Get the fuck out of here now."

The driver then almost turned the limousine over and did crash through the guard rails in front of the port offices, causing Goldman to drop his cigar and burn the shit out of his leg. "You dumbass!" Goldman shouted as he pulled out a pistol. "If I had time, I would shoot your dumb ass right here."

Back in front of the downtown offices

The three FBI agents jumped into their car and then roared out of sight just minutes prior to Goldman's limo slamming into the curb.

Just over the hill from the high rise

"Jonathan?" Rachel asked. "Where are the files?"

"What files?"

"The ones you had the lady get back there."

"Oh, those files. Hell, I have no need for them, so I left them by the elevator. They have probably found them by now."

"Where do we go from here?"

"Let's go back to Spokane and get those pictures of Mrs. Goldman in the paper. We want her giving him hell too."

"Jonathan," Rodney said, "why don't we get him now? He is not fully prepared. It should not be too difficult."

"Timing, Rodney. Timing is everything, son, and now is not the time. You will see in a day or so. It is close but not right just yet."

CHAPTER 23

*Back in Spokane at the offices of the
local rag, the* Radical Times

I walked in first, holding the infamous folder of pics.

"And your name is?" I asked the girl sitting at a small desk smoking a cigarette.

"Sandy!"

"Is your editor in?"

"Yes, Miss Sims is on the phone right now. Would you mind waiting?"

"No," I replied. "And you sure look nice today, young lady."

"Well, thank you, sir!"

"Have you heard of the Goldmans?"

"Heard of? Hell, sir, they run this damn town—or I should say he does."

Rachel and Rodney looked at each other with looks of confusion as I opened the folder and handed the pictures of Mrs. Goldman and the black pool boy to this Sandy.

"What do you think of these? It appears at least that Mrs. Goldman may be a lot of things, but a racist would not be one of them. What do you think?"

"Oh my, sir, are you sure that is her?"

"Well, Sandy, you know her better than I. What do you think?"

"Ah…I believe that it is, sir, or well, at least it looks like…yes, sir, it is her, sure enough!"

"Well, it looks like your editor is still on the phone, so I guess that we will leave and come back later."

"No! No! Sir, let me get her for you."

In no time flat, Sandy had left her desk gone to the editor's office and both had returned with envelope in tow.

"Good to see you, sir," spoke a woman of, say, forty-five years of age. "My name is Marsha Sims and yours?"

"Jonathan—Jonathan Beck, to be exact—and with me are my associates Rodney Fischer and Rachel Jacobs."

"These are some interesting pictures you have here, but why have you brought them to me?"

"Well, you see, Mr. Goldman has developed a bad name through the years of being a racist—you know, by belonging to and promoting so many hate groups and organizations. I thought that it might be a good idea to show the fine residents of this great city that he is down deep inside—or should I say that down deep inside his wife and down deep within his heart—is truly a very tolerant and diverse person. What do you think of that?"

"I don't know, sir. Everyone around here knows of both of their activities outside their marriage."

"Really?"

"Yes, sir!"

"So pictures of Mrs. Goldman hand in hand, cheek to cheek, and belly to belly with her black pool boy would not be a shock around here?"

"I did not say that. You are indeed correct that if these pictures were to become public, it would infuriate this town—and this region for that matter—but I am not sure that I want to be the one to publish them."

"Why? Are you afraid of retaliation?"

"Of course! It is not only that—he would put me out of business the very next day."

"How?"

"You don't understand the dynamics of this region, sir. He controls everything!"

"Let me get this straight, ma'am. The day after these pics hit the newsstand, he would still rule the region and he would still have the racist public of this town behind him? I don't think so, ma'am!"

"I know him pretty well, Mr. Beck, and he is very resilient."

"So you think that he can recover from that quick enough to bury you?"

"His payroll alone controls over fifty percent of the employment in this town, not counting all of the affiliates payroll, etc. This is a port town, sir, and he controls the port and all the other ports from here to southern California."

"Okay, ma'am, then I guess that we will have to look to someone else to publish these pics." With that said, I, Rodney, Rachel, and I headed for the door.

"Wait a minute, Jonathan," Miss Simms said. "Come back to my office, and let's talk about those pictures of my ex-husband's present wife doing a black guy."

"Well," I replied and then looked to Rodney and Rachel and with a slight smile toward Sandy, "this is getting better by the minute."

"Look, Miss Simms, there is more to this than you might think. I believe that your husband is deeply involved with some murders."

"He is my ex-husband, sir, not my husband. My ex is a very powerful man, sir, something akin to the mafia of old in Chicago. He is the Boss, so to speak, of the West Coast, and oh, by the way, who are you? If you plan to take on my ex-husband, you had better be FBI, CIA, or maybe Rambo?"

I was silent for a moment then replied, "Both! Maybe in my younger days all three, ma'am, except Rambo, who was a fictitious character. Here, touch me—I am flesh and blood."

She stepped back a couple of steps and then said, "You are FBI?"

"Not exactly. I am like your husband—ex-FBI and ex-CIA and ex many other things that I cannot talk about that relates to international espionage, etc."

She then asked why I was after her husband, and over the next hour, I gave her most of the details—or at least the ones she needed to know from the day I was brought back to the FBI to head up a team to catch the serial killer or killers to my eventual dismissal and now of my intent to finish the job on my own. I explained the presence of Rodney and Rachel and gave an overview of how her ex-husband was involved. Again, my explanations were all slanted to fit my theory and made to look like facts.

"Look, Mr. Beck, I will publish your pictures as being from an anonymous source with a 'Who do you think this might be?' theme. I will not identify her as being Mrs. Goldman—that will be left up to my readers."

"Agreed, Miss Simms, and I really do not think that you have anything to worry about from your ex. We have him all shook up right now, and he has not seen anything yet. He will not have the time to retaliate against you. He will be too busy trying to get to us." I then reached into my briefcase and handed Miss Simms a bundle of cash and said, "Here is ten thousand dollars in cash. Take a week's vacation to Hawaii just in case I am wrong."

"And after that?"

"It will be all over by then, Miss Simms, no worries!"

Back at Goldman's downtown San Francisco offices

Goldman rushed in his office after frantically leaving the elevator. "Where are the bastards?" he screamed.

"It was the FBI, Mr. Goldman. They wanted our shipping manifest," replied the senior clerk in a shaky voice.

"FBI my ass," Goldman shouted. "You are all idiots, fucking idiots. How have I ever made it this far being surround my morons and fools? What did you give them?"

"The manifest, sir!"

About that time, one of the goons walked in with a box of files in his arms. "Are these the ones?"

"Yes! Where were they?"

'By the elevator. That request was just a front. They did not need the files nor were they FBI."

Goldman then turned to him and said, "Then who are they?"

"I am not sure, boss, but they seem to be playing with us for other reasons, reasons that I have not yet determined."

"I tell you who it is—it's that damn guy that came here looking for the kid. The one I told you dumb asses to kill. Call every one of our associates in this region and tell them the bounty is fifty thousand dollars—no, make it a cool one hundred thousand dollars—to anyone that can get this bastard."

Another one of Goldman's associates walked over and said, "Sir, I have some information on this guy. He is kind of FBI...or at least he used to be. He has a long history of FBI, CIA, and international espionage involvement. His last FBI assignment was to head up a task force for the FBI to solve the killings. However, he was just recently removed from that assignment, at least officially. However, it seems now that he is operating on that same assignment on a freelance basis."

"How do you know this?"

"You recently asked me to get this information, so I did. I was going to call you this evening, then all hell broke loose here. Jonathan Beck is his name. However, he is moving through the region under an alias of John Mays. He has another ex-FBI agent by the name of Rodney Fischer helping him along with some broad by the name of Rachel Jacobs that he picked up along the way. It seems that she was just a barmaid in Spokane when he and she hooked up. I have not determined the details of that meeting."

"Okay, let's regroup, think this through, and instead of being the hunted, let's become the hunter."

"There is more, sir. I got most of my information from sources within the FBI in Atlanta and Washington, DC, and they too are in the region looking for this Beck character. It is also rumored that he was getting close to some of our, ah...some of the patriot groups in this region, and they, too, are after him."

"Okay, let's go back to the port office and my yacht, and let's think this through. We have got to set a trap. It would be great if we could somehow get it set up to where he had a clash with the real FBI and they ended up killing him—or at least maybe we could make it look like friendly fire that got him and his friends."

"I have got to tell you, Mr. Goldman, he is as pro. I failed to mention that during the Vietnam War, he was a world-class sniper and is credited with singlehandedly rescuing maybe a hundred POWs from a camp there. After that, he worked with the guerillas in Nicaragua, an operation where he worked directly under Oliver North and others. This guy is a real-life Rambo!"

"Bullshit!"

"Well, before you get too mad, sir, he has aged and does not have the United States Military, the FBI, the CIA, or any other organization behind him in this mission, and therein lies our advantage if we work smart and carefully. My suggestion is that we wait until he makes a mistake."

Of course, Goldman was not about to wait. It just was not his style, plus he had far more to hide that most of his associates knew. Goldman had always been smart enough in his underground activities to not let the right hand know what the left hand was doing, and if the right hand ever found out…well, it just disappeared in some mysterious boating accident, car wreck, or something. Unknown to these associates, several others that were now only a liability and of no value were being eliminated as they discussed this present plan to trap this Beck guy. By dawn, only the most trusted and most respected of his associates would still be alive.

The photos of Mrs. Goldman hit the papers that morning, and Goldman got an e-mail of them sent to him from his Spokane office. He broke out in a brief fit of rage and then got control calling his wife a bitch, black cock slut, and every other name in the book even though he really did not give a shit. However, he also knew that the people of Spokane and the remainder of the region did give a shit and that this would destroy his ties to the Neo-Nazi, Christian, White Supremacist organizations there—and worldwide for that matter. He would have to assign one of his associates to damage control here, across the nation, and abroad.

Mrs. Goldman was livid, and she was frowned upon everywhere she went after the papers hit the streets even though she tried desperately, to no avail, to deny it was her in the photos.

To put it mildly, the Goldman empire was crumbling by the minute. His offices were malfunctioning, customers were abandoning him, and all his suppliers and worldwide connections were keeping all his personnel busy trying to explain something they knew nothing about.

Goldman and his six most trusted were held up in San Francisco, mapping out a plan of attack to get this Jonathan Beck.

Back in Spokane

Rodney, Rachel and I were sitting leisurely in a small restaurant near the Days Inn by the airport. I had not told Rodney or Rachel as of yet, but it was there at the airport where I wanted it to all come down. By now, I knew that Goldman knew that they were in Spokane, and no way was I going to drive up there; we would arrive via air. *The perfect setup*, I thought, *a mad, confused and frustrated Goldman and his goons rushing to who knows where through the airport*. The only thing that I now needed to get Goldman on the murder charges was to go back to the compound and find the records of his involvement with the Neo-Nazi, Christian, White Supremacist groups, and then dots would all be connected.

This would be an easy task for me. I had now been in the compound on two occasions, a piece of cake, for a man with my experience and background. I only had to wait for the cover of nightfall to get it done. The only question now was where these records and/or documents were located. I knew that they had been in the outhouses at one time for I had seen the evidence when I had the encounter with the dogs at the party. My mind was now racing as I searched my memory, and as I used my thought processes, and then it came to me. They were not at the compound at all. I had seen the traces of where boxes or files had been dragged out of the buildings, but in my mind's eye, I could now see them end abruptly. They had been loaded into some sort of vehicle and moved completely away from the compound, but where to?

By now, Rachel and Rodney had noticed my preoccupation with something.

"Okay," Rachel said, breaking the silence. "What's up now?"

"Just wait a minute," I said as I continued my thoughts. *But where?* I thought again. Then I thought of the day at the Army/Navy store and of seeing that there was a basement. I even thought that I had seen Goldman come out of it maybe. And yes, Rachel had witnessed a fight there between Mr. and Mrs. Goldman just recently. *That's it*, I thought, *the perfect place and much easier to get to.*

"Okay, guys, you two go somewhere, do something. Entertain yourselves until I return."

"No," responded Rachel in a tone that I had become very familiar with by now, a tone that I knew meant that there was no changing of her mind.

"Okay, we will all go! This will not take an expert to accomplish anyway."

"Go where?" Rodney asked.

"All we need now to prove Goldman's guilt is to retrieve the records from the compound, the records that prove his involvement in the Neo-Nazi/Christian/White Supremacist organizations worldwide."

"Okay," Rodney responded. "I have two questions. First of all, where are the records and how will that prove anything?"

"I will answer the second question first," I said, as I leaned toward them across the table of the booth we were in to avoid anyone else in the restaurant hearing me. "The records will show the extent of his involvement both personally and financially in violence against minorities and his own actions, as we speak, of eliminating people in and around his organization as he is trying to circle the wagons. He also has a history of violence against his competitors—that is when there were any. I guarantee you that once his fences have been torn down and when the local police and such feel safe to come out against him, it will all be over. They will also be able to prove that he killed because he was sent by me—ah, the FBI—to get him for his involvement in the mass murders. That is it in a nutshell—opened and closed and his fat ass behind bars, case solved, and we will all be heroes."

Rodney hesitated for a minute, then he spoke up reluctantly because he knew by now that Jonathan had everything figured out and that he would not listen to reason or to anything else. "Look, Jonathan, you do not have one shred of evidence that he killed any of the Muslims that have been grouped into this, ah, what you refer to as the rag head case. It is all circumstantial and you know that!"

"Great, Rodney. I am glad that you agree with me for there are thousands of men and women all over this globe in prison as we speak based on circumstantial evidence. That is all we need here. Goldman's actions past and present will do the rest."

Rodney did not respond for he knew that I was probably right if this thing came down as I planned Goldman would be easily convicted. Whether he was actually guilty or not did not matter for he was now one on one with Jonathan Beck.

The next step was to go to the Army/Navy store and retrieve the records. We would use Rachel as a decoy; no that would have too many risks; we would do it under the cover of night. Regardless of the type of alarm they may have, I could beat it!

However, as they rounded a curve and approached a Stop sign, smoke could be seen coming from the direction of the Army/Navy store.

"Oh shit," I exclaimed. "The bastard is destroying the evidence. Hurry, Rodney!"

As we arrived on the scene, the local police had just arrived along with the local volunteer fire department. At the present, the fire seemed to be contained on the main level. I immediately jumped from the car and quickly flashed my FBI credentials and then moved to the back of the building on a dead run. The local police seemed confused, and the firefighters were more than occupied so no one followed in pursuit. I then noticed a small door in the center of the cinder-black wall out back. It had a simple lock that I picked in seconds. The smoke had not yet reached the basement area, but why? This did not make sense. If Goldman had started the fire, he would have made damn sure that the records, if they were any, burned first. It was too late now for thinking. However, I was to get the records...so I dashed into the dark using the glow of the fire upstairs for light. *Dammit,* I thought, *where are the fucking records? They have got to be here.* But all I could see was inventory, fucking inventory. The floor was starting to squeak, and the fire was beginning to threaten the structure and water, fucking water was everywhere. Then they appeared, just normal-looking storage boxes like you would get from Office Max or Kinkos; however, these had dirt on the bottoms. "There they are!" I yelled out loud. Now how was I to get them out without fire or water damage and then by the authorities? Thank goodness for my credentials. That would work. Other than the IRS, the FBI is the most feared of the government-lettered divisions.

Rodney had driven past the blockade, flashing his credentials and was waiting at the door as I came out with the first of over a dozen boxes. In no time flat, we had the car full of wet boxes and were on our way.

"Did we get everything, Jonathan?"

"I doubt it. However, time was of the essence, to say the least. I do believe that if these boxes contain what I think they do, then we probably have enough. I did not have time to check any of them. However, I did notice dirt stains on the bottom, indicating to me that they did come from the out buildings at the compound. Let's go somewhere safe so we can examine a few of the boxes."

"Where?" asked Rachel.

"Let's go back to the Days Inn."

"Will that be safe?" asked Rodney.

"Probably not. However, I do think that we have a little time to waste before facing Goldman and his goons. It will take some time for them to come up with a plan of attack. I would like to get some of this to the bureau as soon as possible so that they can come down on Goldman too. We need to have him concentrating on covering his ass instead of being able to concentrate totally on getting to us. Beth can help us in that regard. She still has a rapport of some sort with David."

"Yes. She still talks with some of her friends in Washington."

"Great! That's the plan! Now let's get to the motel and make sure of what we have here."

Back at the fire

Goldman had been informed of the fire and had to cut short his planning session in Los Angeles.

Goldman could not wait on a commercial fight because of the fire and of his need to get there in a hurry, proving his concern for the loss. He needed the police to see his concern even though it was he that had hired the arsonist, so he chartered a flight and was on the scene while the firefighters were putting out the last of the flames. It had been a hard fire to fight and had taken much longer than it should have because of the nature of the contents of an Army/Navy store. He was worried because of the recent events in Los Angeles; however, he was feeling better, knowing that all had been destroyed, including the incriminating boxes in the basement. He had a confidant on the scene that had assured him of that.

Jake asked Goldman, "It looks like all is lost. Is that correct?"

"Yes, sir, and I am truly sorry."

The fire chief walked over and offered his condolences.

Goldman showed every possible sign of having experienced a loss.

The chief showed some concern, especially in the wake of the revelations of Goldman's wife's escapades that now had shown up in at least three papers in the region.

"I am sorry, sir. We did our best, but it was not enough to save anything."

"That's okay, sir. I know that you tried. Everything is gone," Goldman said with a sigh that indicated grief for the loss.

"Well," the chief replied, "maybe not everything."

Goldman had his head bowed, but that with statement from the chief, it popped up quickly as he asked, "What do you mean, maybe not everything? All I can see is ashes and burnt rubble."

"You know, sir, the FBI guys."

"What fucking FBI guys?" Goldman yelled, and he tried to regain control of his anger and emotions.

"The ones that came by earlier and removed some boxes from the basement, we think."

"What do you mean *think*? They either did or they did not."

"Well, we were all busy fighting the fire when they showed up and flashed their credentials and then disappeared. We just figured that they were here to check it out. They do that sometimes."

"What about the fucking boxes?"

"Well, we are not sure, sir. We do not think that there was anything in their vehicle when they arrived, but there were some storage boxes in their vehicle when they left. Now we are not sure."

"Not sure about what, dammit?"

"If the boxes were already in their car when they arrived, but we are sure that there were a lot of boxes in their car after they pulled out of here from around back."

"The bastards were in the back?"

"Yes."

"Holy shit! I will check with you guys later."

"But, sir, we will need to complete our report and all."

"See me later, damn it! I have got to go now!"

Back at the motel

"It's a winner, Jonathan," Rodney said as he opened the fourth box. "This shit incriminates the hell out of our guy. You have got him on everything from the interstate transportation of firearms to money laundering, and most likely, the IRS would like to see the records of his offshore bank accounts. Goldman is not only a crook, Jonathan, he is an idiot."

"Okay, now how do we get this stuff to the FBI and the IRS?"

"That's a good question?"

Rachel then spoke up and said, "Can we not take them to the local FBI office in Spokane? They do have one there, don't they?"

"We can't!" Jonathan said.

"I know that, but I still have a few friends left, I think, that might do that for me, at least for a fee."

"Great idea," Jonathan said quickly. "Let's get that done now. The quicker we get the FBI and the IRS on his ass, the better. That, with all of the other shit he is dealing with, will make him vulnerable."

"I have a friend that will do anything for a grand. Is that okay?"

"Yes! However, you have got to meet him or her somewhere secret, and you cannot let him or her know what is going on or where we are. Got it?"

"Yes. That will be no problem, and it is a him. You cannot trust a her with something like this!"

"All right, now here is the plan. He must get it to them without them knowing who he is or why he got it to them."

"What?"

"Have him give an anonymous call to the FBI office telling them that he has something of interest and then let him leave it for them behind a dumpster at the mall or something. Have him call them from a payphone or even better from a stolen cell phone. Can he get that done without getting caught if the bounty is two thousand dollars instead of one thousand?"

"You bet!"

"After that, he must keep his ass quiet!"

"Can we give him another grand for that?"

"Absolutely!"

"Then get it done today."

"Okay, give me the keys."

"Not so fast."

"You have got to go get a prepaid cell phone to call your friend on and then trash it immediately after the call."

"Okay, that is not a problem. Anything else?"

"Yes, you absolutely positively cannot let him or anyone else follow you after you give him the instructions, the address of the FBI office, and the boxes."

"In fact, here's a better idea. Meet him at the mall closest to the FBI offices. I will give you that information and then abandon the car, and Rodney and I will pick you up in the movie theater exactly one hour after you meet this friend."

"Why all of that?"

"I just do not want any mistakes or any openings for a money-hungry opportunist to take advantage of. Understood?"

"Yes."

"Then here are the keys."

Rachel then left on her mission.

A few minutes after she was gone, Rodney looked at Jonathan and said, "Okay, Sherlock, now how do we pick her up there without a car?"

"Not a problem. Let's check out of the motel…no, you check us out of the motel and I will steal a nearby car and pick you up out front."

Goldman was now in his car trying to regroup

"Look, asshole," Goldman said over his cell phone. "The bastards took the boxes from the basement before the fire got them. Why did you not start the fucking fire in the basement, you idiot. Everyone knows that heat rises. By starting the son of a bitch upstairs, you gave them time to get the boxes out."

"Who are you talking about?"

"Never mind, you stupid bastard!" *Clank!*

Goldman was now in a complete state of confusion. He had to do something to draw this Beck bastard out of hiding. He had to kill him and retrieve the fucking boxes before he had a chance to get them to the authorities. If that happened his ass was toast and he knew it. But how could he do that? He had no fucking idea where Beck was? *Think,* Goldman thought. *How can I draw him out? My fucking ex-wife! She is the bitch that published the photos first!* He then wheeled the car around and headed to the offices of the *Radical Times* newspaper. He pulled right up front and parked in the fire zone and then rushed into the office, scaring the secretary. Then he screamed, *"Where is the fucking bitch? Tell me now or I will shoot your fucking ass right now."*

"Ah, ah, sir, she…ah, Mr. ah!"

"Speak, goddammit, before I shoot your fucking head off!" Goldman screamed as he pulled the hammer back on his .38 and held it to her head.

"I am sorry, sir, but she…but…"

"Goddammit, bitch, talk to me now or you are dead!"

"She is on vacation!"

"Where?"

"She, ah…ah…"

"Goddammit, bitch, talk!"

"I do not think that she has left yet, but she has booked a flight to Hawaii."

"Hawaii?"

"Yes!"

"When does it depart?"

"I am not sure, but I think later tonight. She had me come in and get some things together for her."

"Together?"

"Yes! She should be here soon on her way to her mom's before leaving later."

"Great! Now sit your stupid ass right here! No come with me, bitch, while I move my car." Then he grabbed her by the arm and dragged her with him. With his ex's secretary in tow, Goldman ran outside, pushed her into the car from the driver's side all the way across the front, bloodying her nose and almost breaking her left arm on the steering column. He then drove into an adjacent parking facility reserved for the workers of the tenants of the building. Quickly he parked the car and then ran around the car, grabbed her, and then ran swiftly back to the offices, hoping that he had not been detected. He then tied her up and then stuffed her into a closet in the back of the offices and placed a large piece of duct tape over her mouth. Goldman then hid out front and waited. Killing his ex-wife would not only be easy, it would be fun, he thought. Then he had another thought. *I must regroup and rethink. I cannot kill her or the secretary because everyone would come after me at that point.*

Little did Goldman know that at that very moment, Rachel was purchasing a prepaid cell phone, and within the hour, the FBI would be coming after him.

Confusion was everywhere for him! The Goldman empire was crumbling! The only way to save himself he thought was to get this Beck guy first. Maybe then he could alibi everything else!

Back at the motel

Rodney checked out of the motel and walked out front, and sure enough, there I was with a new Taurus, or at least nearly new.

Rodney jumped into the passenger's side and looked at me with sort of a smart-ass smile and said, "Surely you did not get this from the motel lot?"

"Nope! I got it from the parking lot of the bar next door. It was driven by two teenagers, and I doubt seriously if the driver's dad knew they were bar hoping today. They will wait at least a day or so to tell him, plus I switched the tags off of it with another Taurus parked at the motel. The motel Taurus had Kansas tags and the Bar Taurus had local tags, so that should even confuse the authorities for a while."

"Yeah!" said Rodney. "At least until the Kansas folks figure out that they have Washington tags."

"That's right. However, that should work in our favor. How long has it been, Rodney, since you have actually looked at your tags?"

"Okay, I'll give you that point! What do we do now?"

"Let's go to the mall where we are to pick up Rachel in a bit."

Back at the office of the Radical Times

Miss Simms returned to her office, entered the front door, and then immediately felt like something was wrong. Her first response was her best; however, she did not turn and run back out. Instead, she made the fatal mistake of staying and looking around.

It did not take long for Goldman to subdue her and then efficiently and quietly break her neck. It felt good to him, not just because of the pics and all she was—you know, his ex, and if you have ever had one, breaking her neck is always a hidden thought and a desire hidden deep within the dark shadows of your subconscious thought. However, most of us never let that part of our being surface, but today, Goldman did, and it felt good! He then moved on to the closet and again quietly and efficiently, he broke the secretary's neck and then left the building. *Oh well*, he thought, *so much for not killing them*.

Goldman had a lot on him, and his chances of getting out of this unscathed was next to impossible, but at least for the moment, he felt free and relieved at least one of his nemesis is gone, and hopefully, this would draw in the famous Jonathan Beck.

CHAPTER 24

Back at the mall

I instructed Rodney to stay with the car in front of the theater and told him that I was going inside to make sure everything went as planned, and I also wanted to make sure that Rachel was not in any danger.

Reluctantly, Rodney bought the story. However, deep inside, he wondered what my real intentions were as he watched me enter the mall through a door near the cafeteria.

I then moved unsuspectingly through the mall until I found Rachel waiting near a booth that sold dipping dips ice cream. However, I became a little concerned because she was not really waiting; she was talking with a shady-looking character that was sitting in a vibrating chair getting a massage while they seemed to fuss with each other. At that point, I knew what I must do. *That bastard must not breathe another breath after he dropped off the boxes.* The stranger had all the attributes of a swindler…and a professional one at that. I could only see the back of his head and part of his arm; however, I was not impressed with his looks from any angle.

In a few, the two of them left out an exit near the theater but in an area where they could be seen by Rodney, and then they moved quickly to the parking lot, and there they made the exchange. Boxes for cash!

After the exchange, Rachel went back into the mall and the stranger just sat there for a while talking on his cell. He did that just long enough for me to steal another car and then he waited.

It was not long before the stranger pulled out, still talking on his cell, and I followed. The FBI offices were just a few blocks away, a situation that I had planned in advance.

The stranger pulled in front of the office, went inside, and within a very short period, he returned with two guys and a girl, and the four of them removed the boxes from the car and carried them inside. About an hour later, the stranger returned, still talking on his phone. I knew that he was trying to work both ends against the middle. He must go!

I followed him about a block or two, knowing that with his pocket full of cash, he would not go far, and sure enough, he pulled into a local titty bar entitled Pussy Galore" He discreetly pulled around back and parked near the dumpster. It was early, and I was not even sure that they were open, so I made my move and quickly disposed of the stranger and threw his body into the dumpster. Just after pulling away, a large truck came around the corner. It was the waste management people! What a break! Now the body would be taken to the dump, and it would most likely be weeks before anyone found the body, and it would be difficult if not impossible to connect the dots from the body to the mall to Rachel and then to me. *The world would be better off*, I thought. *This joker needed to be removed from the gene pool.*

Back at the mall

Rachel and Rodney had been waiting nervously for at least two hours by now, and they were just about to exit the car and go looking for me, when there I was, just like magic, walking out of the exit near the theater, drinking a fountain drink.

"Where have you been?" Rodney asked.

"Oh, after making sure that Rachel made the exchange without difficulty or danger, I visited a few shops, and look here," I said as I handed Rodney a bag with a fishing shirt and a couple of lures inside. "And I bought these things for my next excursion."

Rodney did not buy this story for a minute, but Rachel did, so he kept quiet, just hoping for the best.

Rodney was getting nervous just thinking about what might have really happened while I was missing. This thing could surely blow up anytime now, and all of them either end up dead or in prison. *Why did I come up here?* Rodney thought. *Then what does it matter now? I must now just survive by the minute and hope for the best in the end.*

Goldman was now riding around town, trying to decide what to do next. *The fire,* he thought, *I must go back there.* He was getting impatient too. He must find this Beck guy; all his efforts must be transferred to him. Why has someone not gotten him yet? The community had several groups after Beck, and his sources had informed him that the FBI, the local police, and others were also after Beck. Plus "my guy," yeah!

"My guy? Why have they not got something on him as of yet?" Goldman decided to go back to his offices and wait. He would like to do battle with Beck on his turf and on his terms.

"What's next, Jonathan?" Rodney asked.

"Let's go have a drink and then wait through the evening before we make our next move."

"Where do we wait?"

"Let's go to the Double Dribble saloon."

On the way, I was thinking that the time was nigh! My only worries were my kids! I could take down Goldman! That would be easy, but what about all of the others in my life? My ex-wife was nothing, just a shot in the dark, another whore along the way. My mother and father had long since passed, and just like everyone else in my life, leaving me nothing but bills. Thinking of my children, I thought, it had been too long since I had a conversation with either one of them. Oh, what the hell, all I had ever been to them was a meal ticket anyway. At times a really good ticket and then at other times, not so good—so is the life of a failing entrepreneur. A thought came to me, a thought that went back to my early days of traveling on the road. "Art is long and life is short, let's have a little snort." That came from the days when "a little snort" just meant a sip of whiskey.

Goldman then thought, *No! I cannot go to any of my offices or ports. This Beck guy now has in his possession all of those files that could easily cause me problems with the IRS and others. By now, he has probably turned them over to the IRS. Beck will do anything at this point to get me for murdering the kid and my ex-wife at the newspaper office. That is, if Beck knew of the murders.* The key now would be for him to get to this Blake guy first, but how? Nobody else has been able to, not even his old friends at the FBI. *However,* he thought, *everyone has a weakness. There must be a way. The girl!* That was it—he could get to them through the girl. How long would it take the authorities to find the bodies and then how long would it take them to look to him as a suspect? Not long! Everyone in town knew that she was his ex and knew of the photos of Goldman's present wife that she had published. That would be enough for them to at least look to him early on. They might, however, hesitate a while just because of who he was and they would not want to be wrong. His mind was now playing games with him because he could actually see a way out. He just had to get to Beck and his traveling companions quickly. Then he could alibi and excuse and lie his way around all the others, except for the IRS stuff. *Oh shit,* he thought. *With my money and influence, he could pay his way out of all of that.*

He then called Max, his closest associate, and most able too.

"Boss! I am glad that you called. The feds are everywhere—in the offices, at the ports, searching and seizing everything in sight—computers, files, and all. What has happened?

"Never mind all of that. I can take care of that later! Where are you?"

"Standing down the hall from the main office with everyone else."

"Get the hell out of there and start walking south on Main Street."

"What?"

"Just do it. I will explain later."

Max left the building and started walking down Main Street as Goldman had instructed him. After about a mile or so, a car pulled up beside Max, and it was Goldman. "Get in quickly," he said.

"What's up, boss?"

"I guess that you have figured out by now that everything that I have worked for is about to be destroyed."

"Yeah, I guess, but—"

"Never mind the details, Max. It would take too long. I need help in taking out this Beck guy if I stand any chance at all of saving my empire. Are you in?"

"Sure, boss. Have I not always been there for you?"

"Yes, you have, Max, and if we get through this, I will reward you greatly. Remember that hunting lodge in Ontario that you said that you would love to own?"

"Yes."

"Well, if we pull this off, and I am able to hold on, it is yours, I promise."

"What's the plan?"

"I am not sure, but first, we have got to find this Beck guy. I think that our best bet to get that done is via the girl that is traveling with him. Blake did not have her when he arrived according to my sources, and there is a guy traveling with them too, and according to my sources, he came up here later from Atlanta. He has FBI connections too."

"Boss, you do know that there is a local girl that was friends of the kid that is now missing?"

"Really?"

"Yes, she worked at a local tavern that is where they met up. Do you think that maybe this is the girl that you say is traveling with this Beck guy?"

"That's it, Max, it must be. I just do not believe that this guy just plucked an associate out of the sky. There had to be a connection, something that got her involved, and that is why this guy is so hard to find. I bet he is traveling on her ID, credit cards, etc."

"Give me a little time, and I can find all of that out."

"No! Time is something that we do not have right now. What is the name of the bar where this girl worked?"

"I am not sure. Let me think maybe it's Double Vision…no, but something like that."

"Could it be Double Dribble?"

"Yes, that's it!"

Goldman then, before thinking, did a U-turn and headed back to the other side of town. "Dammit!" Goldman exclaimed. "I must obey all of the traffic laws because I cannot afford to be pulled over right now." *The cops have got to be looking for me by now*, he thought.

"So you know of this place?"

"Yes, my fucking wife used to hang out there some, trying to find young guys to fuck. It has always been a pickup bar…and a pretty decent one too, I must say, for I have used it from a time or two myself. What is this girl's name, Max?"

"I cannot remember. Let me give Joe a call. I think that he might remember."

At the Double Dribble Sports Bar

Meanwhile, Rodney, Rachel and I arrived at the Double Dribble.

"Why are we going in here, Jonathan?" Rachel asked.

"I don't know, Rachel. I have got a hunch about something, but I also need time to think. I also want to watch a little television to see what, if anything, the authorities are doing or have done with the records."

"Okay," Rachel replied. "However, it will be hard for me not to get into some discussion about where I have been. You do remember that I worked here and that I just all of a sudden disappeared. How will we handle that?"

I then reached over as I got out of the car and held Rachel's hand and said, "Oh, that will be easy. You are with me, the rich guy from the Sierra Club gathering, your sugar daddy of sorts, I guess. We have faked being lovers before, so let's do it again."

Rachel relented, and Rodney just followed along, shaking his head. He knew that there was more to this than I was saying, and from the look on Rachel's face as she looked back at me, she did too. Rachel and I entered the bar hand in hand and with smiles as big as Texas.

Rachel's old boss was behind the counter, and he just stopped in his tracks as he saw her and then turned a little pale. He then stopped what he was doing and almost ran from behind the counter. "Where have you been, girl? We have all been scared to death that you were, ah, I don't know…maybe…"

"Dead?"

"Not so. Here, feel," she said as she let go of my hand and gave him a brief nonsexual hug. "It is me, alive and well. What about some drinks? You still have your liquor licenses, I hope."

"Why, hell yeah! Have a seat in the corner booth, and I will get the drinks. I know what you want. What about your friends?"

I spoke up and said, "Make mine a double vodka on the rocks."

"And for you, sir," the gentleman asked as he looked to Rodney.

"Just a beer, sir. Pour me whatever you recommend that you have on tap."

"That'll work. I will be right back."

Rodney could tell that something was different about me. I had made sure that his face was pointing in the direction of the door and where I could see one of the many televisions slightly to my left. I was right handed, and this allowed me to keep my right (shooting) hand under the table and out of sight of anyone entering the bar or approaching the table. I also had that look about me, the one he had seen only a few times before but had heard about often—the one that led me to get in trouble at the bureau and everywhere else I had ever stayed for long. It was sort of a cross between Rocky and the Incredible Hulk; however, I was masking most of it with a cunning smile. I needed to do that in order to play the part of Rachel's sugar daddy, financer, or something. Rodney had put an extra round of ammunition in his belt and an extra clip in his pocket. He and I were both packing matching military-issue .45s, and we were both great marksmen. Rodney needed to know if Rachel was carrying for if something came down, they would need all of the help they can get.

I excused myself and moved into the direction of the restrooms, so Rodney took this time to ask the question.

"Rachel," Rodney whispered as he leaned toward her. "Are you armed?"

"Yes, I have a .38 in my purse. Why do you ask?"

"I don't know, but I just have this feeling that something is about to happen."

"Me too, Rodney. That is why I really did not want to come in here."

"Whatever it is, Rachel, it has something to do with this place. He did not just select this bar randomly. He knows or, at the least, thinks something is coming down here. Do you have any ideas?"

"No! But you do know that I met Mitch here and Goldman's wife visits here a lot. On a few occasions, Goldman himself frequented this place."

"That's it, Rachel. Jonathan thinks that Goldman has made the connection between you and Jonathan."

"How can that be? We have been with him almost constantly. How could he know something we don't know?"

"That's what makes Jonathan Jonathan. He has been formulating a plan from day one."

"Just look at what he has set up."

"What?"

"Okay, the records that your guy gave to the FBI have not only isolated Goldman they have taken the nutcases out of the 'finding Jonathan' mode because they are now at home, work, or wherever trying to protect themselves from prosecution if, from nothing else, but IRS audits. The FBI and other agencies have now shifted at least most of their attention, if not all, to Goldman."

"What the hell does any of that have to do with us being here? Goldman is running out of places to search and Jonathan, at least thinks like I said before that he has made the connection between, Mitch, you, and Jonathan. It would not surprise me in the least if Goldman came here tonight."

"Do you think that Goldman knows we are here?"

"No! But I bet he has either already been here in the past few days or he is on his way. This is the starting point of it all in his mind if Jonathan is right."

"Then we should not be here. I do not want my friends hurt or involved."

"Too late for that, honey. It is best that we be here when he comes. That is, if he comes and my analysis is right."

"Why?"

"We can protect your friends. If he came wanting answers that he thought they had, even if they did not, he would most likely kill them out of anger and spite."

"Wait."

"What?"

"Check out the television."

"Oh my god, someone has killed the lady at the newspaper."

"Yes, and you and I both know who that is."

"Goldman?"

"Yep! He is doing exactly what Jonathan is doing trying to draw us out for a confrontation. Look, here comes Jonathan."

"Everything come out all right?"

"Yes, did you two see the newscast?"

"Yes."

"It was Goldman, you know."

"Yes, where do we go from here?"

"Nowhere yet, let's just rest and have a few and let me think it through."

In my mind, I knew what was next. The number of players in this game had now been reduced to just me and my crew and Goldman and his. I knew that many of the others were still out there, but their focus had now been shifted in other directions, at least for the moment. What I did not know was exactly where Goldman and his remaining thug or thugs were; however, I had a hunch that they would be paying a visit to the Double Dribble soon. Goldman did not have much time left to get me and try to switch all the crimes in my direction. The feds were most likely obtaining arrest warrants for

Goldman while they sat there and drank their beers. That is, if they did not already have them in hand and looking for Goldman.

About two miles west of the Double Dribble

"Listen, Max! I am going to the bar where the girl worked and put some pressure on her friends to find out where she is staying or whatever information we can get. We must do this quickly because I am running out of time, the feds are probably on our tail right now. You see, Max, if we can get this Beck guy and his partners, I think that I can get out of the big stuff, and then all I will need to do is deal with the IRS and whoever."

"Wait, boss! I think that we need to go there together. This is looking more and more like a setup. You are trying to get to him and he is trying to get to you. At some point, your paths will cross, and it just might be at this bar."

"Good thinking, Max!" Goldman and Max then parked across from the Double Dribble in the parking lot of a Waffle House.

Inside the Double Dribble

"Look, Jonathan," Rodney said. "There is more on the TV!"

The program had been interrupted by an announcement that federal arrest warrants had been issued for Mr. Goldman and his wife. The details of the warrants were being withheld at the present time.

"Great!" I exclaimed as I downed another drink. *To myself,* I thought, we are getting ready for a modern-day shoot out at the OK Corral. If Goldman came there, then the final chapter in this saga would be written. Goldman needed to kill me, and I needed to kill Goldman. That is the only way that either player could make this thing end the way either one wanted it to. Who would survive, me or Goldman?

Rodney then asked the obvious: "You think he is coming here?"

"Yes!" I replied. "He has too! By now, he has made enough connections to put at least Rachel and me together, and most likely, the dots have been connected to you too."

"Look, Rodney, I have a plan. I am going out to the car to wait this out. I want you to get the guy that owns this place to grab Rachel and leave the minute you get a call from me on your cell. Do not tell Rachel what's up. Okay?"

"Okay!"

The stage was being set for the showdown or what might be a modern-day "shootout at the OK Corral"—or I guess I should say at the Double Dribble Salon. At this point, it would be me and Rodney against Goldman and his goon Max.

I moved slowly out to the parking lot, keeping an eye out for anything or anyone suspicious. I was accustomed to going against the odds. However, at this point, I was not sure just how many I might be up against. My instincts had taught me to survey the terrain and to make sure I had everything in front of me as I planned my attack or defense. However, it was not my modus operandi to counter punch. I would attack from a position of strength and move quickly. This situation was somewhat different, and I was concerned. I had really not had the time to know, just how this would come down. Time was of the essence, so I would most likely have to shoot from the hip in this position.

At the Waffle House just down from the Double Dribble

"Boss, we really are not prepared to do anything here other than take everyone out."

"Just wait a minute, Max. We know that our targets are Jonathan Beck, Rodney Fischer, and the Rachel girl. My plans are to move in quickly and try to hit them all in one attack and then survey the situation. We need to make it look like the Rodney guy turned on Beck for the money and that he and the girl were going to split the money."

"Now how can we do all of that with everyone shooting at us?"

"If we play our cards right, the bar will clear out, leaving our targets exposed. We need to kill Beck first and then position the bodies of the others to where it looks like they shot him and were trying to escape. We will shoot them with his gun, setting up the perfect scenario for me. At that point, I can sell the authorities on the fact that we were coming here for drinks and got caught up in the mess. I can then escape the other situations and only have to deal with the IRS or something later."

"That sounds good, boss. It may be easier said than done."

"I know, Max, but I have few options at this point. Fuck, let's kill all three of them and then sort it out from there. We can play switcheroo with the guns or something after the fact. Let's move from here to the 7/11 across the street from the bar and survey the situation before we move."

Parking lot of the Double Dribble

In the meantime, I had removed a rifle from my truck to go with my sidearm and had positioned myself behind a bush, next to an outbuilding in the dark. A couple was in a car near me. However, they were so busy making out that they did not notice my movements. *This was good*, I thought. They would be a distraction when Goldman arrived, taking my attention away from the outbuilding.

It was not long until I saw a car across the street driving suspiciously slow to the side of the convenience store. There appeared to be two men in the car, but they did not get out immediately. The long they sat there, the more, I started to plan my actions.

"What now, boss? I do not see this Beck guy or the girl. Do you want me to go in and look around first?"

"Yes, I will pull over there and wait in the car. Come back to the car after you locate all three of them. I can see the Rodney guy sitting at a table and he appears to be nervous. Let's drive around the parking lot for a minute before you go in to make sure this is not a setup."

"Yes, I have been looking at pictures of all three, and you are correct. That is the FBI guy from Atlanta, Rodney Fischer. I would like to see the girl and Beck. They will not know me, so I should be able to get in and out without any difficulties."

"Be careful, Max. You are the only one left that knows anything about the private parts of my operations now. The others have been eliminated, so you are most valuable, and when this is over, you will be rewarded greatly."

They drove around, and everything appeared to be normal, so Goldman parked in the shadows on the opposite side of the parking lot and let Max out.

I could not believe just how easy this was going to be tonight. There were just two of them, and they were setting themselves up like ducks on a pond.

Goldman smiled as Max entered the bar because he knew that when this was finished, Max would have to die too. Max also did not know that Goldman had positioned another car in the parking lot with two of his smartest and deadliest associates. They were really the ones that would be set up for life in the final analysis.

I moved quickly but quietly to the other side of the facility to a place near where Goldman was waiting in the car for Max. Drawing from my Vietnam and CIA experiences, I moved beside the car, took a towel, and wrapped around the muzzle of my small-caliber rifle and then waited for some noise to hide the sound as I pulled the trigger, shooting Goldman in the back of his head. Goldman died instantly and without movement. *This was good*, I thought, so I opened the door slightly to make sure everything would look normal when the other guy returned. About that time, however, two men came running across the lot from the car where the couple had been making out. In the light, I was exposed and an easy target for the two sharpshooters. One of the shots hit me in the chest just below my left shoulder and the other went into my abdomen. I was able to crawl out of the light and into the shadows as I heard the noise of all the commotion of the excitement in and around the bar. I could also hear the heavy breathing of my attackers.

All sorts of thoughts were running through my mind as I knew I had really screwed this whole thing up for sure. This was not the Jonathan of old. This could not be happening.

Inside the bar, the patrons were frantic, trying to hide under tables, run out the back, and some even coming out the front, trying to get to their cars.

Rodney went out the back and moved quickly into the shadows so he could survey the situation. He saw the two men approaching a car with guns drawn, but he did not see me on the ground near the car. About that time, I started to shoot at my assailants with my side arm. I could not see his rifle, and my injuries were so severe I had little ability to move. I mortally wounded the first one as he came around the front of the car. I then looked over my shoulder and saw the second one standing there with my own rifle pointing at me. About that time, Rachel shot the stranger, but as he fell to the ground, he got off a shot that hit Rachel solidly in the chest. Rodney came up to the car from the shadows on a run and shot the man in the head that had shot Rachel.

We now had four bodies down and mass chaos everywhere.

I was motionless; however, it appeared that Rachel was still alive. Rodney dropped down beside her and saw this small hole in her chest. However, she had the look of a dying woman. Her eyes opened, and Rodney then said, "Why? Why Rachel? Jonathan told you to leave earlier."

She had come running back when she heard gunshots. "I feel very weak, Rodney. I think it is over."

We now have Goldman and two of his goons fatally wounded. I was barely holding on to my life and Rachel is dying, leaving only Rodney and Goldman's goon Max not wounded. Rodney saw Rachel take her last breath, and then something moved in the parking lot… or should I say someone.

Rodney thought, *Oh shit, that is the last man standing for Goldman.* Rodney then moved into the shadows to assess his situation. He was still worried about me, but at this point, he was in no position to check on me.

Back in the parking lot, I was barely hanging on, but I knew that I was at the end of the line. Thoughts of my life were flashing through my mind as my ability to breathe weakened. My mind would take me back to my childhood one minute and then flash to the present the next. I had witnessed the death of many people in my lifetime, and this is exactly what they would say to me was happening as life crept out of their bodies. I worried about my children even though we all knew that in my line of work that I would not die of old age. The phone call to them from whomever would be shocking and sad but not surprising. There was a lot about my life that was familiar and known to them, but no one really knew everything. However, I thought, in reality, no one knows everything about everyone or anyone for that matter, and that is probably a good thing. There were the last thoughts of the infamous Jonathan Beck.

Rodney was still in the shadows and was still not able to determine the location of the last goon standing. About that time, sirens started screaming and bright lights flashing in the distance. This was a good thing, Rodney thought. *I have nothing to fear from the police, so this may actually save my life because the goon would have to get lost and get lost quickly.* Rodney then moved toward the bar through the shadows, hoping to avoid being seen by the goon. He was able to get into the bar, but his entrance shocked the bartender that was hidden behind the bar and he almost shot Rodney. "No! No!" Rodney shouted. "Don't shoot! I am not armed, and I am only trying to find a safe place." The bartender lowered his firearm and then said that the police would be in the building in seconds, so he put his firearm back in the safe.

In a matter of seconds, the police stormed the premises as the first responders followed closely behind them. In their haste, they had run past most of the bodies, including that of Mr. Goldman and his men. Jonathan and Rachel had both expired from their wounds, so the coroner's office had to be summoned to the site to help the first responders deal with the carnage. Rodney was then interviewed and questioned for several hours before he was allowed to leave the scene. He gave them the entire story of what had happened and the details of what led up to this fateful night. The mystery of what had been happening to many Muslims had finally been solved with the death of Mr. Goldman.

CHAPTER 25

The next morning, Rodney called the FBI office in Atlanta and David was elated and happy that Rodney had helped to bring all of this to a successful end. Washington was very excited, and as Rodney was leaving the motel, the head of the FBI and others were on all channels, taking credit for the solving of this mystery that had become known in their circles as this country's largest hate crime. Of course, in Rodney's world, it had been known as the Rag Head Murders.

About that time, his phone rang, and it was Beth on the line with a lot of questions, and finally, he just said, "Look, Beth, I do not know if this thing got solved or not, but maybe it is over for us."

Beth then said, "You do not believe that Goldman was the killer, do you?"

"Look, Beth," Rodney said as he got into his car, "I really do not know. I do know that it will be sold that way, and I know that Jonathan was setting it up that way. I did ask him several times about his proof, but he really had none, and I told him just that. Jonathan was old school, and he knew that the FBI needed this to end, and he also knew that they did not care how that happened. I had a lot of respect for Jonathan and he will be missed by some but not by many. I for one not only questioned his tactics. I also questioned his motives. I told you before that the FBI should not have brought him back."

"But, Rodney, it all worked out in the end, and he will probably be honored by the FBI posthumously."

"I know that, Beth, and we will just have to leave it at that for now. I had the unenviable task of calling his children last night, so I just need to be alone for a bit and get some rest."

"How did they take it? I bet it was really hard on them."

"Yes, it was, but they knew the lay of the land when Jonathan went back to work on this case. They both had pleaded with him to say no, and we all know now that would have been best for them."

"Maybe not, Rodney. I am sure that Jonathan will get some favorable press, and the FBI either has paid or is going to give them a very big check."

"I guess, and I mean I really hope they do for the sake of his children."

"Is David going to bring you back to work?"

"I don't know if he would or not, Rodney, but I think that I need to hunt another occupation. I have had enough stress at the FBI for someone twice my age. I think that a low-profile secretarial job would be welcome now. What about you?"

"I feel the same way, Beth. I believe that I am done and that I need to move on and find something else somewhere else too."

"I am sure that David will offer you, Rodney, after how all of this has come down."

"It will not do any good, Beth. I am done. I am going to start something else somewhere else after the funeral."

Rodney went back to Atlanta to get a few things and then went to Washington to finish the final interviews. about this historic event of ending these horrific hate crimes. This took several weeks to complete with all of the international press and all, but finally, he was not needed any longer. He had a friend in Vegas, so he thought he might go there and get a job tending bar for a while.

6 Months Later

Rodney had settled into a very simple but entertaining life in Vegas, but he thought that it was time for him to pay a visit to Jonathan's son in Colorado. Jonathan did not have the opportunity, so Rodney thought that his son would enjoy Rodney visiting for a day or so and taking in one of his hockey games.

There had not been any more murders, so all was well, and the FBI was planning a celebration or something for Jonathan since he had died in the line of duty while helping to solve the biggest hate crime of our time. They even wanted Rodney to be there to participate and to also receive an honor for his bravery that night. Rodney really did not want to go, but he thought that he should.

Washington, DC

At the White House, things were just getting started, and Rodney and Jonathan's son, Junior, were welcomed with open arms. The President hailed the heroic efforts of his father and said that he would receive the highest award given to a civilian and that the main highway in Knoxville, Tennessee, would be co-named in his father's honor. The highway would now be known as Kingston Pike/Jonathan Beck Memorial Highway. Rodney could tell that this was making Junior very proud, and his sister had just arrived, and this even made her smile. He guessed that neither the president or Junior and his sister knew that Jonathan hated the President and really considered him to be a Muslim at heart.

At the ceremony, Rodney was also recognized for his heroism and bravery, and all in all, it was just a great day for all and for the nation.

Junior took a late flight back to Colorado, and his sister decided to visit here for a day or so before going back to school. The FBI had followed through on their promise and had even doubled the amount of money to be given to them. In a few months, the family would reunite back in Knoxville and have a private celebration of life for Jonathan and then place his ashes in his beloved Clinch River. Jonathan had always said that when he died, it would be time for the roles to be reversed and that the fish could now eat him.

Rodney decided that he should fly back to Atlanta and pay a brief visit to Beth and David before going home, wherever that may be now.

Rodney on the Delta Flight from DC to Atlanta

As Rodney lay back to relax, he started to reflect on the state of the country and on how all of this came down in the end. He had discovered a very deep and wide-reaching movement in the heartland to more of a nationalist view and thought. It was there naturally after 9/11; however, his recent work indicated an even deeper movement, a phenomenon that Rodney knew would come to the surface in some way and somehow in this country. He had also discovered the fact that there were huge numbers of the population that felt left out of the government. They felt that both the Republicans and the Democrats had sold them out in the name of prosperity and had sold their middle-class jobs to China and to other countries that most of them had never heard of before. Many of their jobs had been sent to Vietnam, and that really infuriated them since most of their families had been negatively affected by our failed efforts there during the Vietnam War. They all knew that we only lost because it was a political war and not one led by our massive military. They could not understand why massive amounts of monies were being taken from them in the form of taxes and then sent to Vietnam and others to finance the construction of factories to take their jobs. Rodney knew that the winds of change were blowing, but he also knew that either the politicians did not see it or would not see it. Right before he fell asleep, he whispered out loud, "One day they will see it and it may not be a pretty sight."

The lady sitting next to him said, "What?"

Rodney replied, "Sorry, ma'am, I was just thinking out loud I guess."

FBI offices in Atlanta

David was the nicest he had ever been to Rodney, and David quickly let Rodney know that his job had been saved and that he had even received a raise.

Rodney had visited with Beth earlier that day, and all was well with her, and he told David that he should try again to get Beth back with the FBI. David agreed and said that he would work on it soon and that he thought that he could get her more money since he was definitely not coming back.

After that, they just talked about old times and sports for a few minutes when Rodney noticed something in the corner behind David's desk. "When did you start keeping a rifle in your office, David?"

"Oh, that is not mine. It was found at the shootout, and it was believed to have belonged to Jonathan. I called his son, and he confirmed that it was definitely his father's rifle, so I told him that I would keep it here until he had time to come and get it."

Rodney had never seen Jonathan with a rifle, so he nervously asked David, "What is the caliber?"

David replied, "Oh, it is just a .22."

About the Author

Bunk Russell has been a highly successful businessman, teacher, investor, outdoorsman and writer. He has travelled the world in these endeavors and his vast knowledge and wisdom is always reflected in his writings. Bunk gives us a very unique perspective of life, people and places in the characters and storylines he develops in his fictional novels. Some of his most well known Outdoor Columns are entitled, When The Ducks Don't Fall But You Do" and the Clinch River Chronicles.

Today he is enjoying life with his wife sharing time together in their home in Knoxville, Tennessee and their condo in Clearwater Beach, Florida. His readers are anxiously awaiting the release of his next novel, The Wind in The Trees. This is another politically charged murder mystery novel that will challenge your imagination and keep you focused to the very end.

Visit the author's website at https://www.facebook.com/bunker045/